I0586376

Alma's Loyalty

AMRA PAJALIĆ

Content Warnings

SCAN QR CODE

OR GO TO

www.amrapajalic.com/
themes.html

MELBOURNE, AUSTRALIA

https://www.pishukinpress.com/

Copyright © 2022 by Amra Pajalić

First Published 2022

Pishukin Press

All rights reserved. This book is copyright. Apart from fair dealing for the purpose of private study, research, criticism or review, as permitted under the copyright act, no part may be reproduced by any process without written permission from author.

Cover design: Created using Canva elements

For content and trigger warnings please go to www.amrapajalic.com/themes

Pre-publication data is available from the National Library of Australia trove.nla.gov.au

Paperback Edition 9780645331059

Chapter 1

I was in my room completing my homework when my mother called me. I bookmarked my Maths textbook and walked down the hallway, hearing a conversation in progress. We had visitors, a regular event in our household.

I entered the living room and saw my parents on the couch, with a trio I'd never seen before.

'This is my daughter Alma.' Mum made the introductions in Bosnian. 'This is Arnesa and her husband Nermin, and Arnesa's mother Enisa.'

'*Bože sačuvaj,*' Arnesa said, which meant God Forbid, her mouth formed an O in surprise as she scrutinised my face. 'She looks exactly like Sabiha.'

'Who is Sabiha?' Mum asked.

'Esad's other daughter,' Arnesa said. 'We saw Bahra a month ago in Melbourne.'

I didn't understand what this stranger was saying. My father had another daughter? I looked at my mother for help.

'Esad doesn't have another daughter,' Mum said.

'Yes, he does. Sabiha, from his first marriage with Bahra. She is the spitting image of her father and sister.' Nermin nodded to me.

My legs felt weak. My father was married before? I turned to my father, hoping to get confirmation this was all a lie. His face was white.

'Alma, return to your room,' Mum commanded.

I walked down the hall, hiding in the alcove so I could eaves-drop.

'How could you not know?' Arnesa demanded. 'Bahra was four months pregnant when you moved to Hobart.'

There was an awkward silence before Mum jumped in. 'Bahra told him the child wasn't his.'

'Aren't there tests to find out?' Arnesa said. 'After all, you both know that she wasn't of sound mind.'

'Do you have Bahra's phone number?' my father asked.

'Of course,' Nermin said.

I heard the ping of an SMS. Nermin must have sent my father the phone number in an SMS.

My father passed in front of the hallway and went to his study, closing the door behind him with finally.

'My apologies. Maybe we should reschedule this visit,' Mum said, walking our guests to the front door.

I inched down the hallway and closer to the study. Mum closed the front door after our guests and walked to stand in front of the study door to eavesdrop with her back to me.

Dad initially spoke in a regular voice and then shouted, 'You should have told me she was my daughter.'

Mum opened the study door. Dad was staring at his phone with a distraught face, tears streaming down his face. 'What am I going to do now?' He fell into Mum's arms, his sobbing rending the air.

***

Beep, beep.

I opened my eyes, staring at the glaring white ceiling before me. I lifted my arm and hit the snooze button, discombobu-lated that I was reliving the most traumatic day of my life in my dreams again. Even though it had happened three months before, I always woke up from this dream with the same feeling of betrayal and shock.

I dressed, trying on half a dozen outfits before settling on jeans and a black-and-white striped stretchy top. My new school had no uniform, and I'd debated long and hard about what to wear. Mum's advice was black pants and a white shirt. 'It's a good idea to be smart casual,' she'd said, but I was afraid that was too formal.

I went to the bathroom, washing my face and looking at my frightened green eyes in the mirror. I tried to tell myself that everything would be alright, but if I had learnt anything up until this point, it was that things can always get worse.

I practiced my smile in the mirror until my cheeks were sore. It was important that it looked careless and natural, a mask that I could hide the quiet terror filling me. I stretched my lips wider and pushed my cheeks deeper into my face. That would have to do. It was the first day of term three and I was beginning my third school in year 10.

'Alma,' my little sister Sanela called out my name as she pounded on the bathroom door.

I opened the door, and she rushed in like a tornado. She got her hairbrush from the drawer and handed it to me. I sat on the edge of the bathtub and brushed her hair, while Sanela stood between my legs brushing her Barbie's blonde curls, her little five year old hands finding it difficult to manipulate the tie around the doll's ponytail.

I looked at the clock. Mum was due home soon from her night shift as a nurse. She usually came home before we had to leave for school.

'Done.' I breathed out a sigh of relief. I still had to do my hair and check my outfit one last time before breakfast.

'Now do Barbie.' Sanela thrust the doll toward me.

'I don't have time.' I stopped when Sanela looked at me with pleading brown eyes. It was quicker to tie the doll's hair into a makeshift ponytail than argue. 'Here.' I gave the doll back when I finished.

I carefully brushed my blonde hair back, ensuring that it parted directly in the middle, then stood in profile and smoothed down my top.

My younger brother Ali appeared in the bathroom doorway and met my eyes in the mirror. He and Sanela took after Mum with their brown hair, brown eyes, and round faces. 'Dad's waiting.'

He didn't need to say anymore. I knew Dad was tapping his watch, his patience straining. As a doctor, he was used to being the one who set the schedule.

'Get your backpack,' I ordered Sanela and went to my bedroom to do the same.

As we walked down the stairs, I looked through the round window that was at eye level across from me. Through it I could see the street outside, the roofs of the housing estate we lived in, filling the horizon like little matchbox houses. They all looked alike with their square bricked walls, carefully manicured lawns, and precisely placed plants.

We'd moved to Melbourne three months ago, and I still yearned for our house in Hobart. We'd lived off the beaten track with tall trees hugging our house, cocooning us from the rest of the world. I used to look out the window for hours, my eyes following the leaves as they danced in the wind. Now I averted my gaze from the ugly view that confronted me and continued down.

Dad tried to convince us that the move would be an adventure. He'd given us *carte blanche* to buy whatever we wanted at furniture shops, after our disastrous attempts in transplanting our old furniture: the delicate wrought iron pieces and white wood furniture that looked so perfect and quaint in our brick cottage but had looked wonky and cheap against the multi-coloured feature walls.

'It's no good.' Mum had covered her face with her hand. 'This McMansion defies good taste,' she'd said, her tone full of spite. She'd never been enamoured with the charms of our new home, but she'd been worn down from leaving her family behind and fallen prey to Dad's enthusiasm for space.

Mum had wanted to pack our old furniture in storage, but Dad said we couldn't afford the fees, so we'd sold them at a garage sale. I thought I'd had bad days until then. Among the contenders for the title was the day that I found out about his other daughter, and the day that we moved to Melbourne and I was confronted with the monstrosity that was to be our new home.

'It's got four bedrooms so you don't have to share anymore,' he'd sounded like the eager real estate agent when he showed us around the McMansion.

'But I want to be with Alma.' Sanela grabbed hold of my skirt and tried to burrow into my body.

Even though sometimes I had wished for nothing more than my room, there were too many changes too soon. I wanted things to slow down, but life was fast forwarding at super speed.

'You're big enough to sleep by yourself,' Dad replied to Sanela off-handedly and continued the tour.

But in the end the winner of the *Worst day of my life* was the day of the garage sale when Dad sold every trace of our former life to strangers for pocket-change. As each piece of furniture was sold to an eager bargain hunter, I felt like I was being robbed of a childhood memory.

When we hit the bottom of the stairs, the front door burst open and Mum rushed in.

'Mummy,' Sanela exclaimed with pleasure, holding out her arms.

'*Srce moje.*' Mum picked her up, their dark, glossy hair intermingling together as she kissed her, calling Sanela her heart.

'Let's go.' Dad headed for the front door, briefcase in hand.

Our parents insisted we speak only Bosnian in the house so we maintained our fluency. Mum was much stricter about the rule and ignored us if we spoke English.

Sanela's stomach rumbled.

'Did you eat breakfast?' Mum looked at the clean sink and pushed past Dad. 'Let's fix that,' she said as she rifled through the kitchen cupboards. 'Sit.' Mum pointed to the stool with the wooden spoon she was holding.

As I watched Mum expertly flip eggs and put bread in the toaster, my father's burning gaze drilled a hole in the nape of my neck. Usually I was the one who made breakfast when Mum worked, but this morning I'd spent half an hour changing outfits.

'I'm going to be late,' Dad said, still standing by the doorway.

'Alma, your father will drive you,' Mum told me.

I coughed as the orange juice I was drinking went down the wrong pipe. I'd avoided being alone with Dad since I was expelled from my last school.

'And I'll drive Ali and Sanela,' Mum continued.

My new high school was in St Albans near Dad's medical centre, while Ali and Sanela's schools were closer to home in Sydenham.

When Mum served breakfast, I gulped the eggs down without chewing, only to stop abruptly and cover my mouth as the gooey texture of the scrambled eggs triggered my gag reflex.

'Don't rush.' Mum shot an annoyed look at Dad. He retreated to the living room.

When we finished breakfast, Mum pulled out our lunch bags from the fridge and handed them out. We walked out of the front door and I followed my siblings to Mum's 4WD. Ali got in the backseat and rolled down the window.

'Come on Alma.' Sanela tugged me toward the backseat.

'Alma isn't coming with us,' Mum said gently. 'Daddy will drive her to school today.'

'But who's going to wait with me until school starts?' Sanela was on the verge of tears.

Sanela was in prep and was anxious by herself. I used to stay with her at her primary school until her friends arrived, then undertook the fifteen-minute walk to my previous school, a private all-girls school.

'You'll be all right.' I knelt in front of her and cupped her cheek. 'Your new friend Heidi will wait for you at school.'

Sanela hugged me, her little arms clinging to my neck. She was born when I was ten and I reckon I'd nearly changed almost as many of her nappies as Mum had.

'Let go of your sister now.' Mum grabbed hold of Sanela's arms and gently tugged her away.

'Nooooo,' Sanela shouted, holding tighter.

I took a deep breath and blinked back my own tears. 'You won't be alone.'

'I'll stay with you,' Ali said.

'See.' I made my voice upbeat. 'Ali will stay with you.'

Sanela looked uncertainly between Ali and I. 'Promise,' she demanded from our brother.

'I promise.' He took Sanela's other hand.

'You'll be fine,' Mum said to me with a fake smile stretching her lips, while Ali strapped Sanela into the booster seat. 'You'll make lots of friends.'

As Mum hugged me, I hid my face in her hair, wanting to be a little girl once again and believe in every platitude, but I knew she was just as nervous as I was. I was embarking on a whole new adventure at my first co-ed public high school. Either of those would have terrified me. The two together and I was paralysed.

'Don't forget I'll pick you up after school at Dad's work.' Mum pecked me on the cheek and briskly got in the driver's seat.

I waved as the car reversed out of the driveway. The 4WD was parallel to the house and Sanela pressed her face against the glass window when Dad turned on the ignition to his car. I aborted my waving and jumped into the passenger seat.

We reached the end of the cul-de-sac and Mum's 4WD turned left, while Dad turned right. I watched through the back window until Mum's car wasn't visible anymore.

I looked ahead again, suddenly aware of the silence in the car. The last time I'd been alone with Dad was when I got expelled three days ago and he drove me home, his body taut with seething silence.

Dad took a right turn and cleared his throat. 'There's something I need to talk to you about,' he said, switching to English. He'd lived in Australia for nearly twenty years and had the faintest tinge of an accent when he spoke.

I turned to look at him and clenched my fists. He was going to give me the blasting I'd been waiting for. It was almost a relief after the silent treatment of the past three days. I grabbed hold of the car door handle and fantasised about pulling it open, throwing myself out of the moving car and sliding across the asphalt, my skin peeling like a banana. Surely it couldn't be more painful than what was about to take place in the car.

'It's about your new school.' Dad paused.

I took a deep breath, realising I hadn't exhaled since he first spoke.

'I'm really excited,' I lied. I was full of trepidation about what it would be like to go to a public school. The kids in public schools were rough, and I was told that public schools had less discipline. 'It's got a fantastic academic record.' I recited the facts and figures I'd memorised from repeatedly staring at the school enrolment information.

'It's not that.' Dad waved for me to stop. 'You'll know someone at your new school.'

'Mum told me,' I interrupted again. Mum worked the phones after they enrolled me, calling around the Bosnian community until she tracked down a student who went to the same school. 'Dina Hasanagić.'

'Could you please let me finish?' he snapped.

I hunched into the passenger seat, his words like a slap to the face. My fingers jumped to my mouth, my teeth connecting with enamel, before I remembered myself and sat on my hands.

'I'm sorry.' Dad put his hand through his hair, messing his carefully combed hair.

He was nervous. My stomach clenched harder.

'Your sister goes to St Albans High.' Dad turned to look at me.

'No, she doesn't,' I automatically replied. 'Sanela goes to—'

I abruptly cut out. He was talking about his other daughter. My body lurched as if our car hit a pothole, but the road before us was smooth as glass. It was the same feeling I'd had when I found out about our supposed sister from Dad's first marriage.

After my parents made the family announcement about my father's other daughter, everything sped up. Dad went on a trip to meet his first-born and came back with a job offer and real estate pamphlets in tow. My parents fought over the proposed move. Mum didn't want to leave her extended family who were all within a fifteen minute drive, but in the end it was inevitable. Dad had always wanted to move to Melbourne in order to be more involved with the Bosnian community and have access to greater professional opportunities, and when he found out he had a long-lost daughter, he gained greater familial priority.

Before I knew it we were packing and moving to Melbourne. Dad's attempt to atone for his inadvertent years of neglect were thwarted when Sabiha refused to have contact with him. I wanted to ask him if he knew before they enrolled me. I wanted to shout and scream, but years of habit taught me to keep my lips zipped and my eyes on the floor.

'I know you're probably thinking that I wanted you to enrol at St Albans High because of Sabiha, but that's not true,' he said, as if he'd read my mind. 'It truly is the best school in the area.' Dad peeked at me as he drove. 'I'm sorry. I know this isn't fair to you. If you want to come to work with me, we can find another school for you.'

It was the last thing I expected to hear. 'Do you mean it?'

'Of course,' Dad said. 'It's completely your decision.'

He was tense, his whole body on edge as he waited for my answer. For the first time since we found out about the other daughter, I had his full attention and it was intoxicating. Maybe I shouldn't throw this gift away? Going to St Albans High might be my chance to bring back the Dad I knew, but who'd been missing in action for the past three months.

'What about Mum?' I asked.

'I didn't tell your mother because I didn't want any outside influences to affect your decision,' Dad said.

Anytime there was a reference to the other daughter, Mum stiffened and went on the defensive. She'd fought against the move and lost, and was furious that Sabiha refused to see Dad after our sacrifices.

'I'll tell your mother tonight.'

'But—' I was betraying Mum by even contemplating going behind her back.

'Sabiha is a part of my life now and your mother knows that. She'll see that this is the best decision for all of us.' Dad smiled.

I felt compelled to smile back, even though I didn't agree. There would be hell to pay when Mum found out. Dad stopped the car in front of the school and I looked with concern at the empty schoolyard.

'We're late,' Dad said as he got out of the car.

We were supposed to arrive at the office before the bell, see the coordinator, who would introduce me to Dina, whose job was to show me around the school and take me to class.

Dad reached into the backseat and got out a gift bag. 'I got this for your first day.'

I had a spring in my step as I peered into the bag. He'd bought me a purple organiser, matching pen and water bottle.

When we reached reception, Dad gave me a rushed hug and a peck on the cheek. I closed my eyes, inhaling Dad's cologne, and tried to remember the last time he'd held me. It was way back before we moved to Melbourne.

'Give your sister a chance,' he said before he left.

An admin worker walked me to class and introduced me to the teacher, while the students inside the classroom erupted into chatter.

'Everyone, settle,' Ms Partridge called out as I followed her back into class. 'This is our new student Alma Omerović.' Ms Partridge's forehead wrinkled for a moment and she looked at the back. 'Are you any relation to Sabiha?' she asked.

Time stopped as I followed Ms Partridge's gaze and met Sabiha's eyes. I felt *déjà vu*, as if I was looking at myself in a mirror. We both took after Dad and had his blonde hair, dimpled chin, and high cheekbones. But the longer I stared, the more the differences became apparent. We had different shaped eyes and mouth.

I'd wondered what Sabiha looked like, but at home she was a conversational black hole and I'd had to make do with my imagination. My fantasy revolved around Dad realising he'd made a mistake and casting off his fake daughter. Our lives would return to normal, and we'd go home to Hobart.

There were so many times I wanted to ask Dad if he got a DNA test, how could he be sure, but the questions burnt in my throat, never to pass my lips. Now I knew why he was so determined to establish a relationship with her. There was no mistaking that she was her father's daughter.

'No,' Sabiha spat out, breaking the spell. 'We're not related.'

I had to fight not to run for the door. She looked at me with such anger and disgust; I was scared she'd vaporise me with the scorn shooting from her eyeballs.

'You can sit next to Dina,' Ms Partridge continued, oblivious to the tension in the air.

Sabiha stood and collected her things, her resentment obvious as she slammed her notebook and slapped her pencil case together. She looked like a girl lumberjack; she had on a denim mini and pink leggings, and her feet encased in chunky worker boots. Her outfit should have looked all wrong, instead she looked cool and fierce. I was frumpy in my too-new jeans and bland top and couldn't wait to hide behind the desk.

'Sabiha, quiet.' The teacher shushed.

Sabiha moved to an empty desk in the last row. The two boys in front of her turned around and whispered to her, but she shook her head.

I slid into the seat next to Dina. 'Hi,' I whispered, trying to make eye contact, but Dina snubbed me.

I stared at the teacher stiffly, trying to focus on *To Kill a Mockingbird*, but it was no good. I felt Sabiha's stare like ants walking on my neck. Abruptly, I turned to look behind me, catching Sabiha off guard. I'd expected her to still be staring at me with rage. Instead she looked miserable. I remembered how Dad had implored me to give Sabiha a chance, as if I was his last hope.

Sabiha had determinedly rebuffed his every attempt to establish contact. In the end, their relationship was reduced to him paying weekly child support, a too generous amount that we could barely afford, according to Mum.

After English double period, the recess bell rang, and I turned to catch Sabiha madly packing her things to make a dash for the door.

'Can we talk?' I followed her.

'About what?' Sabiha whirled around. 'How your mother is a home wrecker?'

'No,' I stuttered to a stop, my train of thought evaporating. 'My Mum isn't—'

'Then how do you explain the fact that we're the same age?' Sabiha snapped, turning around again.

Chapter 2

I wanted to slap myself in the forehead. I hadn't even considered how it would look from her end. By this time the class was empty, the only students left were the two of us, Dina and two guys who looked like mismatched salt and pepper shakers.

'We're not the same age,' I shouted.

Sabiha stopped, turning around again, her mouth open to continue her tirade.

'I'm a year younger,' I continued, quietly, since Sabiha was listening. 'I was moved up a grade in primary school.'

When I'd been moved, it had been a point of great pride and honour, but ever since it had become a cause of personal regret and hassle. Dad bragged about my great intelligence and speculated about my future academic career.

Since I began high school, life became even more difficult. I constantly felt out of step. All my friends talked about was getting a boyfriend or keeping one, but personally I couldn't see the appeal. I was forced to pretend I was into the same stuff, even though the chasm was widening.

Sabiha looked at me with suspicion, like she wasn't sure whether or not to believe me.

'It's true,' I insisted, desperate for her to believe me. I told her my birthday.

Her gaze softened, and she looked off-kilter and lost. Her face was so familiar, an almost mirror image to mine, that I felt a certain kinship toward her. I wanted to comfort her, and my arm tingled as I fought the urge to lift it toward her.

'You okay?' Dina put her arm around Sabiha's shoulders.

'I can't do this,' Sabiha muttered and rushed off.

The blonde-haired guy in her group hesitated, looking back at me with an apology in his eyes, but he followed as they all left the room.

Feeling shaky after the confrontation, I sat back down. I was on the first floor of the main building and saw the front of the school through the window. There were students milling around on benches, talking and eating, the noise of a crowd like the buzzing of working bees.

I wished I was one of them, an anonymous student with a clique I could blend into and disappear. The tears took me by surprise and I glanced to see if there were any witnesses. The hallways were deserted. Everyone was outside enjoying the sunshine. I stood to do the same, but realised I had nowhere to go and no one to see.

I sat back down and waited until the bell rang. Mum had packed me snacks for recess, but I wasn't hungry. I took out *To Kill a Mockingbird*. Usually I'd be frustrated at re-reading a book, but it comforted me in knowing what was going to happen. In my experience, nothing good came from being surprised.

When the locker bell rang, I consulted the map on my school diary and walked to my next class. As I walked under the walkway, I passed Sabiha and her friends. Sabiha stared straight ahead and her entourage followed her lead by not making any overtures.

I couldn't help but look over my shoulder when they passed and caught Sabiha glancing back. Our eyes caught for a moment, before she quickly turned forward. I continued walking through the crowded hallway to my class.

I was officially an outcast.

***

When the bell rang marking the end of school, I walked out with relief. I'd spent the day hiding in dark corners, so it wasn't obvious I was a loner, a role that was the equivalent of being a criminal in high school. Dina had been in my class in period five, but she ignored me.

I walked down the main road, enjoying the feel of the weak afternoon sunshine on my skin. I'd wanted to go out at lunch, but hid in the library, watching other students through the window with envy.

As I entered the main shopping strip, I stopped. I didn't know the way to Dad's medical centre. I tried to unscramble my brain and think, but I couldn't even remember the street name. The one and only time I'd been before Dad gave us a tour when he moved into his office and he drove us from home, so I had no point of reference to orientate myself.

I reached for my mobile only to think better of it. If I called Mum, she'd ask questions I couldn't answer. I didn't need to give my parents another excuse to fight.

If only I had internet access on my phone, I could have Googled the address, but Mum had us on a prepaid mobile plan, ensuring that we could only use the phone for emergencies. I'd have to walk the streets of St Albans until I saw something familiar.

I turned, planning on crossing the street at the pedestrian crossing I'd passed, and bumped into someone. I was heading for a spill on the concrete footpath, but muscular arms grabbed me.

I lifted my head and met amused blue eyes. He had slicked brown hair, light stubble on his face showing he was older, and a cigarette dangled between his lips. I was stunned mute. I'd never been this close to a hot guy and something strange was happening. My mouth was dry and my stomach was doing weird somersaults as if a furry critter had invaded my intestines.

'You okay?' He plucked the cigarette from his lips and ground it under his foot. 'Here, sit down.' He ushered me to a street bench and went back to collect my spilled belongings.

Something about the matter-of-fact way he helped me got to me. No one had shown me kindness for a while. The emotions that had been below the surface all day burst forth and hot tears burnt my cheeks.

Mortified that I was crying in public, on a public bench where pedestrians were walking by and while a cute guy watched, made it even worse. The harder I tried to stop, the more the tears came. The cute guy sat beside me. He casually put his arm around my shoulders and sat there, waiting it out.

I reached into my backpack and found disposable tissues, furtively wiping my face. I took out my compact, quickly glancing in the mirror to check I didn't have gobs of snot coming out of my nose.

'Having a bad day?' he asked.

'You could say that.' I looked ahead, not wanting to see his amusement or pity.

'You're the new girl. We go to the same school,' he explained when I looked at him with surprise. 'I'm Alex.' He offered his hand.

'I'm Alma. You don't look like a high school student,' I blurted as we shook hands.

He smiled wryly. 'I'm in year 12. I'll be turning 18 next week. Got a car waiting for me and on my birthday.' He mimicked turning the wheel.

I laughed at his antics.

'You should smile more often. You look gorgeous with your high cheekbones on display.' He brushed my cheek.

I stilled at his touch. He still had his arm around my shoulders, and he held me against his side. I'd never been this close to a guy before and goose pimples broke out on my skin. He was looking at me as if he wanted to kiss me.

It became hard to breathe, and my brain raced. He wasn't going to kiss me. I was imagining it. How to extricate myself from his embrace? There was no graceful way of doing it. I didn't want to be rude after he'd helped me.

'I'd better get going,' I said.

'You sure?' Alex asked. 'It looks like there was something bothering you and I'm a good listener.' He waggled his eyebrows playfully, wrenching a smile from me again.

'My Dad is waiting for me.' I looked away, feeling self-conscious under his intent gaze. 'I can't remember which street his work is in.'

'I'm guessing you're new to the area,' Alex said.

I nodded.

He got out his mobile and pressed a few digits. 'It's actually piss easy to find your way around St Albans. They built the whole place like a grid.' He leaned in and held his mobile in front of me. On the screen was a street map of St Albans. 'We're here.' He tapped his finger against the screen, his hot breath on my cheek.

With his left arm still around my shoulders, and his right holding the mobile, it was like he was embracing me. I had to fight not to hyperventilate. Finally, my eyes cleared and I could see the screen. I followed my path from school and recognised Dad's street.

'Where's Victoria Street?' I glanced at him.

His eyes were on my cleavage. I looked down. As I'd hunched over, my top gaped, allowing Alex to see my bra. I covered my breasts, shifting away from him.

When I gave him a horrified stare, he smiled. 'You can't blame a guy for looking.' He removed his arm from my shoulders and pointed to his left, giving me directions to Victoria Street. 'You okay now?'

I nodded, feeling like a gauche schoolgirl who'd overreacted. I lowered my hands from my chest and bent away from him to pick up my backpack. 'Thanks for your help.'

'I'm always happy to help a damsel in distress,' Alex said.

I braved looking at him.

He was sitting cockily on the bench, wearing a big smile. 'I don't suppose you need some more comforting.' He winked at me suggestively. 'I hear that touch is the best way of healing someone.' He caressed my arm.

'No, thank you,' I said primly and stood.

He stood up, and I had to lean my head back to look at him.

'Until next time, my lady.' He pressed a kiss against my hand. With a quick bow, he turned and walked away.

I watched the way the black t-shirt clung to his wide shoulders, while the skinny black jeans highlighted his thin waist and hips, cupping his cute butt. Realising I was ogling, I looked away. As I walked to Dad's work, I scanned the crowd, looking for Alex's brown hair.

I'd never had such a charged conversation with a boy. The last time I'd been in a Co-Ed School was when I was in primary school and that was one thing I'd been most nervous about. My previous interactions with a boy were at school mixers as we exchanged awkward small talk.

But Alex, well, Alex was a man. He was confident and cocky. He radiated masculinity. I'd had guys crack on to me before and it had been vaguely unpleasant and sordid, with lots of damp hand-holding and nervous eye-shifting. But with Alex, it had all been smooth and light. He'd made me feel good, and he'd given me something else to think about. I was sorry to arrive at Dad's medical centre and have to stop thinking about him.

When I walked inside, it was like coming home. Mum used to work with Dad in Hobart and I'd spent countless hours in the staff room, watching television and doing homework after school.

The waiting room was full and patients who chatted to each other in Bosnian. As Dad was one of the few doctors in the community, they travelled from all over the city to see him and his waiting room became a *de facto* community centre where they exchanged information about all matters Bosnian.

St Albans had a large population from former Yugoslavia that swelled even more after the Balkan war. As a result, Dad had no trouble getting a job and had his pick of medical centres vying for him because of his language skills.

The receptionist answered the constantly ringing phone, 'Victoria Street Medical Clinic,' only to continue speaking in Bosnian.

An elderly woman who was waiting for the receptionist saw me heading behind the desk to the staff room and hailed me. '*Ćija si ti*?' she asked.

'*Esad Omerović mi je Babo.*' I told her who my father was, bemused that the Bosnian way of eliciting parentage translated to *Whose child are you?*

The woman nodded, her curiosity satisfied, and I continued on my way.

I was doing my homework when Dad interrupted.

'Hello Pumpkin.' He sat on the chair opposite. 'How was your first day?'

As I told him about my teachers and classes, I was in heaven. This is what I'd dreamed about, Dad listening to me as if I mattered, but soon his attention waned.

'Did you see Sabiha?' he asked eagerly.

'We had some classes together,' I said.

He nodded, waiting to hear more. Seeing the hope in his eyes, I couldn't bear to disappoint him. 'But Sabiha was in the book club at lunchtime so we didn't have time to talk,' I lied.

'She likes to read?' Dad asked.

I nodded.

'Of course she does. She's her father's daughter.' He kissed me on the cheek. 'Maybe you should join the book club too,' he urged.

'Mmm,' I murmured noncommittally, not wanting to raise his suspicions about our less than enthusiastic reunion.

'I'd better get going.' Dad looked at his watch. 'Thank you,' he whispered, smoothing a hand through my hair.

I used to push him away, annoyed that he'd ruined my carefully prepared hairstyle, but now I put my hand on my scalp, trying to imprint the sensation of his touch on my skin.

I tried to persist with my homework after he left, but I couldn't think. I practiced what I'd tell Mum. She'd want to know all about my first day, and it was impossible to talk about it without mentioning Sabiha.

The receptionist came to the door. 'Your Mum is here. There's no parking spots, so she's waiting for you at the front.'

I collected my belongings and shoved them into my backpack, carrying it against my chest, the top unzipped and contents about to spill out. Mum was double parked. The esplanade was narrow and there was no way for the drivers behind to pass, so they were honking their horn.

I yanked open the back door and jumped in. Mum took off before I had the chance to tie my seatbelt, something she never did.

'This traffic is atrocious,' Mum muttered as she peered through the windscreen.

Ali was in the front seat, his eyes on his hand-held gamer.

Sanela leaned her head on my shoulder. 'I missed you. I haven't seen you since breakfast.' She made it sound as if it was a lifetime ago.

'I missed you too.' I kissed her head. 'Did you have fun today?'

'Heidi had her hair in piggy tails today.' Sanela pouted. 'Can you do my hair in piggy tails tomorrow?'

'You'll have to wake up earlier,' I told her.

When we got home, I yanked my backpack out of the car, forgetting I hadn't zipped it. My books spilled onto the ground.

'Clumsy.' Ali bent and helped me. 'All good today?'

'Kind of.' I looked at Mum, giving him a hint.

'Later,' he said and carried my books inside.

'How was your first day?' Mum threw out the question as an afterthought while we carried groceries from the car.

'Great.' I dumped the grocery bag and rifled through for refrigerated items to put in the fridge. 'I made some friends and had someone to hang with.'

'You'll have to tell me more during dinner.' Mum looked relieved.

I waited for more questions. Usually Mum would demand to know the name of my friends and what sort of students they were. Her motto was: your friends make you who you are. Mum opened a grocery bag and threw packaged boxes in the pantry. She looked frazzled, with dark circles under her eyes.

'Your hair.' I noticed Mum's hair was blonde. Her annual transformation from brunette to brown marked the season change from winter to summer.

'Yes.' Mum touched it self consciously. 'Better late than never.'

I smiled as I prepared sandwiches. Seeing Mum's hair made me feel hopeful, like things were returning to normal. I carried the sandwiches and glasses of milk into the living room.

'What's up?' Ali whispered, when Sanela was engrossed with *Play School* again.

'It's Sabiha's school,' I whispered back, keeping an ear out for Mum in the kitchen.

'For real?' Ali was surprised.

I nodded and swallowed a bite.

'The old man knows?' he asked.

I nodded again. 'He said he'd tell Mum.'

Ali looked sceptical. Dad was all over the place with his working hours at the practice. He didn't get home until late and hardly ever arrived home in time for dinner. After we ate Ali helped me take the plates and glasses to the kitchen. I washed the dishes as Mum pulled out pots and pans to begin dinner.

'Do you need help?' I asked.

'I'll help,' Sanela shouted from the living room. She loved measuring ingredients.

Mum smiled. 'It's okay, go do your homework,' she said as Sanela pushed her foot-stool against the bench top and clambered up.

I was walking to my room when Ali called me from the study. I came to the door, surprised he wanted me to come in. We each had a roster to use the family computer and he was usually possessive of his time.

'Come see this.' He waved at the computer screen.

He was on Sabiha's social media profile. 'How did you get in?' I'd tried to check her profile when we first found out about her, but was too scared to send a friend request.

'I friended her.' He pointed to my name.

I slapped his shoulder. He'd hacked into my account again. It surprised me she'd accepted my friend request, but maybe she was curious about us as we were about her. It lifted my spirits slightly.

'The two of you could be twins,' Ali joked as we read about her likes and dislikes. 'What is she like?' he asked, eyes on the screen.

'Tough.' I'd been struck by her complete lack of fearlessness.

'You mean she's butch?' Ali looked confused.

'No, I mean she doesn't care about what people think.' I was still awestruck at how she'd confronted me, not holding back any of her feelings.

'Of course she does.' Ali interrupted with a frown. 'Everyone cares about what other people think.'

I shared his confusion. Our parents brought us up in a glass bowl under the watchful eyes of the Hobart community. They always cautioned us to be good, to think about how other people perceived us, so it was a foreign concept to not care about other people's opinions.

'I mean, she's a smart arse.' I tried to capture into words Sabiha's *don't hold back* attitude.

'I don't want to see her.' Ali shut down Sabiha's profile with a quick flick of the mouse button and opened up a game, his signal that our conversation was over.

When his session was over, I opened Sabiha's profile again. It was scary how much we had in common. We liked the same TV shows, the same music, we even had quite a few favourite books in common. I wondered whether genetics were imprinted and there was only so much you could do to escape your fate.

Mum burst into the study without knocking. I hit the close icon on the computer screen, but I wasn't quick enough.

Her gaze sharpened. 'Let me see,' she demanded. Mum's rule was we could use the family computer as long as she had our email password and she randomly checked our browser history. I went to my browser history and opened Sabiha's profile, my breathing shallow as I waited to see if her sharp eyes would catch on those four words that would ruin my night.

Mum looked confused as she read it. 'Why are you looking at this?'

'I was curious.' I clicked the mouse to close the browser.

'Wait a minute.' Mum covered my hand. She zeroed in on the Info section of the profile where Sabiha's school was listed. 'She goes to St Albans High School?' Mum demanded.

Shit. I was done for when Dad came home.

'You saw her today,' she said, her voice low, like a rumbling earthquake.

'We're in the same class,' I whispered, wanting to get the worst out of the way.

'This is your father's doing,' Mum muttered and headed for the door.

I reluctantly closed the internet browser. I had thirty minutes left on the computer and had to prepare my schedule to track my assignment due dates. I deleted the old information from my previous school and input my new due dates, the act of creating order lulling me into calmness.

I heard Sanela's squeals and knew Dad was home. As I shut down the computer, my self-imposed calm faded and I was once again a bundle of nerves. I met Ali in the hallway and we exchanged a look. Dad was serious, after all, about telling Mum.

'Mum knows,' I warned Ali in a whisper as we walked to the living room.

'How?' he whispered back.

'Caught me on her social media profile,' I muttered.

'You're so clumsy.' He shook his head in disappointment.

I wanted to defend myself and explain that it wasn't my fault Mum snuck up on me like she did, but he walked past me like I was invisible. When we entered the living room, Sanela's arms were firmly around Dad's neck.

Mum was in the dining room setting the table. She didn't greet Dad, a sure sign she was holding a grudge.

'Thanks,' Ali muttered over Sanela's head. 'Dinner's going to be hell.'

Mum interrupted before I could reply. 'Hands clean,' she said briskly.

'Let's go wash up.' I led Sanela to the bathroom.

'I'm sitting next to Daddy,' Sanela insisted as she washed her hands.

'All right,' I agreed.

'And I want Mum next to me,' Sanela quickly claimed.

I nodded, relieved. Sitting between our parents' tonight would be like being stuck between two sumo wrestlers who were jostling for space.

We sat at the table, and Mum began serving. 'Aren't we going to wait for Daddy?' Sanela asked. The usual protocol was we didn't begin serving dinner until everyone was seated.

'He's coming.' Mum passed the serving dish to Ali.

Dad came in and saw the lay of the land with a glance. He glared at me.

Embarrassed, I looked away.

'What did you do today, Sanela?' he asked. Ali passed the dish to Dad without serving himself.

Sanela took that as her invitation to monopolise the conversation and talk all about her fairy painting that was drying at school. The rest of dinner passed in silence, with only Sanela chattering as she ate. Eventually the tension wore her down too and, by the end, she was playing with her food, pushing her fork into her mashed potatoes and smearing them on the plate.

'Stop playing with your food,' Mum snapped.

'I'm not hungry,' Sanela wailed, dropping the fork with a clank on the table.

Chapter 3

'Yes, you are. You won't be getting any food if you wake up tonight hungry.'

'Leave her alone,' Dad said quietly.

Mum's lips tightened in displeasure, and she didn't speak again. As soon as dinner finished, we pushed our chairs away from the table with relief. Mum retreated to the kitchen, clattering and banging emanating, as she washed the dishes and cleaned every surface and cupboard, her coping mechanism when she was angry.

Dad retreated to his home office and did his paperwork, a nightly ritual that meant that we hardly saw him, whether he was home or not. Ali went to his bedroom, and I did the same. When I returned to Sanela's bedroom to say goodnight, Mum was reading her a story. When Ali and I were small, it was Dad who read to us, putting all his energy into performing the unique characters and sound effects, making us shriek with laughter.

Most nights Mum used to come up too, and she'd sit on the edge of the bed and smile indulgently as she watched us, until eventually she had to call it quits because we kept asking for more books. I used to fall asleep with a smile, my stomach aching from laughter, and a feeling of comfort I could barely remember now.

I returned to my bedroom and read for a little while; before turning off my lamp and going to sleep. I was woken by loud voices. They were fighting again. I crept to my bedroom door and opened it a crack. My parents' bedroom was at the end of the hall and even though their door was closed, their loud voices boomed through the thin plywood and plaster walls.

Sanela's bedroom was right next to theirs. It was convenient for Mum when Sanela was having an unsettled night, but on nights like these when the house shook with their anger, she was the first one to be disturbed. As I crept through the hallway to Sanela's room, I heard my parents clearly.

'None of this would have happened if we didn't move here,' Mum shouted.

'Let it go,' Dad said. 'We're here now and we have to make the best of it.'

'That's easy for you to say when you've got the best of it,' Mum said.

When I walked into Sanela's bedroom, she was already stirring. I picked her up and shushed her.

'Who's yelling?' Sanela murmured sleepily.

'It's the neighbours,' I lied and carried her into the hallway.

Ali was standing in his doorway. I followed him into his bedroom. It was at the opposite end of the hall and the furthest from our parents' bedroom. He'd already pulled out the trundle bed and put bedding on it. I lay down with Sanela in my arms, carefully tucking the doona around us. Ali turned on his iPod, leaving the music low so it muted the shouting.

'This is all her fault,' he said in a vicious whisper. 'Before we found out about her, they never fought.'

'It's not her fault that she exists.' I used to feel the same way before I met Sabiha, but now when I remembered her shell-shocked expression, I felt like I was looking at a mirror. I wondered if she was lying in her bed, staring at the ceiling, feeling like she was being split in two like me.

'You're taking her side,' Ali yelled.

I shushed him and rocked Sanela to soothe her. 'I'm not taking her side. I'm saying it's not her fault. She didn't ask for any of this either,' I whispered.

'Have fun with your new sister tomorrow,' he bitched and turned on his side, making the bed bounce.

As I listened to my parents arguing, I wanted to run into the bedroom and shout 'Stop please, Mummy and Daddy,' the way I used to when I was little. I thought I had a magic touch because they'd instantly stop, hug and kiss each other to prove they were okay, before picking me up and squashing me between them.

I'd tried it once with Sanela while we were still living in Hobart. Ali and I'd hid in the hallway and waited for Sanela to jump out and yell out for them to please stop fighting. Our parents became quiet, and I'd thought that it worked, but then Mum called out my name.

'Take your sister to her room and play with her please,' Mum said, holding Sanela's hand.

Mum wouldn't meet my eyes. That was when I realised that the problems between them weren't something that would go away with a kiss and a cuddle. These were mammoth arguments, the sort of arguments that tore a family apart.

The house was quiet. They had stopped arguing. I stood and collected Sanela. Ali sat up and yanked the doona from the trundle and threw it on his foot post, before using his foot to push the trundle back under his bed.

By the time I reached the door, he'd turned on his side and was asleep again. After I returned Sanela back to her bed, I was wide awake and feeling peckish. The door across the hallway was open again.

I stepped forward and tugged it closed, averting my eyes. Behind the closed door was the same white Princess bedroom suite as in my bedroom, arranged in exactly the same order like a freaky alternate reality. The empty bedroom remained pristine, perfect and untouched as it waited for its Princess to come and claim it. I prayed that day would never come.

I headed down the stairs and into the kitchen and was about to open the fridge when I heard snoring. I tiptoed into the living room and found Dad sleeping on the couch. This wasn't good. In the morning, he'd pretend he was watching an overseas soccer or basketball match and fell asleep during the night, an excuse I'd seen through a while ago.

He slept on the uncomfortable couch, rather than the brand-new, never-been-slept-in-bed that was upstairs. Even when Mum's family visited from Hobart, he'd insisted that I sleep in Sanela's bedroom so they could have my bed. It was like he was keeping it preserved for the night that Sabiha would decide to sleep over and didn't want to sully this possibility by re-purposing the bedroom.

I returned up the stairs. It had infuriated me every time I found the bedroom door opened, thinking Sanela was playing inside, until the day I found Dad standing in the open doorway. As I returned to bed, I wondered what he was thinking about as he viewed the empty room.

Was he imagining Sabiha sitting there with him? The conversations they would have as they bridged the years they'd missed out on each other's lives? I wiped a tear and stared at the ceiling, trying to fall asleep again.

***

The next morning, I was at the kitchen table when Dad walked in with his briefcase in hand.

'Let's go,' Dad commanded as I ate my toast for breakfast.

'But I have to say goodbye to Sanela,' I said, still feeling hungry.

Dad left the kitchen without replying. I looked at Mum, who shrugged her shoulders helplessly.

'You'd better go,' Mum said with a sigh. There were dark circles under her eyes again, witness to a sleepless night.

We were all subdued this morning after last night's big fight. Even Sanela sensed the tension and retreated to her bedroom before school, giving up watching her morning cartoons on television.

Mum handed me my lunch. 'Have a good day.' She kissed me on the cheek, barely touching her lips to my skin, before turning back to the dishes in the sink.

I followed Dad to the car. As he reversed from the driveway, Sanela ran out. I forced a smile and waved through the windshield. Sanela's hands were formed into fists, her little body stiff as she cried. As we drove I glanced at Dad and saw he was holding back his anger.

'I made one simple request,' Dad said when we stopped at a traffic light.

'I didn't—'

He put his finger up, showing he wanted me to be quiet. 'All I asked from you was that you let me be the one to tell your mother about Sabiha.'

'She saw on—'

He put his finger back up, and I bit back the words trying to escape my throat.

'I should know better than to get between mother and daughter.'

My appetite faded and I looked out the window to hide my leaking eyes.

Dad pulled up into the medical centre car park. 'You can walk from here.' He walked to the door without a backward glance.

I walked to school, feeling off-kilter. The whole day turned to shit before I had a chance to greet it. I looked at my wrist and realised I'd forgotten my watch.

The main street in St Albans was deserted and all the shops closed. It was like I was the last person on earth. Everything looked innocuous, with strips of sunshine decorating the footpath. If this was a horror movie, zombies would come out and start nibbling on my flesh.

The first two periods I was with Sabiha and her friends, but sat at the back of class and remained on the down-low. I spent the day like the invisible girl. When I saw Sabiha in class or in the corridors, she pretended like I wasn't there and her friends followed her lead, except for the blonde boy. He always looked at me with regret, even mustering a smile once or twice.

I told Mum I had to do research at the library and avoided seeing Dad at the medical centre after school. I didn't want to face his questioning eyes and have to tell him the truth, that Sabiha was shutting me out just as she did him. Over the next two days, I hung out at the library during lunchtime and began making friends with the chess team.

Who knows how long the standoff would have continued if it wasn't for Alex Payne and his sparkling smile? It was lunchtime on Friday and I was swapping my books at my locker when I saw Alex walking toward me.

His blue eyes lit up with pleasure. 'How's my favourite new girl?' he asked with a grin.

'I'm good.' I grinned back, glad that there were students around watching me having a conversation with a cute guy.

'What'cha doing now?' He put his arm on the wall above my head.

I leaned my back against the wall, butterflies jumping in my stomach at his proximity. 'Going to the library.' I held up my book bag.

'What'cha gonna do that for?' He took the bag and tossed it in my open locker. 'Let's enjoy some sunshine.'

My new friends were waiting for me, but my feet had a mind of their own and followed Alex. He put his arm around my shoulders and led me outside. I saw Dina nudging Sabiha. They watched me leaving with Alex, looking confused. I was like one of the cool girls in TV shows with the high school jock on my arm bringing me instant status and popularity.

As we walked, Alex peppered me with questions about where I was from. I blossomed under his attention. There were pounding footsteps behind us and someone called my name. I turned to see Sabiha and Dina running to catch up with us.

'Where are you off to?' Dina asked, looking suspiciously from Alex to me.

'We're just walking,' I muttered, wondering why she suddenly cared.

'That's right,' Alex said languidly. 'We're enjoying the sunshine.'

With his arms around my shoulders, he went to step around Sabiha and Dina.

'Off school grounds?' Dina demanded, while Sabiha stood beside her, her eyes on the ground like she didn't know where to look.

We were at the side school gate that led to a pedestrian street. I had been caught up in the thrall of Alex's attention that I hadn't noticed where we were headed.

'If you get caught, you'll be in trouble,' Dina said.

I stopped walking. I couldn't get into trouble again. Dad was barely speaking to me now.

'Anyway, I owe you a tour of the school.' Dina stepped forward and took my hand, tugging me away from Alex.

'What's with the intervention?' Alex demanded. 'You jealous?'

'As if,' Dina shot off. 'She's Sabiha's—'

'She's my relative,' Sabiha cut in before she finished the sentence, finally looking up and joining in.

Alex looked at me with surprise. 'Relative?' he asked.

I said nothing.

'We'll finish our walk another time.' He grinned again and kissed my hand before he sauntered off.

'What were you doing with him?' Dina demanded. 'He's the biggest sleaze-bag in school.'

'He helped me on Monday,' I muttered, thick-headed with confusion. 'What do you care?' I asked.

'He was probably taking you to Blow Job Lane,' Dina said.

'What is Blow Job Lane?' I demanded, my voice breaking.

'It's pretty self explanatory,' Sabiha said wryly, barely glancing in my direction. 'And Alex is the one who coined the term.'

I looked at Alex as he walked off. Was it true? Did he really have such bad intentions? I couldn't wrap my head around the fact that the guy who was so sweet to me yesterday could be such a sleaze-bag. I turned to Dina to ask more questions, when her next words stopped me in my tracks.

'Shit, that was a close call,' Dina said, wiping her forehead. 'If you got involved with him Mum would kill me.'

The penny dropped. They didn't really care about me at all. Dina was just covering her arse.

I was about to leave, when Sabiha's other friends joined us.

'So we're welcoming the prodigal sister into the fold,' the brown-haired boy said. 'Introductions are in order. I'm Brian.' He offered his hand. He looked like he was impersonating a hobo. His hair hadn't seen a comb in a week and his clothes were creased like he wore them to bed.

I automatically shook hands with him.

'This is Jesse.' He jerked his head to the blonde-haired guy wearing daggy jeans, and a worn out t-shirt.

'And I believe you know Dina.'

I gave Dina a dirty look, still sore that she'd ignored me after our mothers hatched a plan for her to show me around. Dina looked at me with puppy dog brown eyes. She had gold jewellery dangling from almost every part of her body, and shimmered in the sun. I wanted to turn the topic back to Alex and find out what they had against him, but didn't get a chance.

'You're Sabiha's little sister.' Brian eyed me as if I was an interesting fossil specimen.

'Step sister,' Sabiha snapped.

'Half sister,' I corrected. I did a lot of thinking on the subject. It was important to have the correct label for such a situation because I'd be expected to explain it a lot. 'Same father, different mothers.'

'We're not real sisters, though,' Sabiha said, scoring the first point.

'Of course not,' I replied calmly. 'I already have one of each and don't need anymore.' I enjoyed seeing Sabiha's surprise.

'Burn,' Brian interrupted before Sabiha rallied. 'I see the bitchy gene is hereditary.'

'Shut up.' Sabiha pushed him.

Brian dropped his diary, and I automatically bent to pick it up. I paused with an outreached hand when I saw the collage of male movie stars on his cover, most of them bare-chested with their pecs glistening. I slowly handed the diary to Brian.

'As you can see I'm partial to blondes,' Brian hammed it up, lisping slightly, confirming my half formed suspicion.

I forced a smile. I'd never known anyone who was gay. A squirmy, uncomfortable feeling squatted in my stomach like I'd witnessed someone picking their nose and didn't know whether I should acknowledge what I saw, or pretend it never happened.

Sabiha and her friends began walking.

'Are you coming?' Brian asked.

Sabiha slowed her steps, waiting for my answer.

'I've got things to do,' I said.

'Nonsense,' Jesse spoke for the first time. 'We'd be delighted for you to join us.'

I waited to see if Sabiha would protest.

'Hurry up, I'm starving,' she snapped over her shoulder.

I guessed that was as good an invitation as I would get. I hesitated, unsure whether I wanted to be a charity case, but in the end my curiosity cinched it. I had to know more about my other sister.

'We'll give you a tour of the school,' Dina said.

We walked through the school grounds and they pointed out buildings. There was an awkward silence between Dina's commentary, as if no one could think of what to say.

'I thought they enrolled you at Searers College?' Dina asked.

'I was,' I replied. I'd been practicing my response to this question. 'But my parents decided it wasn't the right environment for me. They thought I needed more academic opportunities.' I breathed a sigh of relief. I'd infused my answer with the right amount of carelessness to forestall future questions.

Dina looked confused. 'I thought they expelled you,' she blurted out.

'Um, well—' I stuttered. I'd desperately been trying to avoid this. I was embarrassed that they had expelled me, especially under the circumstances. I'd always been the student that teachers pointed to as an exemplary role model, yet somehow I'd gotten caught up in a perfect storm and been tipped out of my school. 'Yes, I was,' I admitted, my cheeks flushed.

'Way to go,' Brian said, putting his arm around my shoulders.

'But it's not a bad thing,' Dina protested. 'See.' She reached into her backpack and pulled out a newspaper article.

I looked away. I hated that article and everything it represented. Everyone huddled around it while I stared off in the distance. After they read it they all looked at me differently, like I did something amazing.

The only person who was unimpressed was Sabiha. 'Ever heard of the saying, "don't shit where you eat,"' she said deadpan.

'I didn't think you were the type of person who'd side with the uneducated masses,' Jesse said.

'I'm not,' Sabiha looked flustered. 'But sometimes you have to pick your battles.'

'And sometimes you have to stand for something.' Jesse shrugged.

As they went for it, I was a little uneasy. I hated causing friction. 'I didn't do it alone,' I interrupted. 'A friend helped.' I was stretching the truth, but it did the trick. The tension between Sabiha and Jesse dissipated.

'Of course you did,' Sabiha said. 'You don't look like the type who could do anything alone.'

I gasped.

'What?' Sabiha snapped when her friends turned accusatory looks toward her. She stormed off in a fury.

'Sorry,' Dina muttered and went to catch up with her.

'Don't worry,' Jesse said, putting his hand on my shoulder. 'She'll come around. After all, you are sisters.'

I forced a smile and nodded, even though I didn't believe him. While we were both curious about each other, spending time together was uncomfortable and fraught with tension.

As I continued walking through the school grounds with Brian and Jesse, I wondered what they would think if they knew the true story, the story I'd told no one.

Chapter 4

It began as a joke during media studies. Our assignment by Mr Roberts was to write a letter to the editor responding to an article in the newspaper. I was scanning the newspaper, while my friend Isabella was diligently typing her letter.

Isabella's mother was a CEO of a refugee centre and she was super socially conscious. Even though submitting the letter was optional, she was working on her second letter about the need for better public transport infrastructure in the Western suburbs in response to a tunnel being built.

Mr Roberts was having a conversation with Julia, the class suck up, who was on the computer directly opposite me.

'I want to write about the French government banning the Burka,' Julia said.

'What do you want to say?' Mr Roberts asked.

'That we should do the same thing here,' Julia said. 'Those poor women shouldn't be forced to look like that.'

'Yes, but the article you're referencing is about the Burka being banned because of possible terrorist threats,' Mr Roberts said.

'Did you hear that?' Isabella hissed.

I nodded, not looking up from the newspaper. Ever since she found I was Muslim, Isabella kept going on about the anti-Muslim sentiment. You'd think she was the Muslim.

'He so supports the ban on the *Burka* which is against the rules,' Isabella said. She was also very committed to fairness and following the rules. Last week she'd completed a whole diatribe about people not following the rules when using the school computers and booking them properly. She'd written a letter to the Principal and school librarian and then had follow-up meetings about implementing a proper system.

'What rules?' I asked, not really caring but knowing from long experience that if I didn't indulge her, Isabella would have a go at me about my "supposed" apathy and middle class complacency.

'It's against the rules of teaching. This is supposed to be an exercise in us developing our social conscience in addressing issues we're passionate about. It's not for him to influence who writes about what and how.'

I nodded, even though I thought Mr Roberts was just doing his job in directing Julia to address the assignment, but of course I didn't say that. Isabella acted like any contradictory opinion was a personal betrayal. As she was my only friend at school, I'd learnt to silently agree.

'I'll prove it to you.' Isabella put her hand up. 'I want to write about the *Burka* issue and that it's wrong that they discriminate against Muslim women. Isn't it like against Human Rights or something?'

'Which article are you referencing?' Mr Roberts asked. He scanned the article Isabella was pointing. I looked at it too and saw it was about Muslim women being empowered by wearing the *Hijab*.

'It's a bit of a reach since the *Hijab* and *Burka* are two different things,' Mr Roberts said.

Isabella nodded in agreement and waited until he shuffled off to help another student who raised his hand. 'See.' Isabella was triumphant. 'He is anti-Muslim.'

'No, he's not—'

I was going to tell her the difference between the *Hijab;* the head covering that Muslim women wore, and the *Burka*, which covered a woman's face, but Isabella interrupted me.

'Are you deaf?' Isabella was outraged. 'He wants letters written that support the anti-Muslim sentiment. I'd think you of all people should care. After all it's your people that are being attacked, but if you can't be bothered...'

Isabella turned back to her computer monitor.

I wanted to tell her to take a chill pill and get her facts straight before she launched into conspiracy theories, but if I did, I'd get the silent treatment.

'I think I will write that letter.' I had no intention of submitting the letter as my assignment as I typed it, parroting Isabella's sentences about schools needing to be places for students to develop their social conscience and not be indoctrinated into racism by teachers.

'Good girl,' Isabella patronised. 'Make sure that you include a line about Australia supposedly supporting religious freedom. Here's the newspaper email address.' Isabella flicked open her sent email after she read my letter.

'I'm not going to send it.' I saved my document and removed the memory stick from the computer.

'Why not? I thought you'd want to stand up for your sisterhood.' Isabella narrowed her gaze.

'I want to proofread it again,' I evaded, as I put the memory stick in my pencil case. 'I put my hand up and asked to use the toilet.

When I finished in the toilet, I dawdled as I looked at my watch. I vowed that tomorrow I'd try to make more friends, but it was hard. Everyone in the new school knew each other from primary school. Cliques were firmly entrenched and hard to penetrate. The only reason Isabella took me on as a friend was because she prided herself on her tolerance and the diversity in her friendship clique proved her open-mindedness.

I returned to class thirty seconds before the bell went. I was packing up when I noticed my pencil case was missing.

'Sorry, I had to borrow a pen.' Isabella smiled sweetly and passed it to me.

It wasn't until I was called into the Principal's office the following week I found out Isabella hacked into my email account and sent the letter without my permission, after editing it to include Mr Roberts name as the racist teacher. Naively, I kept Isabella's role a secret, thinking I needed to maintain the friendship.

The school didn't expel me immediately. First, they suspended me as punishment and only after I'd left they sent a letter advising my parents that Searers College wasn't the right environment for me. Dad tried to convince them otherwise, only to find out that a private school had final say in whom they accepted within their hallowed halls and they deemed me not suitable.

***

Now, as the St Albans High school bell rang heralding the end of the day, I ran to the toilets and remained there for ten minutes, ensuring that enough time passed for Sabiha and her friends to leave the school grounds. I'd had enough of the weird vibes that came with being around her and was relieved it was the weekend, so I'd have a reprieve. I vowed that on Monday I'd return to the library and renew my friendship with the chess nerds.

I was at home on the internet when I received a pop-up message. Intrigued, I opened it.

Dina's face popped up on my screen, live and smiley.

'Hi,' she called out.

'Hi,' I said, feeling ambushed. I hadn't really thought through the implications of opening her message and was regretting my impulsive click of the mouse.

'I'm just checking in to see how you're doing,' Dina said.

'I'm good. Everything's good,' I repeated, rushing to fill in the awkward pause and then feeling gauche.

'Oh, good,' Dina said, her face becoming red when she realised she was repeating the same word as me. 'So how are you going with your English essay?' She launched into a monologue about her struggle with the topic while I half listened, trying to find a graceful way to end the conversation.

'Great,' I said when she paused for breath. 'Listen—'

'I'll be seeing you soon,' Dina jumped in before I could end our conversation. 'My parents are planning to visit you tomorrow.'

'Oh,' I said. 'And I'm guessing you want me to tell your mum that you've been helping me out at school,' realising that was the only reason she called me.

Dina's face took on a look of consternation.

The study door behind me opened. 'Who are you talking to?' Mum demanded, walking in with a tea towel in her hands.

'It's Dina,' I said, pushing my chair away from the desk so she could see the screen.

Dina waved at Mum.

Mum leaned over me, her hands on my shoulders so she was visible. 'Thank you for helping Alma settle into her new school,' she spoke in Bosnian.

'No problems,' Dina said, shifting uncomfortably in her chair.

'As you know, she's had a lot to deal with these past few months and it's such a relief that she has one good friend in you.'

Dina smiled queasily.

'Anyway, I'll leave you girls to it.' Mum squeezed my shoulders.

There was a pause after mum left as we waited for the other to speak.

'Anyway, I'd better get going,' I said.

'Okay,' Dina sighed with relief. 'See you later.'

I flicked the screen closed and glared at my computer monitor. I was so angry that she'd called and brought back all the crap feelings from today. As I brooded, I heard voices coming from my headphones. I closed my browser, thinking that a clip was playing from the website I'd been looking at, but I still heard the voices.

A shiver went through me when I realised it was Dina and Brian speaking. I must have turned off the camera so she couldn't see me, but our line was still open and I had audio from her computer. I went to shut down the conference call browser, but when I heard my name and my index finger froze in midair on the mouse.

'I was just talking to Alma,' Dina said.

'So did you neutralise her?' Brian asked.

'Don't be a bitch,' she snapped.

'Anyway, that's not why I called. I have something to tell you,' his voice muted.

'Oh, Brian, what did you do?' Dina sighed.

'I didn't think it would be a big deal,' Brian said. 'I was just going to go stand on the sidelines and watch him play.'

I knew I should click my mouse button and stop eavesdropping, but the itch of curiosity overwhelmed me and my hand moved off the mouse as I listened to Brian's story.

'You should have seen him, Dina,' Brian said. 'He looked like David Beckham, with his torso bare and his washboard stomach glistening from sweat as he effortlessly swatted the ball.'

I'd missed his ex-boyfriend's name and kept picturing David Beckham's face in the role.

Brian's voice was full of painful yearning as he described the way the Beckham look-alike played soccer, as if he were the transistor radio and everyone else was on his frequency, feeling his commands like little bursts of energy.

As Brian watched the object of his affection, his whole body twitched as he fought to control himself from running out onto the field. Brian soon realised that Beckham was just as aware of him. Every time he looked at his phone and sent a text message, Beckham performed tricks and made himself the centre of attention.

Beckham began sneaking glances at Brian. It became like a macabre play of stolen, longing glances being played out where Brian looked at Beckham. Beckham turned away. Beckham looked at Brian, and Brian looked at his mobile.

It became inevitable that there would come a moment when they both looked at each other, a moment when their eyes would meet, and Brian began feeling a sense of anticipation. He knew that when they looked into each other's eyes, he would see if his ex was over him, or if he still wanted him back.

But then the soccer ball rolled to a stop at Brian's feet. It was serendipity. Beckham hit a header that bounced off a player's shoulder. The ball rebounded, and another player kicked it toward the goal. The opposition goalkeeper went to catch it, but the ball deflected off his hand and hit a rubbish bin, before it rolled to a stop at Brian's right foot, inviting him to swing his leg and shoot it straight at Beckham, who was facing him.

Brian looked down at the ball and then his eyes travelled the three metres to look up at Beckham. When they looked at each other, he didn't know what to expect. He knew what he didn't expect. He didn't expect Beckham to show fear for a split second before a curtain of indifference descended.

Brian waited. In the movies, this would be the hero moment. Brian would kick a perfect pass and the ball would fly in a beautiful arc and land in front of Beckham, rolling toward his foot so that all he needed to do was leisurely swing his leg and shoot it toward the goal while it was in motion, catching the opposition goal keeper off guard and rolling it into the net.

Beckham's teammates would huddle into a scrum, jumping and shouting for all to see. They'd pull Brian in to join them and when they stopped celebrating, he would be a member of the team and there would be no more need for their forbidden love to play out.

It took Brian a moment to process the reality of what actually happened. While he was swinging back to kick, Beckham moved. Brian jerked, trying to halt the kick, but his foot glanced off the side sending it jumping like a rock across a millpond, skimming the surface before it stuttered to a stop next to an opposition team player who ran the ball down and scored a goal.

Beckham's teammates huddled together. Beckham muttered something under his breath and they all laughed.

'Thanks fag,' a player shouted, looking over at Brian. The rest of the team laughed, Beckham's booming laugh drowning out everyone else.

Brian was crying when he finished telling his story.

'It's okay,' Dina soothed through her computer monitor.

'You should have seen how he looked at me,' Brian said, his voice barely audible. 'It's like I'm dead, but my body doesn't know it.'

'You know he loves one person and one person only. Himself,' Dina said.

'But he loved me.' Brian's voice was full of pain. 'I know he loved me.'

'Maybe he did,' Dina said gently. 'But once there was the chance the truth would come out about him, he wasn't going to risk his whole life. You know how it is for ethnic boys.'

'Fuck,' Brian cried. 'Why did she have to walk in on us?'

'It's not Sabiha's fault,' Dina said.

My ears sharpened. How was Sabiha responsible for Brian's relationship breaking up? I could understand the pressure a gay ethnic boy would feel to keep his secret hidden. All I had to do was imagine how my parents would react if a son of theirs was gay; the worry about the gossip in the community, the social standing, the religious backlash, and I knew why the Beckham Look-alike was determined to stay in the closet.

But what I couldn't understand was what role Sabiha played in the breakup and why did Brian blame her? I knew that I probably wouldn't get the answer to any of my questions, but at least I found out something important about my sister. She wasn't someone who could be trusted with the truth.

After Brian and Dina finished, I closed my browser and left the study, all the different things I'd heard winding around my head like a strange soundtrack.

On Monday, I entered the school grounds slowly, a mantle of guilt weighing me down after Dina's visit on the weekend. When she finished her conversation with Brian, our dialog box had popped up, showing we'd had a 40 minute video chat and she'd realised I'd been eavesdropping on her conversation with Brian.

'You can't tell anyone about Brian's ex,' Dina had begged me while we were in the kitchen preparing coffee to serve our parents.

I was counting spoons of ground coffee into the *džezva*, coffee pot, and couldn't answer immediately.

'I've got nothing to tell,' I'd said, not able to look her in the eyes as I poured water into the *džezva* and placed it on the stovetop.

She'd gone quiet for too long and I finally worked up the courage to look at her. Her face had a questioning look, like she was too scared to believe me.

'I hope that's true,' she said. 'Because if the secret gets out, a lot of lives will be ruined, including Sabiha's.'

I turned back to the coffeepot just in time. The thick black coffee was frothing and about to spill over.

'I have no interest in ruining anyone, and that includes Sabiha,' I snapped between gritted teeth.

Dina placed the small *džezva* of boiled milk and a glass bowl of square sugar cubes on the large metal tray.

As Dina walked to the cabinet to collect *fildžani*, the small demitasse cups to serve coffee in, I cursed my curiosity in not ending the video call. I carried the tray into the living room and placed it on the coffee table.

'You and Dina can go to your room,' Mum said, as she began pouring coffee.

It was the last thing I wanted, but Mum wouldn't be able to understand my reluctance. Usually, I was desperate and eager to spend time alone with my girlfriends.

By the time Dina collected her handbag, her mother had finished drinking her first *fildžan* of coffee.

'Do a reading for me,' she asked my mother in Bosnian.

Mum was known as kind of psychic because of the accuracy of her readings, something she'd learnt from her mother in the village that she came from in Bosnia.

Mum eagerly picked it up and grimaced as she looked at the sludge at the bottom of the cup. 'Ruin awaits your family,' she said.

Dina looked at me with eyes white with fear, while a feeling of dread settled in my stomach.

'Can I come?' Sanela asked as we began walking up the stairs.

'Of course,' I called out, eager to have a buffer between Dina and I.

After Dina left, I'd spent the weekend feeling a heavy weight pressing down on my chest. Dina's fervent pleas had filled me with fear that I could somehow cause a catastrophic chain of events if I was indiscreet, and now as I walked to school to see Brian and Dina in real life, I wanted to be anywhere but here.

My plan was to avoid the lot of them and renew my friendships with the chess club in the library, but as soon as I began walking across the front lawn of the school, Dina waved me down.

'You're here early,' I said, shuffling my feet nervously as I looked behind her.

'Don't worry, I'm alone,' she said wryly. 'I just wanted to tell you that no one else knows what happened and I want it to stay that way. Everyone would just freak out if they knew.'

'Like I said, I know nothing,' I repeated.

Dina nodded, but didn't reply.

'Anyway, I'll see you later.' I began walking away.

'Where are you going?' she asked. She patted the bench beside her, the look on her face not inviting any arguments.

Chapter 5

I looked longingly at the library. All I had to do was keep walking. Keep as far away from her, and Brian and Sabiha. Try to forget they existed, but I couldn't. I felt shaken up after the weekend and it was just easier to go with the flow. I slid across the bench and sat beside Dina.

'What about Sabiha?' I asked, remembering her tantrum from Friday. I didn't think she would be too eager to welcome me into the fold.

'I've already spoken to her and she's okay with you joining us,' Dina said, not looking at me.

I opened my mouth to ask what changed her mind when I saw Sabiha walking toward us. As she approached I tensed my muscles to prepare for a confrontation.

'Hello,' Sabiha muttered sullenly as she clambered up on the bench beside me.

I looked at Dina in surprise, but she just gave me a blank look.

'Hi,' I replied, my voice barely clearing my throat.

The two of them talked while I stood on the sidelines, feeling like a third wheel. I saw Brian and Jesse appear at the school gates, and as they approached, I examined Jesse closer. He looked nothing like the guy I saw last week.

Dina and Sabiha noticed them too, and their conversation sputtered to an abrupt halt.

'Jesse?' Sabiha said questioningly when he was near us.

Jesse looked like a catalogue model with hair product glistening in his hair, brand new jeans and a white t-shirt that skimmed over his defined pecs. I didn't realise how toned he was until he was wearing fitted clothes, and by Sabiha's awestruck look, I wasn't the only one.

'What's going on?' Sabiha asked.

'Do you like?' Brian almost danced on tip-toes. 'I did a makeover,' he screeched.

Jesse looked bashful, his cheeks pink with all the attention.

'Tell them.' Brian slapped his shoulder.

Jesse took a deep breath. 'My book is getting published.'

His announcement dropped to the ground like a lead balloon.

'Wow, congratulations.' I jumped into the silence after it stretched out too long.

'What book?' Sabiha demanded.

'I've been writing a graphic novel with my friend, Charlie. You know, the artist. Anyway, we met a publisher at a Writers Centre event and he requested we submit and...' he held his hands up.

'I didn't know you were writing a book,' Sabiha snapped.

'We weren't exactly on speaking terms,' Jesse replied softly.

Sabiha looked away, blinking rapidly.

'That's amazing news.' Dina pushed past Sabiha to hug Jesse.

'That's my boy.' Brian slapped him on the arm. 'Tell them the plot.'

Jesse told us about the comic book plot and Sabiha oohed and aahed at the appropriate moments, her waspishness gone.

Brian and Dina separated and began talking to each other about their favourite music and exchanging the CDs they'd burnt. Jesse, Sabiha and I stood awkwardly for a moment, not knowing what to say to each other.

'I didn't have time to talk to you about your article the other day,' Jesse said. 'You're a talented writer. Maybe we can exchange work. Do you write fiction?'

'Um, no, not really.' I flashed to my diary where I wrote about my life like it was a novel.

'You're obviously talented. Isn't she Sabiha?'

'I guess,' Sabiha said grudgingly.

'Writing talent runs in the family,' Jesse said.

Sabiha and I looked at each other with identical looks of scorn. Sabiha turned away and looked at Jesse with yearning in her eyes. 'So, when can I read your masterpiece?'

'I'll email it to you,' Jesse said.

'Great.' Sabiha's smile lit up St Albans like a second sun.

'I'll email you a copy too, Alma,' Jesse said.

Sabiha's smile curdled on her face.

'Have you always wanted to write?' I asked Jesse, eager to change the subject.

He nodded. 'Ever since I can remember. What about you? What do you want to be when you grow up?'

'A lawyer.' I gave my rote answer. I don't know if it was my dream or the one my parents picked for me, but it was what I'd been groomed for since I could remember.

'Really.' Jesse frowned. 'Surprising. What's your passion?'

I paused. If I was to answer honestly, I had none, apart from maintaining my perfect academic record. 'I guess reading,' I finally answered.

'I knew it.' Jesse smiled. 'A love of reading is the first symptom of being a writer.'

Sabiha looked sour. The locker bell rang and gave me a lucky escape.

'What have you got next?' Jesse asked when he saw me examining the timetable at my locker.

'Home Ec.' I looked at the map in my diary.

'I'm going that way.' Jesse gestured for me to go ahead through the crowd. 'Sabiha can come across strong, but she has a soft side,' Jesse continued when we got out onto the walkway.

'I hope you're right.' School was my oasis from everything that was going on at home. I couldn't deal with another battle-front.

'I am. It's been hard on her for the past few months. Suddenly having a father and finding out about this whole other family.'

My eyes stung and I blinked rapidly.

'But I'm sure it hasn't been easy on you either. I'm sorry.' His voice was full of horror.

'It's okay.' I leaned my head forward so my hair shielded my face, but I couldn't do much about my chocked up voice.

'No, it's not.' Jesse put an arm on my shoulder and stepped in front of me. 'Sabiha wants to get to know you. She's just scared about opening herself up. Give her time.'

I bit the inside of my lip until I tasted blood. My eyes cleared, and I flashed my practiced public smile. 'I'm sure you're right. I'd better hurry to class.'

He nodded in relief and stepped to my side. 'It's through those doors and to the left.' He pointed.

'Thanks.' I sped up. When I was safely inside, I relaxed my tense muscles. I had to be more careful about letting my guard down.

It was a relief to spend a double period focusing only on using the correct measuring device for dry and wet ingredients. When the bell rang, I was like a gladiator going back to battle.

As I was getting lunch from my locker, I saw Sabiha finger Brian's wrinkled shirt between her fingertips, her mouth formed into a moue of disgust.

'You used to be the guy who'd change outfits when you had a wrinkle. Now look at you! How long are you going to be impersonating a homeless person?' Sabiha asked.

'As long as you do your lesbian look.' Brian eyed her combat boots.

'Leave him alone.' Dina put her arms around his shoulders. 'He's going through a rough time.'

'So are you,' Sabiha said tartly, 'but you still comb your hair.'

'Better put the girls out on display.' Brian looked meaning-fully from Sabiha's cleavage to Jesse's approach.

Sabiha punched Brian's arm.

Jesse smiled when he reached us, and Sabiha developed a sudden interest in searching through her locker.

'I'll see you guys later.' Jesse waved to a guy across the hallway. 'Charlie and I have to do some revision.'

Sabiha watched him walk away, her face full of disappoint-ment.

My last period I was with Dina, sans Sabiha, and I was grate-ful for the distance. My attention kept wandering from the les-son as I remembered I'd have to give Dad a report tonight. So far I'd avoided talking about Sabiha because of all my "homework," and by drip feeding him a few details here and there, but I knew he would be no longer satisfied.

Tonight he'd want to have a proper chat, and I didn't know what to tell him. I knew I had to gloss over the parts he wouldn't like: Boys who are friends, Sabiha's "take no prisoners attitude," but it didn't leave me with a lot to share.

Dina was doodling "Tony" in her notebook. She closed the cover when she saw me looking. 'My ex,' she muttered and eyed the whiteboard.

I looked back out the window and was relieved when the bell rang.

'Is someone picking you up?' Dina asked as we packed up.

I shook my head. 'I'm walking to my dad's medical centre to wait for Mum.' I purposely dropped my pencil, hoping Dina would hurry and leave.

Instead, Dina bent and picked up the pencil. 'Sabiha and I walk that way.'

I followed her to the lockers, feeling trapped. I didn't want Sabiha to come with me to Dad's, but I didn't know how to get out of it. By the time we stopped off at the library for Sabiha to return some schoolbooks, the crowd thinned. As we walked out of the school, a car shadowed us.

'What if he wants to kidnap us?' I looked around fearfully for an adult. Mum warned me St Albans was dangerous, and that I had to walk from school to Dad's medical centre and nowhere else.

'It's probably some perv with a schoolgirl fantasy. As soon as we confront him, he'll run off.' Sabiha walked to the car and tapped on the window. The window wound down and Sabiha jumped back. I had to fight my feet from running off.

The driver leaned over the passenger seat. 'Don't I get a kiss?'

Dina squealed and ran to the driver's side. The driver stepped out, and they embraced, their bodies meshed against each other.

'Wow, they're really hot for each other,' I muttered, assuming this was the mysterious Tony. It was always awkward watching two people getting it on. I didn't know whether to keep looking or look away.

'Yuck,' Sabiha said. 'That's her brother, Omer.' She stepped forward and shook hands with him.

I blushed. When I looked closer, I saw the striking resemblance. They had the same hair and eyes, and Omer's features were a masculine version of Dina. I was walking away when Dina called me.

'This is Sabiha's little sister Alma,' Dina introduced me.

I nodded and forced a queasy smile. For years, I'd been the older sister. The one who had to take care of my siblings and be the role model, and now I was denigrated to the little sister of a girl I'd just met and didn't know. I wanted to scream that I was my own person. That I wasn't anyone's little anything, but years of practice in being the doctor's daughter meant I automatically plastered a smile.

Omer opened the passenger car door and Dina jumped in. 'You guys want a ride?'

Sabiha walked to the back door.

'No thanks.' I took a step back. 'Dad's waiting.' I couldn't wait for them all to get in the car and drive off.

Omer's car pulled away, Sabiha's hand hanging mid-air as she reached for the car door handle. Sabiha and I stared at each other, dumb-struck. Omer had assumed both Sabiha, and I were going to see our dad together and drove off. It was something neither of us had thought about. To the world we looked like normal sisters—we shared a physical resemblance and had the same surname, but in reality we were two strangers stuck together through circumstance.

We started walking, wordlessly falling into step beside each other.

'Do you have far to go?' I broke the awkward silence first, realising that even though she was my sister, I didn't even know basic facts about her, such as where she lived.

'Across the railway tracks.' Sabiha pointed. 'You?'

'I'm going to my dad's surgery. It's down—'

'I know where it is,' Sabiha snapped.

I flushed, anger taking hold. I was getting sick of being her punching bag. 'Why don't you visit him then?'

It was the question that had been burning inside me every day for the past three months since we'd been living in Melbourne. Just when I thought Sabiha was ignoring my question, she answered.

'It was too...' her sentence petered out as she struggled for words.

I had to fight my instinct to jump in and instead let my silence do the work for me.

'It was too hard,' she finally said. 'I'd spent 16 years thinking he wanted nothing to do with me and then...' She took a deep shuddering breath.

I could just imagine Dad's intensity and strident demands to see his daughter.

'And the timing was really terrible,' she continued. 'Mum was just released from hospital and I was panicked that seeing the husband who'd abandoned her would trigger a relapse.'

'But he didn't abandon her,' I jumped in. 'Your mother left him.'

'Who told you that?' Sabiha asked.

I realised we were getting into dangerous territory and shrugged mutely.

'What a convenient fiction,' she muttered under her breath.

I wanted to call her out, but was too scared we'd ruin our fragile truce. We trudged on in silence, trying to think of another conversational opener, but it was Sabiha who spoke first, probably feeling guilty for her earlier waspishness.

'Why aren't you going straight home?' Sabiha asked.

'Mum's going to pick me up from Dad's.'

'But you can catch a bus home,' Sabiha said after I explained our complicated carpool system. 'There's a bus right next to the surgery.'

'It's too dangerous.'

'No, it's not,' Sabiha said. 'I catch the bus by myself all the time.'

I didn't know what to say. My parents drove us everywhere. I'd never caught a bus or train by myself, and neither had any of my friends in Hobart.

'Doesn't your mum worry?' Whenever Mum saw a child walking on the street alone, she'd cluck her tongue and comment about the dangers it exposed them to and how parents should know better.

'About what?' Sabiha was scornful. 'I know how to get to school and back without someone holding my hand.'

'But something can happen to you.' I repeated the sentence Mum threw at me like a threat and a warning rolled into one.

'The worst thing that's ever happened was being bashed,' Sabiha said nonchalantly. 'But that could have happened anytime, anywhere.'

'You got bashed?' No one I knew had ever gotten bashed.

'Yeah, it happened last year.' Sabiha waved her hand as if it was nothing. 'Some girls slapped me around. No big deal.'

'My Mum said that St Albans was dangerous.' I eyed passers by as possible assailants.

'It's no more dangerous than anywhere else.'

'I guess.' I remained unconvinced.

We'd reached the corner where I turned left and walked a few hundred meters to Dad's medical centre. Sabiha hesitated. I was torn. The only bonus about going to this school was the time I spent with Dad alone, but if I showed up with Sabiha in tow, I would impress Dad.

'Mum's waiting for me,' Sabiha said, forestalling my dilemma.

We looked at each other, unsure about how to say goodbye. Usually Bosnians gave everyone a kiss on the cheek, it was the Anglo equivalent of a handshake, but I hesitated. The situation was weird enough without engaging in some further pseudo-intimacy.

Sabiha must have agreed because she gave me a sharp nod and continued walking. 'See you tomorrow,' she called out over her shoulder.

When I walked into the medical centre, Dad was standing next to the receptionist, talking about a file. His gaze sharpened when he saw me, searching to see if Sabiha was behind me. When I closed the door, he was disappointed, before returning to his conversation. I went to the kitchen and set up to do my homework at the table.

Dad appeared in the doorway. 'How was your day?' he asked as he flicked through the file in his hands.

'I had lunch with Sabiha.'

Dad's head jerked up, and he gave me his undivided attention.

'She and Dina showed me around the school.' I'd omitted Jesse and Brian from the story, as it would raise too many questions.

'Did she ask about me?' Dad was painfully earnest.

I was uncomfortable. I couldn't tell him about Sabiha's anger and disappointment. He'd be crushed. 'We talked about school stuff.' I took the road of least resistance.

Dad looked lost in thought for a moment. 'That's great,' he finally said. 'Keep it light and easy. Don't spook her.'

I nodded, not really understanding what he was on about.

'You've made me so happy.' He hugged me, holding my head against his stomach. 'Thank you.'

I closed my eyes and hugged him back. Before I was ready, he detached himself and left, a spring in his step.

When I got in the backseat of Mum's car, Sanela was determinedly staring out the windshield. 'Where's my kiss and cuddle?' I asked.

Sanela crossed her arms across her chest, her standard pouting position.

'Don't you love me anymore?' I asked.

Sanela shook her head.

I fake cried. It was a game we'd invented when Sanela was two years old. She used to go around smacking us on the face, so we began fake-crying to teach her to stop. Unfortunately, she loved the attention, so we expanded the game and called it "Little Dictator." Sanela would point and say, 'Kwy,' and family members would engage their internal drama queen until she laughed.

I fake-cried and peered at Sanela through my fingers.

Sanela glanced at me, looking worried. She pointed at me and said, 'Laugh.'

I removed my hands and laughed.

She kissed me.

'I missed you,' I said.

It was just the prompt Sanela needed to talk about her day and her adventures with her new best friend, Heidi. I nodded at the appropriate moments, my mind still at school. I looked out at the passing scenery, seeing my reflection in the window.

My stomach dropped. It was as if Sabiha was in the car with me. I turned back to Sanela.

'Are you okay?' Mum asked as we got out of the car.

I forced a smile. 'Yeah, it's just tiring being the new kid.'

Mum nodded, her forehead creased in concern. 'We'll talk later.'

As I let Sanela drag me into the house, I didn't know if that was a good or bad thing. I used to talk to Mum about everything, but since we moved, we lost some of our closeness and I didn't know what to tell her.

Whenever Sabiha was a topic of discussion, Mum underwent a personality transformation. It was like a curtain descended and she disappeared. And if Mum had to talk about Sabiha with Dad, it always ended in an argument behind closed doors while my siblings and I pretended we didn't hear their raised voices.

I didn't know how Mum would react to me becoming friends with Sabiha and if she found out, it would probably lead to yet another argument between her and Dad, but I also needed someone to talk to. Since my last conversation with Dad, I felt weird. I put on a DVD for Sanela and went to the study.

'I've still got twenty minutes,' Ali snapped, his back to me as he stared at the screen.

'I know,' I said. 'I wanted to talk to you.'

'Can't it wait?'

I picked at the doorframe. 'I wanted to talk about Sabiha.'

'What did she do?' He swivelled his chair to look at me.

'Nothing,' I said. 'We hung out at lunch today.'

'So she's your best friend now?' He looked at me with disgust.

I couldn't tell him that the only reason we were friends was because Dina was scared I'd blab about Brian's secret. 'No,' I snapped. 'Dina's my friend and Sabiha hangs around us.'

'So?' He turned back to the computer.

I didn't know how to explain what happened with Dad. The way he made me feel that the only thing he cared about was

Sabiha. It was as if my only function was to reunite them and otherwise I didn't rate.

'Can we talk about this later?' he asked.

I returned to the living room. Mum was in the kitchen preparing dinner. This would be the perfect moment to talk to her under the pretext of helping her cook, but if my conversation with Ali had clarified anything, it was that I couldn't talk about Sabiha to anyone. I sat next to Sanela on the couch, drawing comfort from her warm body. I'd never felt so alone.

Twenty minutes later, Ali exited the study. 'Your turn.' He took his place next to Sanela. 'Do you want to play Guitar Hero?'

Sanela nodded eagerly and put the game on.

I closed the study door behind me. Usually I couldn't wait to get on the computer to send messages to my friends, but the only person I talked to these days was Hanka, my best friend from Hobart, and she was taking dancing lessons.

I logged in and saw I'd received a friend request from Alex Payne. My heart sped up as I clicked Accept. He was on-line.

AlexP "Hello gorgeous."

I heard his deep voice as if he were in the room speaking to me.

AlmaO "Hello yourself."

As I flirted on-line with Alex I could relax. It was nice to have one person where I didn't have to worry about what I said or how I acted.

AlmaO "Dina told me you were taking me to Blow Job Lane."

AlexP "I would never do that to you. You're a good girl."

AlmaO "Where were you taking me?"

AlexP "I wanted privacy because I had naughty ideas about ravishing your lips."

I covered my mouth and giggled. He was so full on.

AlmaO "Who says I would have given you my permission?"

AlexP "I have my ways of persuasion. Wanna find out tomorrow?"

I was about to agree when reason won over. Even though Alex was cute, I was still the doctor's daughter. I'd barely repaired my relationship with Dad after getting expelled, and couldn't risk another setback.

AlmaO "Maybe another time. Have plans with my sister."

AlexP "Sister? Thought Sabiha was an only child."

AlmaO "Different mothers, same father."

AlexP "How come you're the same age? You Mormons or something?"

I held my hands over the keyboard. If I told him they moved me up in class, he might ditch me. He had to believe I was sixteen years old, and there was only one way to do that.

AlmaO "Sabiha was moved up in class."

AlexP "Shit. She's only fifteen years old. She should wear a warning label."

I bit my nail, glad I'd followed my instincts and not told him the truth.

AlexP "So... what'cha wearing?"

I burst into laughter, snorting through my nose. I covered my mouth, relieved no one was around to witness my lack of grace.

AlmaO "A playboy bunny bra and panties, of course."

AlexP "You're wicked. What colour?"

The door opened behind me, and Mum called my name. My hands slid on the keyboard and I quickly shut down the screen. I turned around, putting on my most innocent expression.

'You seemed down when you came home from school.' Mum pulled up a chair and sat next to me. 'Is there something you wanted to talk about?'

It took me a moment to change gears and remember what happened at school. As I mentally flicked through the images, I realised there was nothing I could tell Mum.

'I'm worried,' I said, instead.

Mum watched me with concern.

'About you and Dad,' I continued, thinking as I went along. 'You guys were fighting again last night.'

'There's nothing to worry about.' Mum gave me a quick kiss. 'Married couples fight.' She went to get up.

'But you hardly talk,' I blurted out. Now that I'd finally opened the can of worms about my parent's marriage, I couldn't stop myself. 'Sometimes days go by and you don't talk to each other.'

Mum turned away and flexed her hands. She gave a deep sigh and turned back. 'We're figuring things out. There's been a lot of changes, a lot to process.'

'You mean Sabiha.'

Mum flinched, her typical response when Sabiha's name was mentioned.

'Yes, like that.' Mum avoided repeating her name. 'But there's nothing to worry about.' She patted my knee and got up. 'Your father and I have been together a long time and weathered a lot of changes. This is another wrinkle that will soon pass.'

'I had one more question,' I blurted.

Mum stopped and turned her hand on the doorknob.

'You and Dad met at a Bosnian dance, right?'

Mum gripped the doorknob tightly, her knuckles turning white. She nodded and left.

I watched the space Mum occupied. I'd wanted to ask Mum more questions and put to rest the suspicions Sabiha had raised, but I should have picked a better moment. Mum acted like talking about Sabiha was physically painful and she shut down when she was introduced in the conversation.

I didn't know what was going to happen if Sabiha agreed to see Dad. Feeling that familiar ache whenever I thought about it too much; I rubbed my stomach. I turned back to the computer screen. There was fifteen minutes left before dinner.

AlmaO "Sorry about that. Mum barged in. Where were we?"

Chapter 6

'Wake up, Alma.' Mum threw off my covers. 'Your father is waiting for you.'

I forced my eyes open and turned my head to look at the clock. It was eight o'clock. I'd spent the night daydreaming about Alex, imagining what would have happened if we'd continued our walk. Would he have kissed me? What would it have been like? Every time I thought of him, I felt light and floaty. I couldn't wait to get to school and glimpse him.

I'd fallen asleep in the early hours of the morning and vaguely remembered the alarm clock beeping. My hand had reached for it and I'd flicked the off button before falling back into a deep sleep.

After Mum left, I tiptoed to the top of the stairs and peered down. Mum wasn't exaggerating. Dad was dressed in his suit, his briefcase by his side, and he was impatiently glancing at his watch.

I ran back to my bedroom, panic clawing in my stomach. I wasn't going to have time for a shower. Before pulling on my uniform, I took a few seconds to rub on my underarm anti-perspirant.

When I got to the bottom of the stairs, Mum handed me two paper bags. 'Breakfast and lunch.' She kissed me.

I'd forgotten my jacket and the cool morning wind raised goose pimples on my arms. It was only when I walked into the school library and the librarian gave me a strange look that I looked down and realised I was wearing my old school uniform. Time slowed, and I felt like I was trapped in one of those naked dreams where my limbs were like blocks of cement and I couldn't run for my life.

I looked around to see who else was watching me. The library was still empty. I ran to the bathroom, my mind frozen as I tried to decide what to do. My instinct was to run, but there was nowhere to go. The thought of facing the entire school in my uniform made me nauseous. Reputations were made like this. I'd go from being the new girl to the joke of the school who didn't know how to dress.

I looked at my watch. Mum was dropping off Ali and Sanela. She'd have to go home and get a change of clothes and then come to St Albans High. There was no way she'd make it before class began. Still, if I stayed hidden in the toilets until class and then slipped in right on the bell, I'd minimise the damage. I got out my mobile.

'Alma, what's wrong?' Mum demanded, on alert as she heard my voice.

'I'm wearing the wrong clothes.' I choked back tears as I told her.

'What do you mean?'

'I'm wearing my old school uniform.'

There was silence before Mum gave a heavy sigh.

'Can you please bring me a change of clothes?' I pleaded.

Mum hesitated, she was probably compiling her to do list in her head and getting ready to put on her reasonable voice and ask me to get through the day.

'I can't spend the day like this,' I wailed, panic building at the thought. 'My reputation will be ruined. Everyone will think I'm a loser. I won't have any friends.' My words ran into each other as I contemplated the end of my social life.

'No one's going to think you're a loser,' Mum said briskly.

'Yes, they will. Please, Mum. Please. I promise I won't ask—'

'I'll have to go home after I drop off Ali and Sanela,' Mum cut in.

'That's fine.' I went limp with relief. Feeling shaky, I sat down on the toilet seat and pulled out a book to read. My phone rang, and I answered without checking caller ID, expecting it to be Mum asking about what outfit she wanted me to bring.

'Where are you?' a female voice demanded. I looked at the phone and saw it was Dina.

'Around,' I said, annoyed that she was pushing this fake friendship on me when I wanted to be left alone.

'Come to the front,' Dina demanded.

'I can't—'

'Why is there an echo?' Dina asked. 'Are you in the toilets?'

'Yes, I'm waiting for Mum—'

'Do you need a tampon?'

Dina moved the phone away from her ear and asked if anyone had a tampon at the top of her voice. I covered my face. And to think I was worried about being humiliated.

'Which toilets are you in?' Dina asked.

Making peace with my fate, I told her and hung up. The toilet door burst open with a slam, and Dina called my name. I opened the cubicle and came out coyly.

Dina covered her mouth. 'Talk about dork patrol.' She giggled.

'Here I've got a pad.' Sabiha held up a plastic package.

'I'm hiding because of this.' I gestured with disgust at my uniform. 'Mum is bringing me a change of clothes, but she won't get here until after class starts.'

'Why?' Sabiha asked.

'Because everyone will think I'm an idiot for wearing a uniform to a school that has none,' I said.

'So what?' Sabiha said dismissively. 'You shouldn't care about people you don't know.'

I gaped at Sabiha, not knowing what to say.

'Don't pay attention to her.' Dina took off her jumper and handed it to me. 'She operates on a superhuman level where most people are beneath her notice.'

'And rightly so,' Sabiha said. 'I'm not going to let people who mean nothing to me influence how I dress.'

'You're above the petty concerns of us mere mortals.' Dina sounded like she'd heard it all before.

I put on the jumper and looked in the mirror. It hung past my hips and left a strip of skirt visible.

'Let's go.' Dina tugged me to the door. 'Omer's going to pick me up from school,' Dina continued her conversation with Sabiha as we walked to the front.

'Is he going to see your folks?' Sabiha asked.

Dina shook her head violently. 'I tested them out last night and mentioned his name. I nearly got frostbite the temperature dropped so quickly. They still think of him as a druggy and a loser, even though it's been two years since they kicked him out.' Dina flicked her hair. 'People change.'

I followed behind, tugging Dina's jumper down as I suspiciously eyed everyone we passed. I kept expecting someone to point at me and begin laughing, but no one was paying any attention.

'Where's he working?' Sabiha asked.

'He's between jobs at the moment. He's got a friend who might have something for him, but in the meantime, I'm lending him some money.'

'Do you think that's a good idea?' Sabiha asked.

'He's my brother,' Dina snapped.

'Okay,' Sabiha held her hands up in surrender. 'I'm just saying—'

'I know what you're saying,' Dina said. 'And I want you to stop.'

Sabiha gave her a sharp look and kept quiet. The uncomfortable moment snapped me out of my funk. Dina and Sabiha walked the rest of the way in dead-locked silence, and I was relieved to see Jesse waiting for us at the front.

'Where's Brian?' Sabiha asked him.

'He didn't come to the door when I knocked,' Jesse said. 'I thought he was already here.'

Dina and Sabiha shook their heads.

'I'll call him,' Jesse said, taking out his mobile. 'Hey Bri, where are you?' There was a pause. 'What do you mean?' He pulled the phone away from his ear. 'He told me to jump in my bunker because he's going nuclear.'

'What does that mean?' Sabiha demanded. 'Give me the phone. I'll call him.'

'No need,' I said, catching sight of Brian's approach.

They followed my gaze. The young man from yesterday with the un-brushed hair and un-kept appearance was gone. Brian was wearing skin-tight leather pants, a mesh see-through top, and chunky bikie boots, but it was his face that was the genuine shock. He was wearing foundation, his skin was shiny and blemish free, and his lips were a matte colour.

He had outlined his eyes with eyeliner, dark eye shadow and mascara, making them look like topaz jewels. He looked beautiful. I would have thought that wearing makeup he'd look like a girl, yet with his outfit and walk, he looked more masculine than ever before.

The crowd cleared as he walked. They stood on the sidelines and watched him pass as if he was a rock star that had landed in our suburban high school. Some students watched him with awe and admiration, but there were others who looked disgusted that he was parading his private life so openly.

The group next to us laughed. 'Where's the homo brigade?' one girl said loudly enough for Brian to hear as he drew alongside them.

Brian stopped and gave the girl a once over. 'I can dress straight, but you can never change ugly.'

The girl gasped and everyone else laughed. Things settled, and they all returned their eyes to their respective groups. The moment for ugliness had passed, for now.

'Hello beautiful people,' Brian said cheerily.

'What brought this on?' Jesse gestured at his outfit.

'I figured if people were going to call me a faggot, I might as well live up to their expectations,' he said with a smile full of bravado.

'You look like a gay cliché,' Sabiha said.

'This is what they expect, isn't it?' Brian said.

Sabiha rolled her eyes. 'It doesn't mean you have to lower yourself to their expectations.'

They had a staring contest until Dina stepped in and slapped Brian's shoulder. 'I hope you brought a change of clothes. If you go home like that, your dad will go nuts.'

'That's not a problem,' Brian said flatly.

'Of course it is,' Dina insisted. 'Your Dad is always on your back about you being not blokey enough. If he saw you in make up he'd blow a gasket.'

'Don't be a spoilsport,' Sabiha said.

'Shut up,' Dina snapped. 'Not everyone has a mum like yours who doesn't get on your back about everything. The rest of us have parents whose love has boundaries and if we cross them, we're out. No second chances.' She turned back to Brian. 'Do you have a change of clothes?'

'No,' Brian said.

'For fuck's sake, Brian—'

'He said it won't be a problem—' Sabiha interrupted.

'Because my dad already saw me,' Brian continued in a regular conversational tone.

Dina and Sabiha were struck dumb.

'How did that happen?' Sabiha asked.

'I was in my mother's room putting on makeup after everyone left the house when his ute pulled up in front. I thought about hiding. When I was experimenting by myself, I did it before. I had enough time because he went to the backyard to collect his toolbox before he came into the house. All I had to do was duck into the bathroom and remove my makeup and he wouldn't have known what happened.' He stopped, his voice breaking as he began losing control. He cleared his throat and continued.

'I couldn't do it,' Brian said. 'I couldn't keep lying and hiding, pretending everything in my life was normal and great while all along I feel like I'm drowning. So I stepped into the hallway and he saw me.' He sounded like he was going to cry.

Sabiha put a hand on his shoulder to comfort him.

'It was like I was watching my death.' He put on his bravado like an armour and his voice returned to normal. 'He stepped back as if I was contagious or something and went off his nut, screaming the usual crap. "You're not my son. Wish you were dead. Never come back to this house."'

'I'm sorry, Brian.' Sabiha hugged him.

He accepted her hug for a millisecond before detaching himself. 'Them's the breaks.'

'What are you going to do now?' Dina asked, on the verge of hysteria. 'Where are you going to live?'

Brian looked dazed, as if he'd only realised he was homeless.

'He'll be fine.' Jesse put a calming hand on Dina's shoulders. 'He'll stay at my house.'

Dina took a deep, gulping breath.

Brian's face cleared. 'Thanks. I'll talk to my brother Greg tomorrow and sort something out.'

Jesse nodded. 'However long you need.'

There was a pause as everyone processed. Brian's gaze caught mine. 'What do you think, Alma?'

All eyes turned to me. It was like I was facing an initiation ceremony where I was thrust naked into a wintry landscape to either freeze to death or find suitable shelter. I looked at Brian and the words were easy. Even though he was puffed up with bravado, his eyes were full of yearning. I knew the feeling of being torn between two impossible choices. Sometimes you had to burn your bridges in order to move forward.

'I think you're very brave,' I said. 'Coming out at high school isn't easy, but lying about who you are isn't either.'

'Let's hope he did it for the right reason,' Jesse added archly.

Brian gave him a dark look, but said nothing else. It was times like these that I was confronted with the fact that I was the outsider. They were old friends, and I was the newbie excluded from their secret world. Remembering what was happening at home, I realised my good fortune. They didn't know my secrets either, and that's how I wanted it to remain.

'What have we here?' Brian demanded as he saw me tug Dina's jumper down, trying to cover my uniform. 'Is this a fashion *faux pa*?'

I flushed. All I wanted was to blend in, instead, all I did was stand out.

'Who you gonna call?' He sang the Ghostbusters theme. 'Fagbusters,' he yelled, taking hold of my arm.

'Where are we going?' I tried to hold back, but he was dragging me along in his wake.

'I'm going to transform you,' he said dreamily. 'You will be my masterpiece.'

I looked over my shoulder and mouthed help to Dina for rescue.

'What are you jabbering about?' Dina demanded.

'Just wait and see.' He got to the female toilets and yanked it open. '*Queer Eye Rescue* coming through.'

There were two girls washing their hands at the basin. 'You can't be in here,' one of them said, catching sight of Brian.

'It's not like I'm going to ravish you, my dear.' He fluttered his hands toward the door. 'Off with you.'

The girls scuttled out.

'What if they dob you to the teacher?' Dina demanded.

'Stop them if you're worried.' Brian rifled through his backpack.

'Let's go.' Sabiha grabbed Dina's arm. 'You get the girls. I'll make sure no one else comes in.'

'It's good they're gone,' Brian said. 'Now I can get my groove on.'

'They're worried about you,' I said, as he did something to the back of my uniform.

'You don't need this anymore, do you?'

I shook my head and was horror-struck when I heard a ripping sound. Mum was going to go off at me. We always donated our clothes to the mosque, and she'd be furious that I'd ruined a brand new uniform.

'I know they're worried, but sometimes you want to come to school to forget about your problems, not be reminded of them.'

I knew the feeling. School used to be my refuge, the place where I could get away from the drama at home, but now it was a double-edged sword. It got me away from my parents, but it put me directly on the path of my biggest drama, my other sister.

Brian spent what seemed like forever playing with my uniform, but he wouldn't let me see until he was finished.

'Don't overdo it,' I said nervously as he put makeup on. 'I don't want to look too...' I let the sentence die out, so I didn't offend him.

'I'm guessing you were going to say slutty,' Brian finished, and moved me toward the mirror. 'No chance of that.'

I looked at the stranger's reflection. It took me a moment to comprehend that I was looking at myself. Brian had somehow made the uniform fitted, so it outlined my body, making my waist look impossibly small. My top button was undone and my cleavage was on display, but it was my face that was his true masterpiece.

I looked fresh-faced, but pretty with my eyes doe-like, while my lips were pouty and plump. I looked down at my feet. My hem was lifted above my knees and Brian tugged my socks up over my calves.

'I look like a naughty schoolgirl.' I tugged on my pigtails.

'Isn't it great?' Brian stood.

'I don't know if this is the look for me.' I kept my eyes on the mirror. It was like I was staring at an amusement park mirror that reflected a distorted image. If I moved, the image would shift and I'd recognise myself again.

'Go outside for five minutes,' Brian pleaded. 'If after that time you don't like the look, I'll take it all off and let you hide under this.' He held up Dina's jumper.

'I don't know if I can.' I finally met his eyes.

I'd never worn a miniskirt in my life. Mum bought all my clothes and only permitted modest outfits. Even though most girls my age were used to flashing boob, I might as well have been wearing my bra over my clothes. It all felt wrong and strange that I couldn't imagine letting anyone see me. Brian's eyes entreated me more than any words could. He'd already been rejected publicly once. I couldn't do it to him again.

'I'll give it a try.' I forced the words past my frozen lips. I took a deep breath and stepped out of the toilet.

Sabiha was standing guard in front of the toilets. 'Don't go in there,' she said to the two girls. 'My friend's puking up her hangover.' The girls turned away like seagulls diving into the ocean.

'I'm done,' I said to Sabiha's back.

Sabiha turned, and her eyes widened.

Dina clapped. 'You are a genius.' She kissed Brian. Her whoops caught the attention of passing students and they imperceptibly slowed with the girls giving me what seemed like jealous looks, while guys were openly checking me out.

'What do you think, Jesse?' Brian asked. 'You like?'

Jesse's eyes went up and down, and he looked slightly dazed. 'You look amazing.'

Sabiha frowned. 'She looks okay.'

'This is my masterpiece you're talking about.' Brian was indignant, as if I was his painting and he was being slighted.

'She's young for that get up,' Sabiha said.

'You remember your Wonder Woman costume for my Comic Book party?' Brian asked archly.

'Yes, I remember,' Sabiha snapped. 'You were the one who hired it and I was the one who got burnt by it.'

They both looked embarrassed. Brian looked away first. 'Maybe she is young.' He yanked me to the side of the hallway and, with a twist of his wrist, re-did my front buttons, and loosened my skirt. 'There.' He flipped me around like I was a Barbie doll. 'Do we get the Big Sister stamp of approval?'

Sabiha nodded. 'Much better.'

As we walked to class, I enjoyed the frisson of energy that my appearance created. Even though students in the hallway looked busy taking out their schoolbooks from lockers and rushing to class, everyone was slower as they watched from the corner of their eyes.

I intercepted quite a few looks from guys, their eyes full of warm approval, a small smile tilting their lips when I made eye contact. Each time I looked away and blushed, fighting the grin that curved my mouth, but I couldn't. I was light and effervescent as if I'd drunk soda and the fizzy bubbles and sugar-hit buoyed me.

While I was used to being the centre of attention, this was the first time they actually saw me. Because Dad was a community leader, there was always a stir when we attended Bosnian community events. Everyone attempted to come and meet him, to kowtow to him or ask a favour. I was always Dad's daughter, the doctor's daughter, never Alma. This was the first time I was stepping out of Dad's shadow. No one cared I was Esad Omerović's daughter. All they saw was Alma, the new girl, and they liked me.

I saw Alex at the end of the hallway. He licked his finger and touched his skin, miming that I was hot. I smiled at him before Sabiha whisked me away.

Chapter 7

Enveloped in the heady feeling of being admired, I forgot all about Mum coming to the school until a student walked into class and asked for me. I followed the student's pointing finger to the door and saw Mum peering through the window. I waved and stood. Mum's smile was replaced with horror as she caught sight of my outfit.

'What are you wearing?' Mum hissed when I was in the hallway.

I shifted uncomfortably, painfully aware of the fact that everyone in class was watching us. Mum must have realised the same thing because she bit her tongue.

Mum stepped into the classroom. 'I need to speak to my daughter for a moment,' she told the teacher.

I looked in and saw Sabiha staring at us. Mum turned her head and locked eyes with Sabiha. Time stopped as the two of them eyed each other. Finally, Mum tore her gaze away and began walking.

'You didn't tell me she looked like him?' Mum briskly walked down the hallway.

I followed, not knowing what to say.

Mum stopped abruptly in front of the female toilets at the end of the hallway. 'Here.' She handed me a plastic bag as she looked at the stairs.

I took the bag and peered inside at the black pants and a white shirt.

'I'll see you tonight.' Mum walked down the stairs.

'Mum,' I called.

Mum stopped, and I saw she looked shell-shocked. I wanted to say something comforting. Something to ease her devastation, but no words came.

'Thanks.' I held up the bag.

Mum nodded and continued down the stairs, her high heels making a clacking sound.

I went into the bathroom and closed the cubicle door behind me. I took out the shirt and pants. They looked like an outfit you'd wear as a uniform in a supermarket. I smoothed down my school uniform and remembered the admiring glances I'd been receiving all morning. In the end, the decision was simple. I put the bag Mum brought into my locker and returned to class.

***

'So that was your mum,' Sabiha said at lunchtime.

I nodded.

'Why aren't you wearing the clothes she brought?' Dina asked.

'Because she wants to look hot,' Brian interrupted, twirling in front of them. 'Like me.'

'Brian, can I please speak to you?' Mr Sheen, our Maths teacher beckoned.

Brian lifted an eyebrow as he joined Mr Sheen. They walked away so that we couldn't hear them.

'I think he's in trouble,' Sabiha said as we watched their pantomime.

Mr Sheen gestured at Brian's clothes. Brian put his hand up and stalked off, his strides long and lithe, as if he was practicing for the catwalk.

'What happened?' Sabiha demanded.

'He's a homophobe,' Brian said.

'Why?' Dina asked.

'He said I need to wear more appropriate clothing.' Brian undid his top button to expose more chest. 'Which is code for I need to dress straight.'

'Maybe he's right. You are creating a stir everywhere you go.' Dina nodded her head to the gaggle of girls on our right. As soon as the girls noticed they were being scrutinised, they quickly turned away and pretended they were engrossed in talking to each other.

'Is that such a bad thing?' Brian formed a moue with his mouth.

'Yes, it is,' Dina snapped. 'This isn't a game, Brian. You're playing with your life.'

'You're right, Dina,' he snapped back. 'This is *my* life.'

'I think someone wants to speak to you,' Sabiha said in a sotto voice as one girl ventured toward him.

Brian broke his staring contest with Dina and looked over.

'You're Brian, right?' the girl asked when she was within speaking distance.

'That's my name,' Brian said, putting on his sparkly persona.

'We were wondering if you could do your Queer Eye Rescue for our friend.' She pointed to a girl with dark kinky hair who was shyly peeking from the back of the group. 'She's been dumped and could really use a lift.'

'You bet. I've got my bag of tricks right here.' He patted his bag and, with a quick wave, walked off.

'You need to back off.' Sabiha faced Dina after Brian left. 'He's got it hard enough without you riding him.'

'I'm trying to help him.' Dina yanked her hair off her face impatiently. 'He's gone off the rails and doesn't realise it.'

'That's not how you help him,' Sabiha said firmly. 'He's come out of the closet now and there's no changing that. All we can do is support him.'

Dina looked over at Brian. 'I'm scared he'll disappear from my life like my brother,' she whispered. 'I can't lose anyone else.'

Sabiha put her arm over her shoulders. 'We won't lose him.'

Dina nodded and turned away from Brian as she wiped her face. 'I've got to wash up.'

'We'll come with,' Sabiha said.

'No.' Dina shook her head emphatically. 'I need a few minutes alone.'

It was just Sabiha and me, shuffling our feet uncomfortably as we tried to find a topic of conversation. 'Where's Jesse?' I asked.

'He's in the computer room working on his graphic novel.'

There was another uncomfortable silence.

'Your Mum looked angry when she saw me,' Sabiha finally said.

'She was angry with *me*.' I lied. 'This is not my usual wardrobe.' I gestured to my outfit.

'I thought for a moment that she didn't know we were going to the same school.' Sabiha searched my face.

'She knew.' I fought to keep impassive.

'But was she okay with it?' Sabiha persisted.

I finally met her gaze. 'No.'

Sabiha nodded as if she already knew. She turned away to look at Brian, who was leaving with the group of girls. 'Where are you going?'

'We're going to the oval to show Rodney what he's missing,' the kinky-haired girl shouted, full of bravado as she modelled her new look.

Sabiha followed them and I ran to catch up with her long strides. Sabiha positioned herself next to Brian as we walked, while I followed in the back. The girls headed straight for a group of boys who were in the middle of a match.

'Rodney,' the kinky-haired girl yelled. 'You're a two-timing asshole.'

The game came to a halt and a guy who resembled the Incredible Hulk with a bulky body and fly-away brown hair detached himself from the team and walked over.

'This is not the time,' Rodney said to the girl. 'Now beat it.' He walked off.

The kinky-haired girl swore at him, going through an impressive list of profanity, before moving onto comparing his penis to a straw. While their Jerry Springer revival was going on, Brian was looking around the oval like he was searching for a ghost.

'Piss off, you fag hag,' Rodney said. 'And take your homo brigade with you.' He pushed Brian, who didn't see him coming.

Brian started falling, but Sabiha grabbed his arm and kept him upright. Sabiha threw herself in front of Brian and shoved her face into Rodney's. 'Fuck you,' she shouted, red with rage.

I stepped forward, my familial instinct kicking in, but hesitated.

'Bring it on, homophobe,' Brian shouted, coming out of his daze.

'Come on,' Sabiha urged, as she tugged his arm off the oval.

I fell in step and took Brian's other arm, helping Sabiha walk toward him.

'Let go.' Brian shook us off.

Sabiha glanced behind and I followed her gaze. Rodney was back in the middle of his soccer fray. His girlfriend and her posse were sullenly walking behind us.

'You need to stop letting these bitches involve you in their bullshit games,' Sabiha said loudly enough so the girls behind us could hear.

The kinky-haired girl looked wounded, while her gal-pal hugged her shoulders and gave Sabiha a dirty look. They veered away from us and Sabiha watched them go moodily.

We reached the portables, and Sabiha stopped in the recessed doorway.

'It's got nothing to do with them. It's everything to do with me.' Brian gestured at himself, his look of frustration saying it all.

'Tone it down then.' Sabiha sipped from her water bottle.

'So even my best friend is blaming me for a homophobe attack,' Brian snapped.

As they shouted at each other, their bodies moving in jerky spasms as anger raged through them, my hands clenched as if I were fighting off an attack. School was my one haven, and now even that was falling apart.

'That's not what I'm saying,' Sabiha argued back. 'I'm just saying you don't need to be in their face about who you are.'

'Really?' Brian demanded. 'And if you were me, what would you be doing?'

Sabiha paused in consternation, the water bottle halfway to her mouth. 'I'd add fake eyelashes to make my outfit pop,' she finally said nonchalantly.

Brian's face went blank for a moment as he processed what she said. 'You're right,' he finally replied, peering into the window glass. 'I'll have to buy some tonight.'

'Dina's probably freaking out about us abandoning her.' Sabiha walked to the front of the school.

I followed, bemused. Five minutes ago, they were acting like they'd kill each other, but now they were back to being best friends. I didn't know what to make of Sabiha's unrestrained emotion and her volatility made me slightly uncomfortable.

The rest of the day passed uneventfully, and I walked by myself to Dad's, with Sabiha, Brian and Dina electing to stay behind at school and admire Jesse's artwork. Jesse had invited me to stay, and while I'd been curious to see what he was doing, Sabiha's stiffened pose gave me the impression that my company was not desired.

I'd barely set up for homework when Dad appeared and made himself a cup of coffee.

'How was everything at school today?' he asked.

Something about the considered way he asked made the hairs on my skin stand up. Had he found out about Rodney and the fight on the oval?

'All good.' I stared down at my Humanities textbook.

'So you didn't tell me about your new friends?' He sat down across from me. 'Who do you hang out with?'

'Just Sabiha and Dina.'

He hesitated, like he wasn't sure whether he should continue. 'A patient talked to me today about Sabiha.'

The penny dropped, and I was on safe ground. 'Let me guess, she's hanging around with boys. We're at a Co-Ed School, Dad.' I hated this aspect about the community. Everyone was always gossiping and sticky-beaking into other people's business.

'Yes, but this patient saw her kissing a brown-haired boy.'

'That's Brian,' I said. 'They're friends.'

'Just friends?'

All I had to say was that Brian was gay, but I hesitated. I remembered the way Sabiha had flicked me off after school, like I was a pesky fly.

'I don't feel comfortable spying on Sabiha,' I said.

Dad looked frustrated before he smiled. 'I'm glad you're friends with Sabiha and that you're looking out for her.' He kissed me on the head.

Dad hated tattle-tails. He always went on about how brothers and sisters had to look out for each other because he had a horrible relationship with his brother and sister. If he caught me fighting with my siblings, he'd punish all of us equally.

He stood to return to work and gently squeezed my shoulder. 'I'm very proud of you.'

I nearly dropped to the ground and begged for his forgiveness, but it was too late. He was already out the door.

I couldn't concentrate on my homework after he left, and I packed up. I was waiting outside the medical centre when Mum pulled up, the 4WD breaking sharply. Mum stared out the front of the windshield, tapping her fingers on the steering wheel as I got in the car. I listened to Sanela's chatter with one ear, my stomach jumping with nerves as we pulled up into the driveway.

When we walked into the house, I followed Mum to the kitchen, while Ali and Sanela drifted off to their rooms. I waited by the kitchen counter for the lecture about my outfit to begin. Instead Mum opened the kitchen cupboards and pulled out pots listlessly. Mum turned to put the pot on the stovetop and jumped when she saw me.

'I thought you wanted to talk to me.' I bit my lip and waited for Mum to collect herself into her usual fireball. When Mum was on the warpath, she squared her shoulders and maintained eye contact, as if she were conducting a lie detector test and her eyeballs were the conduit.

'Yes.' Mum looked like she was trying to remember what she wanted to say. 'About this morning, you know I don't approve of clothes like that.'

'I know,' I said meekly. 'The girls were helping me out.'

'Okay.' Mum nodded absent-mindedly.

I waited to hear if she had anything else to say. I'd spent the day dreading a lecture and didn't know whether to consider myself lucky that I'd finally caught a break or be worried about Mum's out-of-character behaviour.

'I have to make dinner before I got to work,' Mum said.

'Do you want help?'

Sanela ran into the kitchen holding a notebook. 'Alma, I need you to help me with my English homework.'

I followed Sanela to her room with relief. By the time I finished helping her and we came back downstairs, dinner was ready and Mum was packing her work snacks.

'Your father said he'd be home by now.' Mum looked at her watch in concern.

'I'll call and check where he's at.' I ushered her to the front door. 'You get going or you'll be late.'

Mum kissed us and stepped out.

'I want to call Daddy,' Sanela demanded after I closed the front door.

'Later.' I led her to the kitchen table where Ali was already serving himself. 'Let's eat first.'

After dinner, Ali remained in the living room watching television while I gave Sanela a bath and put her to bed. When I stepped into the hallway, I saw Dad coming up the stairs.

'I just put her to sleep,' I whispered.

He nodded wearily and pushed open the bedroom door. Sanela was lying on her side, her hand on her cheek, the nightlight casting a glow on her cherubic face.

'There's dinner in the microwave,' I told him when he closed the bedroom door. 'I'll warm it up while you have a shower.'

I was in the kitchen when the phone rang. It was Mum calling to check in with Dad. 'He's upstairs,' I told her.

'Oh, good,' Mum said. 'He's putting Sanela to bed.'

'Mmm,' I lied. Mum did three night shifts a week on the proviso that Dad spent the evening at home and put Sanela to bed, but he didn't always make it in time.

'Love you.' Mum blew a kiss down the phone line and hung up.

'Who was that?' Ali shouted from the living room.

'Mum,' I shouted back.

Ali came to the kitchen door. 'You didn't tell her about Dad.'

I shook my head. 'She thinks he's putting Sanela to bed.'

Ali nodded his approval. We agreed that our parents didn't need any more reasons to argue. When Dad came downstairs, I had served his dinner. I made myself a cup of tea and sat across from him.

'Can I get one?' Ali asked when he came in.

I ignored him. With a sigh, Ali made himself a cup of tea and sat down at the table too.

'Sorry I came home late,' Dad said between bites. 'I left you in the lurch.'

I flushed with pleasure. 'I know you couldn't help it.'

Dad sighed heavily. 'I had to tell a woman her five-year old-son has leukemia.'

I nodded sympathetically. Usually, it was Mum that he would confide in. They used to stay up late at night talking to each other while lying in bed. I loved hearing their voices when I got up to go to the toilet, Dad's deep baritone melding with Mum's voice, until they used up all their words and fell asleep curled in each other's arms.

'I spent all afternoon thinking about Sanela,' he said. 'And then I came home too late to be with her.'

These were the toughest days for Dad, when he had to deal with a sick child. He always sought the comfort of his children, as if he needed our touch to reassure himself that we were still present, still breathing, and would stay that way.

I looked over at Ali and we both got up. Ali stood behind Dad and wrapped his arms around Dad's neck, while I knelt on the floor and put my arms around Dad's chest. As Dad rubbed Ali's hands and kissed my head, we were once again a whole family.

Sabiha didn't exist in this world and as I closed my eyes and gave myself up to Dad's embrace, I wished it would stay that way permanently. We spent the evening watching a reality TV show. Dad sat in the middle, his arms on the back of the couch as Ali and I snuggled on each side. I felt hopeful that the Dad I knew would return to us.

For a few hours, I erased Sabiha from my mind and enjoyed the family moment. When Dad turned off the television and I had to go to bed, I was too tired to stand up and wanted to curl up and fall asleep where I was.

'Come on.' Dad tugged me by the arm off the couch. In the end, Dad and Ali half carried me between them to bed, where Dad tucked the covers around me, before kissing me on the forehead. I fell asleep floating on a cloud of contentment and bliss.

Chapter 8

I woke up holding the happy feeling inside me, like a secret I was hiding from everyone, not knowing that the bubble would burst within a few hours. It all fell apart during lunch.

We were waiting in the canteen line. Brian was wearing yet another provocative outfit. It was like he didn't want anyone to forget for even a minute that he was gay. Today he was wearing a see-through mesh top and skin-tight leather pants, with the zipper area diamante studded.

He'd already received two warnings and detention. The school tried calling home, but his parents didn't care. The teachers were at a loss. They didn't know what to do with a kid who didn't fear consequences.

Being in Brian's presence meant being the centre of attention and we'd all taken care with our appearance. Dina and I brought our outfits to school and changed in the female toilets, with Brian doing our make up.

Sabiha was the only one who had the freedom to leave the house as she pleased and instead of taking advantage, her only concession to beautifying herself was a slash of lip gloss and mascara.

I wore black lycra figure-hugging tights. I'd wanted to wear a skirt over them, but Brian demanded I take it off. I'd given in without a murmur, feeling trepidation and excitement as I walked out of the safety of the girl's toilets. Soon enough, my trepidation faded when I was bathed in the warm approval of guys checking me out as I passed.

Alex walked past me and slipped a note in my hand.

I was waiting on-line for you yesterday.

I glanced over my shoulder and caught him checking me out. He'd included his mobile number. I sent him an SMS message that I'd be on-line tonight, feeling a delicious thrill as I pressed send.

'Aren't you supposed to be in detention?' Dina asked Brian.

'That's right.' Brian giggled. 'But I have plans.'

'Pimping yourself out to bitches who will make fun of you tomorrow,' Dina said.

Brian spent recess continuing his Queer Eye Makeovers and Dina was getting progressively more pissed off as each girl emerged with her new look.

'I'm guessing you're feeling neglected.' Brian hugged her. 'I can make you look fabulous. A few snips here.' He grabbed her hair and made scissors with his fingers. 'And you'd look like a dyke.'

'Shut up.' Dina pushed him away and laughed.

'Where's Jesse?' I asked.

Sabiha looked at me with suspicion.

'He's doing his comic book thing with Charlie,' Brian said. 'I don't know what I'm going to do,' he sighed heavily. 'I can't live off Jesse forever.'

'What about Greg?' Dina asked. 'You said he'd take you in.'

Greg was Brian's older brother. He was in his last year of uni and had offered Brian a room in his share house.

Brian shrugged, saying nothing.

'Brian!' Dina demanded. 'What happened?'

'Nothing.' He held out his hands straight, the same way Sanela did when she was lying.

'What did you do?' I asked, mimicking the tone of voice I'd use on Sanela in the same situation.

Dina and Sabiha looked at me with surprise, but kept quiet. They turned back to Brian.

'We had a fight.' Brian looked at the ground. 'He wasn't happy that I came out to my parents. He said I broke Mum's heart.'

'Aha.' I made a go on gesture.

He gesticulated with his arms. 'And he had an entire list of rules for me moving in, like how I had to dress and what grades I had to get. It was worse than a Siberian camp.'

'So?' Dina said. 'You had to follow rules when you lived at home.'

'Exactly.' Brian gestured with his hands. 'And I couldn't take it anymore. This is the first time in my life that I've been free to be myself. And I'm not giving that up for anyone,' he said fiercely.

'That still doesn't change the fact that you can't stay at Jesse's forever,' Dina said pragmatically.

'Maybe you could get your own place,' Sabiha said.

'He'd have to pay the first month's rent and a deposit. It's at least $2,000. My brother is looking for a house to rent,' Dina elaborated when she saw our questioning looks.

'That's not a problem,' Brian said. 'I was saving for a car. The issue is I'd have to get a job so I can pay the rent.'

'You should work as a hairdresser,' I said.

'I'd have to do an apprenticeship,' Brian said.

'Then you'd have to leave school.' Dina was horrified at the possibility.

'So.' Brian shrugged. 'It's not as if there's anything holding me there.'

'What about us?' Dina argued.

'We'd still see each other,' Brian said.

'Yeah, right.' Dina looked dejected and shuffled her feet as she moved in line before she halted. Her face cleared, and she smiled. 'I have to make a phone call.' She thrust her money into Sabiha's hand and told her what to order, before breaking out of the line.

'Who are you calling?' Brian shouted as she ran off, but she lifted her hand to wave without stopping.

As we walked out of the canteen after ordering, Rodney detached himself from his group and headed toward Brian. 'Fucking faggot,' Rodney said, hunching over Brian.

Brian showed no fear. He looked up at him with a smirk. 'Be careful, you might catch my gay germs.' He breathed out with each word, blowing his breath into Rodney's face.

Rodney wiped himself and shoved Brian, sending him backward to land hard on the ground. He went to follow up with a kick, but Sabiha picked up a rubbish bin and threw it at Rodney, hitting him in the side and making the rubbish paper float around him like confetti.

'Fucking bitch.' Rodney headed for Sabiha.

'Let's see how tough you are hitting a girl,' Sabiha shouted, not moving as he got closer.

The crowd pushed me in front of Rodney. I looked up at him and clenched in fear, trying to make myself as small as possible. Rodney gave me a quick once over as he nudged me out of the way.

As Rodney continued toward Sabiha, Brian threw himself forward and grabbed Rodney's feet, making him topple to the ground. Rodney turned around and tried to hit Brian, but Sabiha threw herself forward and grabbed his arm, pinning him under her body. They all writhed on the ground, Brian and Sabiha grabbing an errant arm or leg as Rodney attempted to punch or kick.

A crowd gathered. I wanted to jump in and help, but I was scared. Things were finally good with Dad. If I got in trouble, he'd be angry with me again. While I was debating, Mr Sheen came on the scene.

'Nothing to see here,' Mr Sheen said firmly, throwing himself into the melee, he pulled Sabiha to her feet first. 'Enough!' he shouted, forcing them to stop moving.

Rodney and Brian stood.

'What happened here?' Mr Sheen asked.

'He attacked Brian—' Sabiha said.

'The fucking fagot—' Rodney said at the same time.

'Enough.' Mr Sheen shut them both down. 'What do you have to say for yourself, Brian?'

'He owes me twenty bucks for ruining my shirt.' Brian held up his top and poked a finger through the tear.

'You were due in detention fifteen minutes ago,' Mr Sheen said.

'This isn't Brian's fault,' Sabiha interrupted. 'Rodney attacked him. Brian was only defending himself.'

Rodney slouched and said nothing.

'Brian, you've been told that you attire is unsuitable for school—' Mr Sheen said.

'According to the straight police,' Brian replied.

'We are enforcing the school standards. Girls are not allowed to wear see-through clothes, so why should you receive any exemptions?' Mr Sheen asked.

'You're being a homophobe. This entire school is homophobic,' Sabiha shouted, looking at the crowd that was still lingering in the vicinity.

'This doesn't concern you, Sabiha,' Mr Sheen said. 'Move on.'

I tried to drag her away, but this incensed Sabiha more.

'I'm not going anywhere,' Sabiha shouted.

'I don't have to take this shit.' Brian headed toward the front gates. 'I'm out of here.'

'Come back here this instant,' Mr Sheen shouted.

Brian lifted his middle finger in reply.

'You're suspended,' Mr Sheen shouted.

Brian didn't slow down his pace.

Mr Sheen turned back. 'You two are going to see the principal.' He grabbed Rodney and Sabiha's arm and tugged them along.

Dina appeared at my side as Mr Sheen left.

'Shouldn't we go help Sabiha?' I asked, after I caught Dina up.

'She'll be fine,' Dina said dismissively. 'Sabiha will find a loophole.' She pulled out her mobile.

'Who are you calling?' I asked.

'Brian.' Dina frowned, as if I was asking a stupid question. 'If he doesn't come back, he'll be out of school for good.' The phone rang and then re-routed to voicemail. 'He turned it off.' She was outraged. 'And I have some big news for him. My brother wants Brian to move in with him.'

When the bell rang I went to class, all the time feeling like I'd left something undone. Ten minutes into class and I was called to the principal's office. I walked down the corridors sweaty and anxious. I did nothing wrong, so why was I in trouble?

Sabiha was sitting in front of the Principal's office. 'Good, there you are,' she said with exasperation. 'Give me Dad's phone number.'

'Why?' I asked.

'Because the principal is insisting on calling Mum and I don't want her involved.'

'Are you sure you want to call Dad?' I got his business card out of my purse. 'He's going to freak out that you're in trouble.'

'I've got no choice,' Sabiha said, worry darkening her eyes as she took the business card. 'There's talk of a suspension.'

I stepped away as she returned to the Principal's office, rubbing my fingers where Sabiha brushed against my skin. It was the first time we'd touched. I should have been elated that she was going to contact our father. Dad was going to be happy that I'd succeeded where he failed. Instead, I was exposed. My two lives were merging and soon there would be nowhere to hide.

I remembered Rodney's look. Animal desire muted even blind rage. If only everything was that simple and I could face the rest of my life in my battle armour, using my sex appeal to shield me from all the messiness of life.

I trudged through the corridors and back to class, my concentration shot as I tried to imagine what was happening in the Principal's office. Would Dad greet his prodigal daughter's transgression with anger and disappointment, or would he contain his emotions and welcome her back into the fold?

I kept imagining scenarios between them, alternating between their reunion being a love story music video, to it resembling a sumo wrestler match, all awkward groping and jolly posturing. When the bell rang, I rushed to my locker and found a deflated-looking Sabiha waiting for me.

'What happened?' I asked.

She paused, her face going through a few moods as if she was trying to find the right words. 'I'm not being suspended,' she said, as if I was supposed to celebrate or something.

'With Dad,' I almost growled, my curiosity like a physical pain.

'We didn't really get the chance to talk. He was too busy fending off Mr Sheen's version of the event. I apparently reacted 'aggressively' when he intervened,' Sabiha said, making quotation marks.

I had to bite my lip from telling her I agreed with Mr Sheen.

'So now I have to go to the medical centre so Dad and I can talk,' Sabiha said.

I felt let down by her matter-of-fact synopsis of the events, but her face was preoccupied and didn't invite further questions. I exchanged my books, and we walked side by side out of the school gates. Sabiha kept clenching and unclenching her fists.

'There's nothing to be nervous about,' I said, the words escaping even though I'd vowed to let her suffer in silence.

Sabiha let out a harsh laugh. 'Easy for you to say. You're not meeting your father for the first time.'

'You met him.' My brow furrowed in confusion. 'He came from Tasmania to see you as soon as he found out.'

Sabiha stared ahead. 'He came into the house and talked with my grandfather, but I stayed hidden in my room, eavesdropping through a crack in the door.' She looked at me from the corner of her eye. 'I know you think I'm a bitch, but I couldn't do anything else.'

'Why?' I burst out in frustration.

'I'd spent so long thinking that he'd ditched me, that he purposely ignored my existence, it was hard to suddenly shut off all that anger and rage.' Sabiha shrugged.

'Weren't you curious?' I'd been dying of curiosity ever since I'd found out about Sabiha and only the fact that my parents were in such discord over the topic had prevented me from asking questions.

'Of course,' Sabiha said. 'But I had to protect my mum. If I spoke to him, it was like I was choosing him over my mum and I couldn't risk her feeling rejected like that. She might have had a relapse and ended up back in hospital.'

I nodded, shying away from the admission about her mum. I'd heard the hushed whispers about her mother being mentally disturbed. The story about her public breakdown in a shopping centre and being taken into custody by police had made the rounds.

Whenever Dad spoke about his other daughter, he always focused on the disadvantage she'd had to not only miss out on having a father but also to be raised by a mentally unstable mother. Since I'd met Sabiha I didn't see that this was any great liability. She seemed to be fine.

'Why did you change your mind?' I asked.

'The first time he came to see me I thought it wasn't real, that he was putting on a show, but now.' She looked at me from the corner of her eye.

But now he's proved his sincerity by jumping the minute you called, I finished her sentence in my head.

'Won't your Mum be upset?' I asked snidely.

Sabiha looked at me with surprise. 'She's been okay lately. Plus, she's been telling me I need to see him. That it's no good to let all these emotions fester inside.'

I bit my lip and swallowed my angry tirade. I wished I had the luxury of being able to act on my emotions and do what I wanted. Instead, I was always fighting to keep the peace and make everyone else happy.

When we walked into the medical centre, the receptionist looked at us, mentally comparing our physical similarities. As I led Sabiha to the kitchen area, I wondered if this was going to be my future from now on.

'Dad will be here when he finishes with his patient.' I sat at the table.

The staff room was half full with dirty boxes and Sabiha nervously paced, her boots scuffing the cardboard as she twirled in the small space.

The door opened and Dad walked in. I stood.

Chapter 9

Dad's eyes glanced past me and searched out Sabiha who was leaning against the kitchen bench, her slouching posture belying her earlier nervousness.

'Sabiha,' he said her name like a prayer.

'Dad,' Sabiha said it with a question mark.

He reached for her, but she shied away. I saw his pain as he watched Sabiha like he was trying to imprint her image on his brain. There was an awkward silence as they tried to think of what to say. Sabiha was avoiding looking at him. She looked like she regretted coming.

'I've got something for you.' Dad quickly left.

'You okay?' I asked.

Sabiha nodded. 'It's stupid.' She ran her hands through her hair. 'I didn't expect to feel...' her hands flailed as if she couldn't describe the overwhelming emotion.

Dad came back holding a gift bag. 'Alma told me you liked to read.'

Sabiha took the bag gingerly, as if she expected it to be full of squirming snakes. She took out the books and stacked them on the kitchen bench; her face transforming into one of transcendent joy. 'Wow.' She cleared her throat. 'This is too much.' She looked like she was contemplating returning it.

'You're my daughter.' Dad covered her hand with his. 'I wish I'd been there while you were growing up.'

Sabiha closed her eyes and breathed through her mouth. Dad reached for her again. It seemed like she would bolt, her body stiff and on the verge of moving away, but then she squared her shoulders and stood her ground. Dad hugged her, his hand cupping the back of her head as he held her tightly against him.

I saw him over Sabiha's head. There was pain in his eyes as tears seeped down his cheeks, but then there was also unbound joy as he looked down at Sabiha. He never looked at me like that and vicious jealousy cut off my breath.

Sabiha tore out of his resisting arms, surreptitiously wiped her eyes. She stepped back and nearly tripped over a box. 'Fuck,' she swore as she righted herself.

I stiffened, expecting Dad to tell her off, but he acted like she'd said nothing. He gestured to the sofa and Sabiha went and sat.

'What happened today?' he asked as he sat on the sofa next to her.

Sabiha gave him her version of events in which was a loyal friend protecting Brian from a homophobic attack.

'You should have got a teacher's help?' Dad said. 'They could have hurt you.'

'There was no time,' Sabiha said like it was obvious. 'Anyway, Mr Sheen is such a homophobe. He's been picking on Brian all week.'

She was glossing over the truth. Brian wasn't wearing proper clothes and had received two warnings already, but she was making him sound like a victim of a homophobic institution.

I expected Dad to come down with his whole "you have to follow the rules" speech. Instead, there was silence.

'All that matters is that they didn't hurt you,' he said.

'So what's with the boxes?' Sabiha asked after an uncomfortable moment's silence.

'I'm cleaning out a spare office,' Dad said. 'We have another doctor beginning next week and all these old records need to be shredded.'

I was relieved when Sabiha scrunched up her nose. Dad told me about the job weeks ago and while it was mind-blowingly tedious to be anchored to a shredder for two hours a day, I was looking forward to the alone time with him.

'The pay isn't that great, only $10 an hour,' Dad continued. 'But if you're interested, the job is yours.'

Sabiha became very interested. 'Ten bucks,' she repeated back, eyeing the boxes and calculating how much dough she could make.

'There's probably at least twenty hours of work here,' Dad said.

I felt like he'd slapped me. I knew from bitter experience that there was about ten hours of work involved. He was adding on extra hours to entice Sabiha.

'I'll do it.' Sabiha smiled.

'That's great,' he said.

'When do I start?' Sabiha asked, her voice cheery.

I zoned out as they worked out the details and pretended to be doing my homework, but I couldn't look away from them. They looked like a flirtatious couple, eyeing each other when the other one looked away and I was the third wheel.

After she left, he looked dazed, his eyes out of focus as he stared out the door that Sabiha walked out of. 'I'd almost given up that this day would come...'

I didn't know what I was supposed to say, so I kept silent.

'You don't mind Sabiha doing the shredding work?' He finally met my eyes.

'No.' I played the part of the obedient daughter while inside I was screaming in pain.

'It will give us the opportunity to get to know each other and get her away from bad influences like Brian.'

He paused and gave me a sideways look. I squirmed, waiting for him to call me out on not telling him about Brian being gay.

'I'd better call your mother and tell her about what happened today,' Dad said, and left.

My stomach hurt after he left. I felt like he was having a go at me with his last sentence by making a point of updating Mum before I had the chance to "blab" on him.

While Mum was driving, she kept glancing at me in the rear-view mirror, her forehead creased with worry. When we got home, Sanela and Ali ran upstairs, but Mum gently took hold of my arm and led me to the kitchen.

'You're probably feeling left out because your father has asked Sabiha to work at the office, but he needs this time for them to get to know each other,' she said, sounding like a B-grade actress delivering lines in a bad movie she regretted signing up for.

'I know.'

Mum squeezed my hand. 'Promise me you won't let Sabiha lead you astray.'

'You've got nothing to worry about.' Mum blamed Sabiha for my provocative school outfit. I tamped down my guilt. Anyway, if I told Mum the truth that it was Brian who was responsible, I'd open a bigger can of worms. Mum was religious and not known for her support of "alternative lifestyles."

'Sabiha isn't someone who's lead I'll be following,' I said.

Mum smiled.

I reviewed my last comment and realised she thought I was siding with her against Sabiha, when I was commenting on Sabiha's dress sense. Mum hugged me. I inhaled her scent and tried to recapture the sense of comfort that I usually received in her arms, but it wasn't working today. I was like a spinning top, twirling round and round, hoping I could keep up the pace.

I forced a smile for Mum, pretending she'd soothed me. She let me go with a fake smile of her own. I could barely wait to get to the computer and message Alex. Whenever the bad feelings overwhelmed me, I thought of him and felt a thrill of anticipation. His flattery and smooth charms were the balm that I needed to soothe the sting from Dad's displeasure.

I logged into my computer, feeling butterflies dancing in my stomach.

AlexP "I've been waiting for you, gorgeous."

I felt a thrilling, squirming sensation in my stomach, knowing that as I was thinking about him, he was thinking about me.

AlmaO "Sorry. Home drama I had to sort out."

AlexP "Sister trouble?"

AlmaO "Yeah. Dad's given her the job at his office he promised me."

AlexP "Bummer. On the plus side, maybe we can see each other now?"

As I thought about my reply, I bit my fingernail. I'd been stalling, meeting with him, using homework and my part-time job as an excuse, but now I couldn't think why I'd been so hesitant. I'd feared my father's reaction if he found out, but after seeing him today with Sabiha, all my fear had muted and it didn't seem life and death anymore.

AlmaO "Okay."

I typed, holding my breath as I took my fate in my hands.

AlmaO "I'll sort something out."

AlexP "Can't wait. By the way, did I tell you how hot you were today? I couldn't take my eyes off you."

I made a little squeal under my breath.

AlmaO "Thank you."

AlexP "Can't wait to see what outfit you're going to model for me tomorrow."

AlmaO "I'll keep that a surprise."

As we flirted on-line I felt like time stopped and I was enveloped in a safe cocoon. All my worries tipped out of my head and floated away. When it was time to end our on-line chat and return to the real world, I felt a wrench near my heart. I wanted to remain in this moment forever.

I sat on the chair staring at the blank screen as I worked up the motivation to get up. Mum called my name, finally breaking my inertia. When I exited the study, I walked past Dad's office and saw him working at his computer.

I went to the kitchen to help Mum with dinner. Mum made *sarme*, minced meat and vegetables folded into boiled cabbage leaf like a parcel.

'Dad's home early,' I said as I set the table.

'Mmm,' Mum said noncommittally.

I frowned. This was a sign of bad things to come. They proved me right during dinner.

'She was on the train for two hours.' Dad was telling us a story about a patient of his who had arrived in Australia a few months before and went for her first train trip. 'She began walking up and down, the carriage attracting the attention of passengers by calling them *majmune* as if it was their name.'

I frowned, wondering why this woman would call the passengers monkey.

'She did this for about half an hour and finally she reached a male passenger and called him *majmune*. He stood, completely offended. "How dare you call me a monkey?" he demanded of her.' Dad looked at us to check we were paying attention. '"Oh, good, you speak my language," the woman said. "I'm lost and need you to help me."'

We exploded into laughter as we realised her clever ploy to get help in a tricky predicament.

'Well, I've got one for you,' Mum said. 'It's a changeover at my workplace.'

In Mum's job as a nurse, she had to spend fifteen minutes with the nurse on the previous shift to receive information about the patients.

'Anna calls me over to read the notes from her changeover and they say: "John was hungry and ate the staff. He was still hungry and ate his family."'

We broke into laughter.

'Why did John eat his family?' Sanela was perplexed.

'He didn't, sweetheart,' Mum said between bursts of laughter. 'She wanted to write John ate *with* his family.'

'Well, there's a perfect example of why a preposition is important,' Dad said wryly.

I looked around the table at everyone's smiling face and a feeling of wellbeing descended over me. We were a normal family again, before the prodigal daughter entered the picture.

When we lived in Hobart, we used to eat dinner together every weekday; the room echoing with laughter and conversation as we shared stories about our day. On the weekends Mum worked the night shift, and we'd lounge on the couch, eating takeaway while we watched TV with Dad. I didn't realise how much I'd missed these markers of normalcy.

There was a lull after Mum finished her story.

'I was thinking we should invite Sabiha to lunch this Saturday.' Dad lifted a spoon of *sarma* to his mouth.

Mum dropped her fork, the clatter of metal hitting porcelain clanging in the silence. All eyes turned to her. She picked it up again. 'That's a great idea,' her voice was uneven as she gracelessly cut through the cabbage.

Ali tossed his fork down. 'I don't want her here.'

Dad frowned, his eyebrows joining, a sure sign of his displeasure. 'That's not an option.'

Ali's hands tightened on his cutlery. He looked between our parents, deciding whether to protest further. Mum shook her head. Ali returned his attention to his plate, tossing his food around. My appetite faded too, and I listlessly moved my peas.

The only one who was unaffected by our father's announcement was Sanela. 'I'll get to meet Sabiha,' she screeched, as if she was talking about a rock star.

'That's right.' Dad smiled encouragingly.

'I want to make her an invitation.' Sanela squirmed in her chair. 'Can I Mum? Can I please?'

'Of course.' Mum's smile was forced.

'Can I do it now?' Sanela was already halfway off her chair.

'Finish your dinner first,' Mum said.

'Okay.' Sanela shovelled food in her mouth.

The next few minutes were excruciating in their awkwardness. I wanted to be anywhere but here. My thoughts drifted to Alex again, and I spent the rest of dinner mentally planning my outfit for tomorrow.

'Finished.' Sanela held out her hands.

'Okay, you may leave the table,' Mum said.

She didn't have time to finish the sentence before Sanela clambered off her chair and sprinted for the stairs. Soon after, we stopped pretending we were eating anymore and Ali and I were on dishwashing duty.

'Why did he have to invite her?' Ali whispered viciously.

Dad was in the study writing patient notes, while Mum mumbled something about doing a load and disappeared into the back of the house where the laundry was. While I was folding the linen a few days ago, I'd found a packet of cigarettes hidden amongst the pillowcases. Mum was probably furtively smoking with the laundry window open, the iron board leaning against the door preventing anyone from coming in.

'Because she's his daughter.' I was feeling anaesthetised after immersing myself in my usual daydream about Alex. We were at a dance together, out in public like any normal girlfriend and boyfriend. All eyes were on us, the girl's eyes jealous and cutting as Alex gazed at me adoringly.

'Traitor.' Ali turned away from me.

I snapped out of my daydream and scrubbed the pot harder. 'I'm trying to see it from his point of view.'

'She ruined everything.' He had tears in his eyes. I put my hand on his shoulder, but he shrugged it off. He quickly wiped his hands and left me to finish the dishes alone.

I stood in the kitchen feeling the weight of the silence in the house pressing down on me. Once upon a time, we used to all scrunch up on the couch in the living room after dinner, watching a movie or reality TV show together. The house was full of shrieks of laughter and pulsed with life. Now we were becoming estranged in this monstrosity of a house.

I caught my reflection in the kitchen window and noticed my cleavage looked especially enticing in the bra I was wearing. I tilted my head to the side and tried a different pose. Maybe I could alter the red silky top for tomorrow. As long as Mum never found out about my secret alterations, I'd be fine.

Sanela yelled my name. I walked into the living room and saw her leaning over the balustrade. 'I need your help,' she said and disappeared.

'Just a minute.' I returned to the kitchen and rinsed my hands.

I spent the rest of the evening doing my homework in Sanela's room, giving her advice and help about her invitation card.

'Time for your bath,' Mum said to Sanela as she came in.

I picked up my books and passed her by, catching a whiff of cigarette smoke as I passed.

After reading in bed for a while, I turned off the lights, but I couldn't fall asleep. A heavy weight of expectation hung in the air, the feeling of the other shoe dropping. Sure enough, I heard raised voices echoing through the walls. I leaned over the bed and saw it was ten o'clock. As usual, my parents waited until they thought we were asleep before tearing into each other.

I covered my head with the pillow, trying to drown out their shouting. The pressure built behind my ears as I fought to breathe through the foam. I threw the pillow off and gasped in oxygen. The screaming stopped when I was about to go to Sanela's bedroom. I heard Dad's footsteps heading down the stairs.

The silence was even more oppressive than the shouting was. I thought about Alex and the need to contact him built. I couldn't go downstairs and message him on the computer because Dad was sleeping on the couch or watching television until he cooled off and returned to the bedroom, but there was another way.

I got my mobile, and after debating various messages, I typed. AlmaO "U awake."

My thumb hovered over the send button. Was I being desperate to send Alex a message? We'd only chatted on the computer a few hours ago and here I was chasing him again. In the end, my need was too strong and my thumb hit the send button. Within thirty seconds, my phone beeped a reply. With shaking fingers, I opened the message.

AlexP "I was dreaming about you. In my dreams, I got to caress every part of your body. I hope my dream comes true soon."

I lay on the bed and replied.

AlmaO "I dreamt about you too."

I wanted to write more. I wanted to tell him about the swirling dreams I had about him, full of bright colours and soft sounds. How my body was alive in anticipation of his touch, as if I was sleeping beauty and he had awoken me, but I was too shy and embarrassed.

He sent a photo of himself. He was lying bare-chested in bed, his hair tousled and shadows highlighting the pecs on his chest.

AlexP "I'm lying in bed, imagining you with me."

My breath caught in my chest. I hugged my pillow and imagined that it was Alex who was lying next to me. I could hear his deep voice as he spoke.

AlexP "I want to see you. I want to imagine that we're lying side by side."

I turned on my lamp and checked myself in the mirror above my vanity. I was wearing a daggy nighty I'd had for years. It was so thin from washing it was almost see through. I took it off and rummaged through my wardrobe until I found my spaghetti-strap summer nighty that hugged my body. I arranged my hair to flip over my shoulder and frame my cleavage. I quickly smeared lip gloss on my lips and lifted the phone toward the mirror, snapping a full body shot.

AlexP "You are so beautiful that you make me ache."

I swept away my reservations under a wave of happiness.

AlmaO "I wish you were here with me. I want your arms around me."

Time became suspended as we sent messages back and forth. He wanted to call me, but I told him he couldn't. It was too risky that the sound would travel, alerting my parents. My phone beeped.

Alma: "I have no credit left. We'll have to talk tomorrow."

I lay down in bed, but I couldn't sleep. It was as if every nerve ending was alive. My phone beeped again and I read the text message that my credit had been recharged.

AlexP "Now we can keep texting."

I lay back in bed and smiled.

AlmaO "How can I ever thank you?"

AlexP "Being able to SMS you is thanks enough."

I hugged the phone to my chest, tears burning my eyes. He was the sweetest boy I'd ever met.

We texted until my fingers ached. When we finished, I turned off my light and lay in the dark room and tried to sleep, but no matter how much I tossed and turned, I couldn't get comfortable. I felt warm and sweaty, and there was a damp tingling between my legs.

Without realising I was doing it, my hand brushed against my panties and I felt a burst of pleasure shoot through me. My fingers reached inside and brushed again more deliberately and I had to bite my lip to keep from moaning. As I touched myself, I thought about Alex, imagining that he was with me in the bed, kissing me, touching me.

The pleasure built and built. My hand moved quicker and suddenly an overwhelming sensation washed over me and it was like my whole body was floating on a cloud. I opened my eyes, and the room looked all foggy and out of focus. I closed my eyes and drifted off to sleep, Alex' name a sweet taste in my mouth.

Chapter 10

I was in the girl's toilets doing my morning makeover and changing out of the jeans and top I'd left the house in, and into a denim skirt and red silk top I'd hidden in my backpack.

I should have been exhausted. I didn't fall asleep until 3 o'clock in the morning, but I was invigorated, my whole body alive. Alex had sent me a message as I was leaving home.

AlexP "Can't wait to see what sexy outfit you'll be wearing today."

I'd altered my top by snipping at the v-neck to make my cleavage stand out more. I checked myself out in the mirror above the sinks. It was such a bummer there was no full-length mirror, so I had to stand on my tiptoes to see as much of my outfit as possible.

'Who are you dressing up for?' Sabiha asked wryly. Now that Brian wasn't coming to school, she'd reverted to her butch ways, even forfeiting lip gloss.

I was struck mute, my blush a dead giveaway.

'Who says she's dressing up for anyone else?' Dina answered for me. She was also changing into another outfit and putting on makeup. 'Some of us just like to look good.'

'You mean some of you are vain and shallow,' Sabiha countered.

'Ha, ha.' Dina fake laughed. 'Says the girl who gets mistaken for a lesbian daily.'

'Fuck you,' Sabiha snapped and stormed out of the toilet.

Dina and I met each other's eyes in the mirror and giggled helplessly. When we exited the bathroom, Sabiha was moodily staring out the window.

'You know I love you,' Dina said to Sabiha, giving her a bear hug.

'Suck up.' Sabiha smiled.

As we walked down the corridor to class, I saw Alex standing on the side, scanning the crowd. He saw me and mimed there was an exploding mine in his hands, flailing as if he would fall down. I grinned and looked over my shoulder as I passed to see him checking out my arse. There was a spring in my step as we continued walking.

'We should go visit Brian tonight. Help him settle into his new place,' Dina said.

'Can't.' Sabiha looked pained at missing out. 'I'm working for Dad.'

I stifled a smile. It was her first day of the job and she'd been pumping me for information about how everything worked and diligently took notes. I thought she'd only cared for the money, but all her questions were about how Dad wanted things done and I'd realised how desperate she was to impress him.

'What about you?' Dina turned to me.

'No, I can't.' I automatically refused. I only visited friends' houses that Mum knew about.

'Why not?' Dina said. 'Aren't you supposed to be hanging around until your Dad finishes, anyway?'

I nodded. Thursday night's Ali did karate, so I had to stay at Dad's and go home with him.

'Say you're going to the library with me. My brother will drop you off afterward,' Dina said.

I was stunned speechless. It had never occurred to me to defy my parents and lie to them about my whereabouts. I was always mindful of doing the right thing, respecting my parents, and living up to their expectations of me.

'I don't think that's a good idea,' Sabiha said. 'Dad is old school.'

Dina looked at her with surprise. 'Since when do you advocate respecting parental authority?'

Sabiha visibly squirmed, uncomfortable at being caught out as a hypocrite.

'I'll come.' I made the snap decision, my primary motivation wanting to get at Sabiha.

'Good.' Dina put her arm around my shoulders. 'And you can cover for us,' she told Sabiha. 'If her "old school" Dad twigs onto something, you give us the heads up.'

I gained satisfaction from Sabiha's stony face, then had a moment of disquiet. I'd never flouted my parent's rules like this, but why should I be missing out on all the fun? It wasn't as if I was scoring any brownie points in being the dutiful daughter. It even seemed that Sabiha was benefitting by getting into trouble and getting Dad's undivided attention.

I called Mum and got permission to stay at the public library near Dad's work to do my homework. During recess, I ducked into the toilets and sent Alex a text message.

Alma: 'Can't chat tonight. Going to Brian's.'

My phone beeped. I looked down and read.

Alex: 'Ok.'

His matter of fact reply left me let down. I thought he'd at least suggest we try to meet up.

At the end of school, we parted company at the school gates. Sabiha turned left toward St Albans centre, while Dina and I turned right. The thrill of doing something illicit made the adrenaline surge through my body. I skipped to expand my energy.

'Where are you going, Bunny?' Dina laughed and ran to catch up to me.

'I'm so excited.' I spread my arms wide.

'Gees, you don't get out much.'

Dina said it as a joke, but it cut through me. 'No, no, I don't,' I said soberly, realising my parents controlled so much of my life.

'Don't worry.' Dina grabbed my hand and skipped with me. 'You've got me to corrupt you.'

We got to Brian's house out of breath and laughing maniacally.

'Welcome to my humble abode,' Brian said as he opened the front door. He bent over at the waist and extended his arm in an invitation for us to enter.

Dina pushed past him, and I followed, taking in every detail. The house was weatherboard and the walls inside were scuffed and smudged, as if a thousand handprints had marked them. Our footsteps echoed on the hallway floorboards. When we entered the living room I examined the matted sofa only to gasp when I saw Alex sitting on it.

He gave me a grin as he lifted a beer bottle. 'Well, hello,' he said, imbuing his voice with surprise. 'Fancy meeting you here.'

'Who invited the riff raff?' Dina threw herself on the beanbag.

'Settle.' Omer tapped his cigarette on the full ashtray. 'Alex is a mate.'

Dina rolled her eyes, but refrained from further comment. After Brian gave me a tour of the house, we went back to the living room. Brian sat next to Omer, leaving me to sit in the only spot available—next to Alex.

'Now that everyone is here, we can start the party.' Omer pulled out a cigarette from his pocket. Everyone cheered.

I wondered what the big deal was. It was only a cigarette.

Omer lit up and took a deep breath. 'This is top shit.' He passed it to Brian.

As Brian took a drag, I twigged. I looked around the circle. Everyone was smiling as they waited their turn. When Dina took a drag, I got panicky. What was I going to do when they passed it to me? I wanted to be cool and blend in with everyone, but Mum was a nurse, and Dad a doctor. I'd listened to hundreds of stories about medical emergencies that resulted from illegal drugs, not to mention the constant warnings that my parents knew all the signs of intoxication.

Dina passed the joint to Alex, who took a deep breath and let out a blissful smile as he exhaled. 'None for you, young lady.' He leaned over my lap and passed the joint back to Omer.

He was treating me like a child. I was about to demand a drag when he squeezed my thigh and winked. He was looking out for me. He must have noticed my panic, and he'd given me an out. I smiled tremulously in reply. As the drugs took hold, everyone descended into hilarity. I leaned back on the sofa and watched, feeling like I was an anthropologist studying a newly discovered tribe.

'How can you be sure you're a fag?' Omer asked Brian. 'Play both teams before you can decide.'

'I have,' Brian said, taking another puff.

'Really,' Omer stirred. 'You've been with a girl?'

'You bet I have.' Brian smirked.

'If she's a dog, it doesn't count,' Omer said.

'Sabiha isn't a dog,' Dina cut in.

'You fucked Sabiha.' Omer hooted, slapping his knee.

I looked at Brian with surprise. I knew something wonky happened between them, but I didn't think they'd had sex.

'I didn't fuck her.' Brian gave Dina a dirty look.

'Then it doesn't count,' Omer said flatly. 'Only if you did the full deed.'

'They did—' Dina started.

'Shut up.' Brian threw a cushion at her. 'Sabiha will kill you if she finds out you blabbed.'

Dina sobered up for a second, realising his threat wasn't without merit.

I was sorry Dina hadn't finished.

'I wonder what they did.' Alex whispered in my ear. 'First or second base.'

I screwed up my face. I was equally curious and disgusted.

'It must be gross thinking about your sister's sex life.' Alex smiled.

I nodded.

The toke passed to him again. He took another drag. 'That's it for me. I've got plans tonight.' He leaned next to me so that our shoulders were touching. 'How's your first week as the new student been?'

This was the first time he'd asked me a serious question. Usually we flirted madly on-line, keeping it light and fun. He'd become my soft place to fall. I wondered if he was really interested or if he was making small talk. I was going to give him the usual response about being glad that I had new friends, but something about the way he was intently watching me, like he was interested in every word, made me stop.

'Weird,' I ended up saying instead.

'It's not everyday you find out you've got a long-lost-sister,' Alex said.

He got it. He really understood what it was like. My words cascaded like a dam that burst its banks. I told him all about what had happened since I began school. About the way I would sometimes look at Sabiha and get the strangest feeling of *déjà vu*, as if I was looking at myself in the mirror. About how, when I watched Dad and Sabiha, I wondered if he would ever look at me like that again. And about how my parents' marriage was strained with them acting like strangers.

And as each shameful confession burst out of me, Alex listened. He maintained eye contact and made me feel like the most important person in the world. I cut off mid-sentence as Omer's raucous story got everyone screaming with laughter.

'I can't believe you did that.' Brian laughed so hard he fell off the sofa, setting them off again.

'Let's find somewhere where we can talk.' Alex went to Brian's bedroom door and held it open for me.

Before I entered, I hesitated. I wanted to go in and be alone with him, have the chance to put some of our flirtation into practice, but now all I could see was the enormous bed and the possibilities it suggested. I remembered the way he'd made me feel the last time we'd talked, and the way I'd touched myself under the cover of night and blushed from excruciating embarrassment.

I looked at Alex. He was watching me with a smile, patiently waiting for me. Laughter boomed from the living room behind us, reassuring me I had nothing to fear. The house was full of people. Feeling sheepish, I sat on the bed, and Alex sat beside me, leaving a comfortable margin of space between us. I tugged my skirt past my knees. Everything had been easy in the living room, but now an awkwardness had descended.

'Anyway, I've talked enough.' I forced a laugh. 'Have you got any siblings?'

'Kind of.' Alex looked down at the floor as he bunched up the bedding in his hands. 'A little sister Amy.'

I was caught up on the words kind of, but before I had the chance to ask, he continued.

'It would have been her eighth birthday next month.' He gulped. 'She had leukaemia.'

'I'm sorry.' I grabbed hold of his hand and rubbed his back with my other hand.

'Thanks. I get what you're going through.' His lips formed into an imitation of a smile. 'I've been going through a hard time too.'

'What was she like?' I leaned on his shoulder and half hugged him.

'She was like most little sisters, a pest.' He laughed. 'She was a great kid, though. Anyway, things have been tough at home since it happened. My parents aren't doing well.' He wiped his face with his hands and tenderness filled me. 'She was Daddy's little girl and since she's been gone, he's checked out. He's either at the pub or if he's at home he's drinking in his man shed.' He stared blankly at the wall in front of us. 'We used to be like mates–going to the footy every week to watch the Doggies, but now he's missing in action.'

'I'm sure he'll come back to you.' I rubbed his back.

He put his arm around my shoulders, and we hugged. It was a while before I noticed the hug had changed from mere comfort to something more. I realised I was in a bedroom alone with a boy. That I was sitting on a bed alone with a boy. That I was hugging a boy while sitting alone on a bed with him. What if he'd assumed that by coming into the bedroom, I was agreeing to something?

'Anyway, you probably want to leave now.' He turned away from me and rubbed his eyes.

My stomach sank. He was crying. I'd underestimated him. Damn, why did I over think things? Of course, he wasn't making underhanded plans.

My hands cupped his shoulders. 'It's going to be all right.'

He didn't turn toward me. I'd ruined it. I'd had a nice guy, someone who got me and I could talk to, and I let suspicion get between us.

'Thank you.' Alex covered my hand with his. 'I've got no one else to talk about this stuff. My mates aren't the sensitive type and my ex ran off when things got too heavy with Amy.'

'I'm not going anywhere.' I squeezed his hand and waited.

He turned around after a few moments. 'I'm sorry about that.'

'It's okay.'

Our eyes caught, and the moment softened, changed into something else. He nudged his head forward, slowly, looking from my lips and back to my eyes again. I knew he was going to kiss me. I had time to process his intent as his head slowly descended. By the time his lips touched mine, I was breathless with anticipation.

At first I was stiff and nervous, wondering if I was doing it right. I kept wondering if my mouth was open too much, did I use too much tongue? The boys I'd kissed before were my age, but Alex was older, sophisticated and I was being measured against all the girls that came before.

He knew what he was doing and soon enough, the sensation of our mouths melding together set off delightful explosions in my body. As we kissed, he kept his hands on the bed beside me, our lips the only things touching. He was letting me set the pace. When my body was too weak to hold myself, I put my hands on his shoulder and leaned into him. I was awash with sensation. My lips tingling, my skin supersensitive as he put his hands on my waist. I lost time and the next thing I knew, his hand was under my top, cupping my breast. I broke the kiss.

'Are you okay?' His lips moved to my neck.

Trying to work through an answer to his question, I stared up at the ceiling. I'd never gone to second base with a boy. I didn't know if I wanted to stay or go.

Alex stopped kissing me and looked at me. His face tightened at whatever he saw there and he removed his hand.

I tugged my top down, feeling self-conscious.

'You can go,' he said tonelessly.

I looked at the door. All I had to do was stand up and take two steps. Two steps and I'd be out of this excruciatingly embarrassing situation. Two steps and Alex would go from my future to my past. I realised I had the answer to his question.

'I'm okay.' I leaned over and kissed him.

'Really?' His arms wrapped around me.

'Really,' I whispered against his lips.

His hand went under my top, and he caressed my bare back. Tingles followed. He took control of the kiss and went back on top. His hand moved to my breast again, and I stopped thinking.

My vision became blurry, and I wanted to be closer, to merge my body with his. He flipped me on top of him and cupped my bottom. Then he put his hand between my legs. Before I protested, he'd removed his hand, and I relaxed back into the kiss.

He moved my hand down. It took me a moment to process that he'd placed it on his penis. I froze and came out of my trance. I hesitated, surprised at the softness of his skin, before turning my head.

'I think we need to stop.'

'Come back.' Alex lifted his head and tried to kiss me, but I moved away.

'No.' I lifted myself off him.

'I thought we were having a good time.' Alex followed me to the edge of the bed and brushed my hair away from my face before leaning in.

I moved away. 'We were.' I buttoned my shirt. 'But things are going too fast.'

Alex lay on the bed and groaned. 'So. You're a girl, I'm a guy. We're alone with a bed. This is what we're supposed to do.'

'Maybe, but I'm not ready.' I stood and tucked my top in my pants.

'I am.' Alex took a condom out of his pocket.

I looked away, my cheeks flushing with embarrassment.

'Are you blushing?' Alex peered at me. 'Most sixteen year old girls have seen a condom before.'

I jerked my head to look at him. He didn't know that I had just turned fifteen, and I had to keep it that way.

'Shit, are you a virgin?' he whispered the last word like it was a disease.

I stared at him like a deer in headlights.

'You are.' He laughed.

My eyes filled with tears, and I grabbed the door handle.

'Don't.' Alex stood and put his hands on my shoulders. When I kept tugging the door handle, he hugged me, pulling me against him. 'I'm sorry. I didn't mean to laugh. I'm just surprised.'

He turned my reluctant body until I was facing him. 'Of course you want things to be special. We'll take it easy.' He put his hand under my chin.

I kept my eyes on the wall beside us as he lifted my head.

'And when the time is right, we'll take that step. I'm falling for you.' He tucked my hair behind my ear.

My eyes snapped to his.

'I want you to be my girlfriend.'

I gaped in shock.

'Don't you want that?' His voice hurt when the silence stretched out too long.

'Of course I do.'

'Good.' He smiled gently and kissed me.

I kissed him back, but I wasn't able to let go. My brain was in overdrive as I tried to process what had happened. I now had a boyfriend.

'We can't tell anyone,' I said when he broke the kiss. 'No one can know that we're together. If it gets back to my Dad—'

'Of course.' He rubbed my shoulders. 'We'll keep it on the down-low.'

'We can't be together at school.'

'But we can be together after school.' He smiled.

I fake smiled, not knowing how to let him know that this event, me coming to Brian's house instead of being at Dad's surgery, was an aberration, a one-off event that would be impossible to replicate. 'I usually get to school really early,' I said hopefully.

'How early?'

'Eight o'clock.'

He winced.

'I'd better get going.' I lifted my hand awkwardly toward the door.

'When can I see you?' Alex asked as I headed toward the door. 'Omer's lent me his spare keys.'

'I don't know.' I stalled.

'Please.' He bent and kissed my cheek before returning to my lips. 'Don't keep me hanging.'

'I'll text you.' I opened the door.

'You go first,' Alex said. 'I'll be out in a minute.'

I ducked into the bathroom to put on the jeans and t-shirt I'd left home in this morning. As I packed my trampy clothes in my bag, I caught a whiff of cigarettes. I'd have to put them straight in the washing machine so Mum didn't touch them.

When I got out, Jesse was in the hallway. 'I didn't know you were coming?' I said with surprise.

'I had a few things to do after school,' Jesse said.

Dina entered the hallway. 'I was wondering where you disappeared to.' She looked at me.

'I'm right here,' I said.

'Oh.' Dina looked confused. 'Oh,' she said again suggestively when she saw Jesse.

Omer called her and she returned to the living room, a concerned look passing over her face as she left.

'So,' Jesse said.

'I'm leaving.' I gestured to the front door.

'Me too,' Jesse said.

'You just arrived.'

'The interesting people are leaving. And anyway, this isn't my kind of party,' Jesse said ruefully, peering into the living room. 'See you tomorrow.' He closed the door behind himself.

I entered the living room. 'I have to go.' When Dina didn't respond, I kicked the beanbag.

'Already?' Dina threw herself backward and looked at me upside down from bloodshot eyes. 'Shit!' Dina fought her way out of the beanbag. She walked to Omer who was dozing on the couch. 'Come on.' She slapped his arm. 'Drive us.'

'Is that a good idea?' I asked. 'We could get into a car accident.'

'Nah.' Dina waved her hand. 'He's used to it.'

I didn't find her statement reassuring, but I didn't have a choice. If I walked, I'd be late and raise Dad's suspicions.

Dina made Omer a coffee. 'We'll leave in a minute,' Dina said, as I nervously paced.

I looked at the time on my mobile and bit my nails. I glanced at Brian's bedroom door and wondered if Alex had already left without saying goodbye. Omer slugged back the last of the coffee and grimaced. He picked up his keys, and we went to the hallway.

Alex exited Brian's room, looking relaxed.

'Did you rub one out in there?' Brian demanded.

Alex shrugged ruefully.

'Tell me you didn't stain my bedspread.' Brian pushed past him and examined the room. 'Payne!' he yelled with outrage.

'And that's my cue to leave.' Alex ran through the front door.

I blushed with embarrassment, feeling like what we did together was a seamy postscript. As I got into the backseat of Omer's car, Alex was halfway down the block. Omer drove fast. I kept seeing images of his car wrapped around an electricity pylon featured in news footage. Either way, I'd be dead. If the accident didn't kill me, my parents would. Omer stopped with screeching tyres a few shops up from Dad's medical centre.

I went to get out, but thought better of it. 'Listen.' I put my hand on Dina's shoulder. 'There's no need to tell Sabiha about me talking to Alex or all the other stuff that happened.'

Dina turned a blank face toward me.

I mimed smoking.

'Oh.' Dina nodded. 'So you don't want me to mention Jesse either?'

I nodded, realising Dina didn't know I'd been alone with Alex.

Dina nodded and turned to the front.

I entered the medical centre and headed straight for the kitchen. I was pouring myself a glass of water when Sabiha walked in and closed the door.

'You're cutting it fine,' she said.

I gulped the whole glass before answering. 'Does he suspect anything?'

'No. He asked me to go see how you were doing half an hour back and I "pretended" to check on you. By the way, you were having trouble with the photocopier.' Sabiha sat on the kitchen counter.

'Thanks.' I wiped my mouth with my hand, then stopped, horror stricken when I remembered I'd touched a penis. I poured hand-wash lotion and scrubbed it under the tap.

'He's a really dedicated Dad.'

'What do you mean?' I dried my hand with a paper towel.

'I mean, he's thinking of you the whole time, even when you're not here.' Sabiha sounded confused, as if this was a strange phenomenon she hadn't encountered before.

'So what?' I threw the paper towel in the bin and sat on the couch.

'You take it all for granted.' Sabiha's face was screwed up with disappointment, as if I had committed a grievous crime.

'He's your Dad too.' I wanted Sabiha to shut up and give me some time to process what happened with Alex.

'Not really,' Sabiha said, but I had stopped listening.

Would Alex think I was a slut now because I'd let him touch me? We'd gone way past what I'd thought I would do with a guy, and now I was feeling embarrassed and uncomfortable at the thought of seeing him again.

'You ready?' Dad asked from the doorway.

I nodded.

'Did you get your assignment done?' Dad asked as I walked past him.

'Just have to type it.' I could buy myself more computer time to chat with Alex.

Sabiha and I waited by Dad's car while he turned off all the lights.

'What did you guys do at Brian's?' Sabiha asked abruptly.

'Nothing.' I didn't want to tell Sabiha about the joint. I didn't know what her moral compass was with those things. 'We hung out and talked.'

'Sounds like you're hiding something.' Sabiha demanded.

I shifted nervously away from her. 'Why would you think that?'

Dad saved me from further interrogation. He pressed the car alarm. Sabiha and I reached for the passenger car handle. I hesitated and Sabiha opened the door.

'You're getting dropped off first,' I said. 'So you should sit in the back.'

Sabiha gave me a stricken look and sullenly passed by to sit in the back. I sat down next to Dad, enjoying the triumph of winning.

Chapter 11

I spent the night tossing and turning and woke up feeling tired. I'd tried to message Alex in the afternoon, but he wasn't on-line. The thought of seeing him at school filled me with nervous trepidation. How was he going to act toward me after yesterday? I wished I had someone to talk to about these confusing feelings, but there was no one to trust.

Dina and Sabiha were already at our regular spot when I walked up, their eyes glued to a piece of paper. I collapsed on the bench and yawned. How was I going to get through the day without falling asleep?

'I'm bringing chips and dips. What about you?' Sabiha asked Dina.

'I'm on dessert duty so I'll get biscuits and a cake,' Dina said.

'What's going on?' I asked, the cobwebs clearing as my curiosity peaked.

'We're coordinating food for Brian and Omer's housewarming.' Sabiha's attention was on the list in her hand. 'Did you tell Jesse that he's doing drinks?'

Dina shook her head. 'I'll track him down at recess.'

'When did this happen?' I asked.

'After you left the living room,' Dina said.

'Where were you?' Sabiha asked.

Dina looked up at me, her eyes like saucers radioing SOS.

'Jesse gave me a tour of the house,' I said.

'Jesse was there?' Sabiha demanded, looking cut.

Dina gave me an apologetic look.

'He wasn't there for long,' I lied. 'We had a quick walk in the backyard. That must have been when you guys decided about the party.'

'Sure,' Dina said. 'That must have been it.'

'When's the party?' I asked.

'This Saturday,' Sabiha said.

She continued to write her list as I waited for her to say more. My eyes blinked. I wanted to storm off and stick it to them for not inviting me, but as I looked around at the stream of students walking in groups past us, I remained glued to the seat.

Noticing my reaction, Dina said, 'you're invited.' She looked at Sabiha. 'Isn't that right, Sabiha?'

I smiled my relief, my despondency fading. I didn't even begin planning my outfit when Sabiha doused my enthusiasm again.

Sabiha was frowning at her list. Noticing the silence, she looked up. 'Brian invited you, but I told him you couldn't come.' She shrugged carelessly. 'It's a grownup party.'

'So,' I demanded.

'So, your parents would never let you come,' Sabiha said slowly, as if she was speaking to someone intellectually challenged.

'And your Mum will?' I demanded.

'She's giving me permission to go.'

'What about Dad?' I asked, wanting to put a dent in her confidence.

'If he asks, I'll tell him I'm sleeping over at Dina's,' Sabiha said.

I looked at Dina for confirmation.

'Unfortunately, I'm not that lucky,' Dina said. 'I have to sneak out while my parents are sleeping.'

'So we're covered,' Sabiha said. 'What's going to be your cover story?'

Usually there would be no way in the world that I could ever contemplate going to a party without my parent's knowledge. Mum insisted on knowing every detail and she'd drop me off and pick me up afterward, ensuring that I was where I said I was.

But since Mum started working night shift she'd slowly been increasing her work hours. At first she was only working twice a week, but now she was doing on average three shifts and she was rostered on this Saturday. Mum took on the shift, assuming Dad would be home, but he had a conference and was delivering a talk.

After a long discussion with Ali and I about responsibility, they made the decision that we could stay by ourselves for the night. I was filled with disquiet at the thought of betraying my parent's trust, but Sabiha's superior attitude goaded me into continuing with my story.

'I don't need one.' As I explained why, I felt a frisson of joy as Sabiha's superior look faded.

'Aren't you supposed to babysit your little sister or some-thing?' Sabiha asked.

'Not a problem.' I snapped my fingers. 'My little brother will take care of her.'

Sabiha and Dina exchanged a look. 'Are you sure it's a good idea to go?' Sabiha looked at me with concern. 'This is going to be a full on adult party and you're young.'

I lost the power of speech, but my furious look spoke for me.

'She's mature for her age.' Dina gave Sabiha a warning look.

As soon as I sat down in first period, my adrenaline faded and I regretted saying I would go to the party. I'd never flouted my parent's authority. They always knew my friends, and I'd only been to outings that they approved.

There were so many logistical aspects to attending the party, I didn't even know how to address them. How was I going to leave the house? And even though I'd boasted that Ali would take care of my little sister, that was a big stretch. While he helped me on the nights that we were home alone, I was the one that did all the heavy lifting with Sanela.

Then there was ensuring Sanela didn't know what was going on. She didn't understand the concept of a secret, and anything she heard was passed around to all sundry. Not to mention transport.

I imagined myself catching a taxi to the party and back, but now that I actually thought about it, I was reminded of every single headline I'd read that featured a young girl alone in a taxi being taken advantage of by an unscrupulous driver.

Maybe I should ditch the whole idea. All I had to do was report back on Monday and tell Sabiha that my little sister was sick. No harm, no foul, but the thought of eating crow and having Sabiha establish her superiority even more made me sick to my stomach.

Plus, there was the fact that once again I'd be marked as the outsider. Dina, Jesse and Sabiha would return to school on Monday full of stories about their night of sin and debauchery and once again I'd be the dorky fifth wheel, the one who had no stories to share apart from how many times I'd watched *The Gruffalo* in a weekend with my little sister.

Still, was it worth risking everything to get back at Sabiha? If my parents caught me sneaking out, there would be no telling what would happen. I'd done nothing this bad that I couldn't even contemplate what suitable punishment they'd dream up.

There was the devil's voice telling me it didn't matter if they caught me. Because if I went down so would Sabiha and Dad could no longer close his eyes to the reality of what Sabiha was really like.

I spent the first two periods weighing up the pro's and cons of attending the party. At recess, I received a text message from Alex. I had to read it three times before I understood. Ten minutes into period three, I asked the teacher for a toilet pass. As I walked into the toilets, my stomach was full of nervous butterflies.

I pushed open the doors to the cubicles slowly. 'Alex,' I whispered. I reached the end of the cubicles and was pulling out my mobile to text him when the toilet door next to me opened and arms dragged me in. A hand covered my mouth as I tried to scream. I struggled as I was pressed up against the cubicle wall, my hands gripped.

'It's me.' Alex let me go.

'You bastard.' I put my hand on my chest as I fought for breath.

He put his hands above my head and boxed me in. 'I missed you.' He gave me a kiss that stole what little breath I had left.

'We can't.' I gestured to the door where anyone could enter.

'No one will come.' Alex kissed me.

I was reluctant. It seemed kind of sordid to be petting in the school toilets where anyone could come in, but as he continued kissing me, thinking became harder. I got swept away in the moment of passion. He picked me up, my legs automatically wrapping around his waist to hold myself up. He pressed my back against the wall.

As he kissed my neck, I cupped his head, feeling a thrill that he could hold me with such ease. It was like every romantic fantasy I'd imagined. The strong, hunky guy and the feminine, dainty heroine. I glanced over at the toilet and the romantic pall faded. Alex lifted his head and kissed me again.

I broke the kiss and turned my head away. 'I have to get back to class.'

'Shit.' He set me down and held me, his breath puffing against my forehead.

My legs were wobbly, and I had to clutch the wall until I regained my balance.

'Are you going to Brian's party tomorrow night?' He adjusted his jeans.

'I don't know,' I said. 'Sabiha said I shouldn't go.'

He peered over the toilet cubicle. 'What's it to Sabiha? Do you want to go or not?'

'I want to, but—'

'But what?' Alex urged. 'It's our chance to be together properly.'

My eyes popped open. Properly? Did that mean?

Seeing my shock, Alex twined his hands through mine. 'I mean, where we can spend time together like a proper couple.'

I looked at our joined hands and felt a thrill. My boyfriend and I were holding hands. 'I don't have any way of getting there,' I finally said, remembering one of my logistical constraints.

'That's easy. I'll pick you up. SMS your address and the time.' He gave me a kiss before he left.

I spent the rest of the day in a daze. Things were moving too fast, and I was on an express train, destination unknown. I'd been enjoying my flirtation with Alex and had only thought as far as the next day and the opportunity to get some thrills. Now that we were officially a couple, there were certain expectations attached.

Whenever I'd thought about having sex, I'd always imagined it in the longed for future. It would be when I was married and, of course, on my wedding night. My husband would slip off my satin wedding dress and we'd gaze at each other adoringly as we entwined our hands, our matching gold wedding bands sparkling under the hotel chandelier.

But now that daydream belonged to someone else. Some girl I once knew who didn't understand the reality of desire and need. Who didn't know about the urgency that gripped you when you were caught up in the moment's passion and nothing else mattered but satisfaction? A girl who didn't understand the thrill that went through your body when a guy gave you that look, the one that said I want you, I need you, I can't be without you.

I left behind the girl who believed in happily ever after in Hobart. That girl had parents that made her dream in a fairy tale. But now, as I watched my parents battling through the darkness of a marriage gone wrong, that fairy tale dream seemed like a novelty joke.

It was time for me to bury that girl forever. I had to take Dad's lead in wiping the slate clean and letting go of my old life and become the new me. I was a girl with a boyfriend. A boyfriend who had expectations. And I was going to fulfil those expectations properly. I got through the rest of the school day in a daze. I was consumed with one thing and one thing only—how to get to the party.

When I went to meet Sabiha after school, there was a crowd gathered in the corridor. I pushed through the crowd and saw Sabiha standing in front of her open locker, Dina beside her. There were condoms spilling from it.

Sabiha slammed the locker door shut. There was a crude graffiti drawing of a penis on the front with a mouth on the tip. 'What the hell are you staring at?' she demanded at the rubber-neckers.

'What happened?' I asked, as the crowd dispersed.

'What do you think?' Sabiha said. 'It's someone's idea of a joke.'

I bent and picked up a note.

"I hear you're very talented. Meet me in BJ Lane after school."

Sabiha snatched it from my hand and read it, her lips curling into a bitter smile. 'Someone's been talking.'

Dina took the note. 'Don't be paranoid.'

'It happened last year, but I'm copping flack now,' Sabiha said.

'It's probably a smart arse spinning shit to get at you,' Dina said.

Sabiha bit her lip and turned to stare at her locker. I waited for her to get moving. Seconds passed, but Sabiha still stood as if frozen. Dina and I looked at each other helplessly.

'We should get going,' I said.

'I can't,' Sabiha replied. 'I can't leave my locker like this.'

Dina put her hand around Sabiha. I expected Sabiha to push her away, but she listlessly leaned her head on her shoulder.

'Of course.' I wanted to smack myself. 'I'll go find some stuff to clean it.' The only way to contain this rumour was to remove the evidence.

When I returned ten minutes later with a bottle of graffiti cleaner, the condoms were gone and Dina and Sabiha were sitting on the floor. I got to work scrubbing the locker. A few minutes later, my arm was aching and my movements were slowing.

'Here.' Dina appeared at my side and took over. 'Okay, I think it's gone,' Dina said, panting slightly.

After we'd washed our hands, we walked to the school gates and split in opposite directions. Dina was going to Omer's and Sabiha and I were going to Dad's medical centre.

'Are you okay?' I asked after we'd walked in silence for a few minutes.

'Everyone's going to be pointing and staring at me.'

'It will pass until something new comes along.'

'I guess,' Sabiha sighed. 'It's just that I get sick of always being the circus freak show.'

I glanced over at her and was surprised to see the pain on her face. She was usually always so tough and impenetrable, acting like she didn't give a stuff about other people's opinions that it had never occurred to me she was faking it.

I'd never really thought about what her life was like being the daughter of "that crazy woman." When Mum and Dad told us about her mother, their voices had been full of pity, and the Bosnians acted like anyone with a mental illness was destined for a fate worse than death. I couldn't even imagine the gossiping and backstabbing that we have subjected them to.

I wanted to say something comforting, something that would get across my newfound understanding, but before I could find the words, Sabiha increased her pace as if she regretted showing her vulnerability and was attempting to run from it.

When we got to Dad's medical centre, Sabiha told him we were late because we were borrowing books for a school assignment. Sabiha sorted boxes, while I did my homework, the sound of the shredder filling the small kitchen.

Dad came into the kitchen and helped Sabiha sort the papers, even though it was obvious there wasn't much help needed. Sabiha took his help in stride and soon enough they were laughing and talking, as the pace of shredding slowed significantly.

'Don't you have to be with a patient?' I asked after fifteen minutes passed and he made no sign of moving.

'I've cleared my schedule for the next two hours.' Dad opened another file.

I looked back at my homework, dry-eyed. The blows kept coming. When he'd proposed that I take the job I'd hoped to have some alone time with him, but accepted that the most I could hope for was snatches of minutes between his appointments. Yet now that it was Sabiha doing the dull and ridiculously simple job, he had no problems clearing his schedule for her.

'I have something for you.' Dad returned to the kitchen holding a plastic bag that he handed to Sabiha. 'I know your birthday isn't until next month, but you need this now.'

I watched curiously as Sabiha took out a box from the bag. 'A new mobile phone,' Sabiha squealed and gave him a hug.

I frowned. Our birthdays were three months apart? How did that happen?

Dad hugged her back, breaking into a smile. 'I've put you on the same plan as the rest of the family and you can call any of us for free.'

Sabiha opened the box and took out a mobile phone that was identical to the ones Dad bought for Ali and I. 'It's even got internet,' Sabiha said with a hushed whisper as she pressed buttons.

'No it doesn't,' I jumped in. When I'd received my mobile Mum and Dad purposely disabled the internet.

'Yes it does. Look.' Sabiha brought it over and showed me the website she'd opened.

I felt like I was sucker-punched in the gut. Dad was watching Sabiha with an indulgent smile.

'Why does she get internet and we don't?' I demanded abruptly.

Sabiha looked at me with surprise. 'You don't have internet?'

We both waited for Dad to respond. He tugged at his shirt cuff, his tell that he was uncomfortable. 'Because your mother has very strong ideas about what young people should and shouldn't have access to.'

I packed up with shaking hands. He was such a liar. He and Mum made that decision together and now he was sandbagging Mum to look good in front of Sabiha.

'Where are you going?' he asked.

'I'll wait for Mum outside.'

He called my name, but I didn't stop. When Mum picked me up, I had to fight the urge to tell her about Sabiha's mobile, but in the end, I swallowed my words. If I did, I'd be responsible for my parents having another fight. Instead, I stared out the window and daydreamed about Brian's party.

In my fantasies, Alex and I spent the night dancing. I was wearing a sexy, red dress, and he was in tight black pants, his shirt unbuttoned to flash his six-pack. Everyone watched us with envy while we danced. All the girls perved on Alex, but he had eyes only for me.

'I'm lucky to be with you,' he said as he dipped me.

I smiled as Mum turned into the driveway, all my anger fading. I couldn't wait to speak to him again.

Chapter 12

I didn't have time to sleep in on Saturday morning. Mum woke me by barging into my bedroom and ripping the curtains open. I sat up in bed, blinking in the bright sunshine.

Mum bent over and picked up clothes from the floor. 'Do you have any more washing?'

I shook my head.

'Change your bedding before you come down.' Mum left.

Sanela rushed in, still wearing her nighty, and threw herself on my bed. 'Mummy's cross.' She covered us with the doona.

'It's a big day.' I lay back on the bed for a few minutes. 'Sabiha is coming for lunch.'

'What's she like?' Sanela asked. 'Is she nice?'

I was surprised. Out of all the adjectives that could apply to Sabiha, nice wasn't anywhere in the top ten. 'She's, well...' I stuttered to a stop. I didn't know how to finish the sentence. The first words that sprung to mind were selfish, superior, harsh, bitchy, underhanded. 'Yes, she's nice.'

Mum shouted my name from the hallway. Sanela jumped out of bed with a gasp and ran to her room to get dressed.

Mum was in a frenzy of cleaning, demanding that each nook, and cranny was spotless. Dad and Ali spent the day outside, mowing the lawn and trimming the bushes, while Mum and I cleaned the house with Sanela trying to help.

After we cleaned, Mum and I prepared food for the BBQ. I sliced eggplant and zucchini for the charcoal on the grill and prepared the salads. We were having a regular garden salad with oil and vinegar dressing, and a *šopska* salad with tomato, cucumber, roasted peppers, onion, topped with grated white brine cheese and parsley sprinkled on top.

Mum prepared the meat. She'd already marinated a whole chicken in olive and sunflower oil and rubbed it with garlic. Last night she'd marinated barbecue lamb chops in *vegeta* and garlic, and now she was making marinated chicken and beef skewers by threading capsicum and mushrooms.

In the fridge was *pljeskavica*, spicy Bosnian beef patties that are flatter and thinner than hamburgers, and *ćevapi*, skinless sausages. Now all we had to do was take the condiments out, *ajvar*, a Bosnian relish, *kajmak*, churned cream and *kefir*, a fermented drink.

I set up the table in our alfresco area using real cutlery and glasses because Mum hated plastic, and covered the table with a cloth to protect it from the elements, and then went to get ready.

After we all dressed, we waited in the living room, bunched up by the window, for Dad to return home from picking up Sabiha.

'How long until they come?' Sanela demanded as she peered past the curtain. She wanted to catch the first glimpse of Sabiha.

'At least another ten minutes,' I said patiently and bit my nails.

I just wanted to get through the lunch unscathed. Until now, each sphere of my life was completely separate, but now they were converging and I was worried that the ripples would reveal too many things I wanted to hide.

'Get away from the curtain,' Ali snapped.

Even though it was a barbecue Mum made us all dress up in our best and Ali was slouching on the couch in a nice shirt and jeans, acting like he didn't care, even though he was tapping his foot in a nervous rhythm that I recognised.

'Why?' I demanded.

'Because it's going to look like we can barely wait to see her.'

'So.' I crossed my arms. 'We can barely wait.'

'I don't want her to know that.' Ali stood and tried to lead Sanela away.

'No.' Sanela stomped her foot. 'I'm waiting here.'

'Come here.' Ali tugged her sharply, but Sanela grabbed hold of the curtain in her hands and gripped for dear life. 'Let go.' He lifted her fingers one by one.

'You're hurting me,' Sanela whimpered.

'Let her go.' I threw myself between them and dug my nails into the soft skin on top of his hands.

'Ow.' Ali snatched his hands back and let Sanela go.

Sanela fell to the ground.

'Bitch.' Ali pinched me on the side, making my flesh burn.

'Ow.' I screamed, lifting Sanela with one hand while I rubbed my side with the other. 'Bastard.' I slapped him on every part of the body I could reach.

'Meany,' Sanela shouted and slapped him too, her hands mostly hitting his legs and knees.

'Stop it.' Mum's scream echoed round the room.

We broke away from each other and saw Mum standing at the top of the stairs, her body stiff with rage. She'd been on edge all day as she demanded perfection from everyone considering Sabiha's first visit. She was like a volcano on the verge of eruption.

There was the sound of a car pulling up and Mum looked through the round window on the stairs landing facing the front of the house. 'They're here,' she rushed downstairs.

We frantically tried to repair our clothes and hair.

'Here we are,' Dad said in English as he held the door open for Sabiha to enter.

Sabiha followed him. She looked fresh-faced and somehow vulnerable. Her clothes weren't the usual scuffed and worn clothes that screamed attitude, instead she looked like a Target catalogue with a perfectly pressed shirt, A-line skirt and shiny feminine shoes that she carefully removed in the entryway.

'This is your brother Ali,' Dad said.

Ali automatically offered his hand, but he pulled it back at Dad's look of annoyance.

Sabiha noticed their interaction and put her hand out. 'Nice to meet you, Ali.'

'And this is your little sister Sanela,' Dad said after she shook hands with Ali.

'Hello.' Sanela threw herself at Sabiha's legs and hugged her thighs.

Sabiha stiffened as she looked at the top of her head.

Dad reached for his hand to pull Sanela away. 'Sanela's friendly.'

Sanela looked up in confusion as he pulled her away. Dad had told us to treat Sabiha like family before he left and she was only following his instructions.

Noticing her hurt, Sabiha leaned down and cupped her cheek. 'You're gorgeous.' She gave Sanela a brief peck on the cheek.

Sanela brightened and smiled.

'And this is my wife, Jasminka.' Dad jumped over me to Mum, who was standing on my right.

'Nice to meet you.' Sabiha offered her hand again.

'We're glad you visited us,' Mum said, her voice holding an edge of displeasure. She'd switched to Bosnian, as per her rule that we all speak it at home.

Sabiha's smile faded. She thought Mum was having a go at her for not seeing Dad before, but Mum was still in anger mode from our little tiff and it was hard for her to switch gears.

'You have a beautiful house,' Sabiha said after an awkward silence, peering at the high ceiling. It was the first time I'd heard her speak in Bosnian and her accent was apparent. Her slow choice of words marked her as a novice speaker.

'Thank you. Lunch will be ready in fifteen minutes,' Mum said in English, and briskly gestured for me to help her.

Dad went outside and fired up the barbecue while Mum and I carried out the meat. Ali and Sabiha awkwardly stood in the doorway together, trying to make small talk.

Sabiha nudged closer to Dad. 'Wow, that's a lot of meat,' she said, examining the plates to be barbecued. 'I thought it was just us.'

'It is.' Dad squinted as he flipped the *pljeskavica*. 'Why don't you give Sabiha a tour of the house,' Dad said when he caught Sabiha curiously peering through the sliding door.

'I'll come.' Sanela clasped Sabiha's hand.

'Why don't you go too?' Dad nodded at Ali.

'Let's go upstairs.' Sanela tugged Sabiha. 'I want to show you my dollhouse.'

We couldn't all fit on the stairs. Sanela led Sabiha up, while I walked next to Ali, who watched Sabiha's back moodily. I nudged his side and mimicked he put a smile on. He nodded and eased his frown lines.

'See, this is where she lives.' Sanela was hogging the conversation, going into the life of her dolls.

'My turn.' I led Sabiha to my bedroom.

'It's so tidy.' Sabiha said it like it was a bad thing. 'You told me you had a poster of Ian Somerhalder on your wall.'

'I do.' I opened my walk-in wardrobe. Taped on the inside of the doors were my posters and photos in a colourful mosaic.

'Oh.' Sabiha peered at the photos. 'My poster is above my bed so I can see him first thing in the morning.'

'Mum doesn't let us mark the walls,' Ali said.

'She's a neat freak,' Sabiha said.

'No, she's house-proud,' Ali retorted, as if Sabiha was having a go.

'What's your room like?' Sanela asked.

Ali and I perked up.

'It's smaller. My entire house is much smaller than this,' Sabiha said wryly. 'And I don't have a built-in wardrobe, just a regular wooden one that I have to fit everything into. I have a big bookshelf with all of my books and I covered every wall with something that has meaning to me.' She brushed the clean walls, her lips formed into a moue of disgust.

'Do you want to see your room?' Sanela asked.

'My room is in my house,' Sabiha said.

'It's across the hall.' Sanela took her hand and dragged her across. 'See, this is your room for when you sleep over.'

Sabiha looked around the room with wonder. She gingerly stepped across the threshold and gently touched the white princess' furniture with her fingertips.

'Dad bought it as soon as we moved in. He wouldn't let anyone sleep in it,' Ali said accusingly.

Sabiha turned around. She looked awestruck, with tears seeping out of her eyes.

'Lunch is ready,' Dad called out.

I turned around and saw his head peering over the stairs.

'Sabiha is crying,' Sanela said to Dad.

He ran the rest of the way. 'What happened? Did someone say something?' He brushed past Ali and I in the doorway and collected Sabiha in his arms.

'Nothing's wrong.' Sabiha wiped her face. 'They were showing me my room.'

'Do you like it?' Dad asked quietly.

'I love it.' Sabiha hugged him and they clung to each other.

'Why don't you all go downstairs?' Dad ordered.

I shuffled down the stairs, feeling deflated.

'What was that about?' Ali asked.

I shrugged. 'That's how it's been since they started speaking.'

Mum came out of the kitchen, wiping her hands on a tea towel. 'Where's your father?' she asked as we walked out to the alfresco room.

'He's hugging Sabiha because she was crying.' Sanela sat at the table.

'Is she all right? Should I go upstairs?' Mum asked, looking up the stairs with concern.

'I think they want to be alone,' Ali said, his tone caustic.

Mum stopped, undecided. We trooped out and sat at the table to wait. We sat for five minutes in silence, the tantalising smell of cooked meat wafting in our nostrils from under the foil covered trays. Mum kept waving away the flies, aiming for the salad.

My stomach growled, and my irritation rose. Ali tapped his fingers on the table. 'Stop that,' I snapped.

He tapped harder, giving me an arch look. I slapped his hand. He elbowed me.

'Stop it. I've had enough of you,' Mum hissed.

'Mummy, I'm hungry.' Sanela tugged on her arm.

'I know,' Mum said. 'Dad and Sabiha won't be much longer.'

'I want some chicken.' Sanela nudged the foil.

'Don't,' Mum said. 'We have to wait.'

'How much longer?' Sanela whinged.

'I'm sure they won't be long.' Mum's face was losing its calm façade and was getting creased with irritation. We waited a few more minutes. 'Go get them.'

When I walked up the stairs, I heard the quiet murmur of their voices. My footsteps softened, and I crept down the hallway.

'She kept me from you all these years,' Sabiha cried.

They were talking about Bahra, Sabiha's mum. It seemed she finally believed Dad's version of events between her parents.

'Don't blame your mother completely. We were both at fault. We weren't happy in our marriage and she wanted out. She was scared that if I knew about you, then I wouldn't have wanted to get divorced.'

'Really?' Sabiha asked.

There was a silence. I held my breath.

'Yes, I would have done everything in my power to be in your life,' Dad said.

My eyes burnt, and my legs were shaky. I leaned against the wall and breathed through my nose. If Dad didn't divorce Sabiha's mum, he wouldn't have married Mum. Which meant that Ali, Sanela and I wouldn't be born.

Ali had it right all along when he called Sabiha the enemy. I had thought that by getting along with Sabiha I could get closer to her dad, recapture the man that he was and heal our family, but now I knew that was a myth. The man that I knew was gone.

Mum's frustration wafted upstairs like a presence, and I had to interrupt. I crept down the hall backwards and then scuffed my feet on the wooden stairs as I climbed the last step. When I reached the doorway, they were sitting on the bed. Dad had his arm around Sabiha's shoulders and she listed against him.

'Mum wants to serve dinner,' I said.

'We'll be right down,' he said.

As I went back downstairs, I caught sight of my reflection in the hallway mirror at the landing. My eyes looked large and shocked. I thought I'd passed the worst of it with Sabiha. That the shock-waves from our reunion were over with, and yet each time I got knocked down again. I took a deep breath and smoothed out my face to look pleasant.

'They'll be right down.' I kept my head down as I unfolded the napkin on my lap.

They came in five minutes later. 'We thought you got lost.' Mum tried for a light-hearted tone, but sounded biting. She'd spent all morning cleaning and preparing food only for the entire meal to be ruined.

'We were talking,' Dad said.

Sabiha and Dad sat, and we finally began serving ourselves. I was shaking from hunger because I'd been saving myself for the barbecue all morning and barely had breakfast.

'Wow, I thought this was just a barbecue, but it's a feast,' Sabiha said with a nervous laugh.

'You're a special visitor,' Sanela repeated Mum's warnings. Everything had to be special.

Sabiha looked disappointed.

'You're not a visitor. You're family.' Dad shot Mum an angry look.

'Yes, but this is a special occasion,' Mum snapped. 'After all, it's Sabiha's first time visiting us.'

Dad looked chastened. The lamb chop I was eating became hard to swallow as an uncomfortable silence descended and we were all reminded of our strange circumstances.

Mum took a deep breath, like the kind you do before diving off a high board. 'Sabiha, what sort of things do you like to do?' Mum asked her softball question she used as an icebreaker on all of our friends.

'Sabiha loves writing,' Dad answered for her.

Sabiha nodded.

'What sort of things do you write?' Mum passed the salad around.

'Articles. In fact.' Dad used his fork as a pointer. 'She's going to be a journalist.'

This was the first I heard of Sabiha's ambition. I looked at Sabiha and saw she was frowning at Dad.

'Actually, I write short stories,' Sabiha said tentatively, as if she feared contradicting him.

'Of course. She's developing a portfolio of different samples,' Dad said with approval.

'No.' Sabiha dropped the salad bowl on the table and it landed with a bang. She looked embarrassed as she attempted cleaning vegetables off the tablecloth. 'I enjoy writing short stories.'

'Of course you do,' Dad said. 'But you have to think about a proper job.'

Sabiha looked down at the table, her fork beside her plate. Dad's face creased in consternation as he realised he'd overstepped, but he didn't know how to fix it. Dad looked to Mum for help, his usual gambit for her to keep the conversation going.

Mum stared at him. My stomach dropped. Just when the silence went for too long and it seemed she was going to leave him hanging, her manners took over.

'You've made Alma's transition to her new school effortless,' Mum said. 'She's thrilled there.'

Sabiha looked up.

'We were nervous at first,' Mum continued. 'Alma only went to all girls' private school's so there were a lot of adjustments to be made.'

'Really?' Sabiha's gloomy face faded as she looked at me curiously. 'You didn't tell me that.' She picked up her fork. 'No wonder you're such a dork around boys.'

Dad breathed a sigh of relief while my fists clenched as I waited.

'Boys.' Mum's ears sharpened. 'You didn't tell me about any boys?'

I wanted to close my eyes the way you do when a speeding car comes at you. This is exactly what I'd feared would happen and now that my worst fears were coming true, I was a hapless bystander.

'They're just some guys we hang around with,' Sabiha said off-handedly.

'I hope you girls know you're too young for boyfriends.' Mum had been lecturing me about waiting because my schooling was the most important thing for my future. Guilt squatted in my stomach like an unwelcome visitor when I thought of Alex.

'We're friends.' Sabiha was annoyed. 'It's Brian and his best friend, Jesse.' She turned to Dad. 'And you know we have nothing to worry about with Brian.'

'Why?' Mum was puzzled.

I closed my eyes momentarily, wishing myself away.

'Brian is gay,' she said.

'Gay.' Mum repeated, as if she'd announced he was an alien, and to her he might as well be. 'You didn't tell me that.' She looked as if I had stabbed her.

I looked at my plate, gripping my cutlery so tight my hand hurt.

'Dad didn't have a problem with it when he found out.' Sabiha said. I peeked up and saw she looked perplexed at the commotion her over sharing had caused.

'You knew about this too?' Mum looked at Dad, her voice accusatory.

I sunk into my seat. This was exactly what I'd feared would happen.

'Let's talk about something else.' Dad put on a fake smile, giving Mum the signal that they should talk about this later. Mum gave him a death stare and thinned her lips as she stabbed her *ćevapi*.

Dad waited a beat for Mum to introduce a new topic of conversation, but she turned her attention to her food.

'Did you have time to read those books I gave you?' Dad asked.

'Yes,' Sabiha said uncertainly.

'What books?' Ali demanded.

'I bought Sabiha the books I loved reading when I was young,' Dad answered. '*Call of the Wild, White Fang, Old Man and the Sea* and *All's Quiet on the Western Front.* Which one did you read first?'

'Um, well,' Sabiha said. 'I'm still reading them.'

'Sounds like you don't like them,' Ali needled.

'It's not that I don't like them.' Sabiha was flustered and her face flushed. 'It's just that they need to be read properly.'

'So which one have you started?' Ali asked.

'Well, *White Fang* is very elemental,' Sabiha said hesitantly.

I'd read all the books that Dad gifted her. He'd insisted that we all read the classics, so that we had a "well rounded" education like the one he'd had in former Yugoslavia, and I knew what her concern was. They were all boy books with dark themes and made for heavy reading. I would have chimed in to help her, but after she'd landed me in the shit about Brian, I was enjoying her discomfort.

'So you've read none?' Ali concluded with a happy smirk.

'That's enough,' Dad snapped.

Ali looked at Sabiha with resentment before stuffing his mouth with a lamb chop.

'So who are your favourite authors?' Dad asked.

They spoke to each other as if they were the only ones in the room, while we looked on in silence. When it was obvious no one could eat any more, Mum stood and wordlessly collected the large serving dish and carried it to the kitchen.

'We'll have ice-cream in the living room,' she said curtly.

I began stacking plates and Sanela got the breadbasket and carried it. Usually Ali was hit and miss when helping with cleanup, but this time he collected the cutlery, which said a lot about how much he wanted to avoid spending time with Sabiha.

Sabiha had followed Dad to the doorway, but she stopped and watched us for a moment. 'I'll help.' Sabiha returned to the table and collected dirty plates.

'You don't have to do that,' Dad said. 'You're a guest.'

'I thought she was family,' Ali said with a raised eyebrow.

Dad foolishly stood in the sliding door doorway. He had one leg out of the alfresco room and one in. His face lined with consternation. He didn't know what to do. 'You're right, Sabiha. The sooner we finish, the sooner we can all sit down.' He began helping too.

Soon we were all trooping to the kitchen to put the dishes onto the kitchen bench. Mum bit her lip to keep her frustration from spilling over. All we were doing was transferring the mess from one room to another.

'Kids, take Sabiha upstairs while I wash up and we'll have ice-cream in a little while. You can stay and help,' Mum told Dad when it looked like he was going to follow.

I knew he was going to get a "what for" with Mum hissing her frustration at him under the cover of the banging dishes as they stacked the dishwasher. When we got upstairs, Sanela went to the toilet and Ali disappeared into his bedroom, leaving us alone.

Sabiha's phone beeped. She looked at the screen and smiled. 'Brian's all pumped about the party. Are you still going?'

'Why?' I sat on my bed and grabbed my cushion, squeezing it to contain my anger. I couldn't look at her. I knew I was going to cop it from Mum when she left.

'Maybe it's not a good idea,' Sabiha said. 'I mean, your Mum was even freaking out about you being friends with Brian.'

She was such a hypocrite. The only thing she cared about was making sure I was out of the way so she could do what she wanted. Well, I had my own plans that were nothing to do with her.

'You're not going then,' Sabiha said, sounding relieved, assuming my silence was a no.

'I didn't say that,' I said.

'But your parents—'

'Are my parents and I'll make my own decisions?' I stood and threw the cushion at the wall.

Sabiha's eyes widened. 'I'm trying to look out for you.'

'That's not your job,' I said flatly.

'Did I do something—' she was asking, when Sanela burst through the door again.

'I found it.' Sanela brandished her Glamour Barbie.

Sabiha gave me one more confused look, before she gave Sanela her attention. They talked until Mum called us down.

'It's time to take you home,' Dad said to Sabiha after we all had ice-cream.

'Thank you very much for having me to lunch.' Sabiha gave everyone a kiss and hug. The only person who hugged her wholeheartedly was Sanela. She came to me last, giving me a hurt look when I gave her a perfunctory hug and air kissed her cheek.

'I'll go straight to the city,' Dad said before he left.

'You'll be home as soon as the plenary session is finished,' Mum said.

Dad nodded, saying nothing.

Ali and I exchanged a knowing look behind Mum's back. Dad would stay at the conference for the cocktail party afterward. He always said that networking was a necessary evil and we knew he wouldn't be back until midnight.

'Ali, Sanela upstairs,' Mum commanded as soon as the front door closed. 'Alma, with me.'

When I entered the kitchen, Mum was behind the counter. The kitchen was her domain, and she was tough and impregnable behind it. She put her hands on her hips and I knew I was in deep shit.

'What's this about you being friends with boys?' Mum demanded in Bosnian. Now that Sabiha was gone, she reverted to her mother tongue.

I needed time to think things through, but if I hesitated in answering her, she'd think I was lying.

'We all hang out together.' I erred on the side of simplicity.

'Who's we?' Mum demanded.

'Me, Dina, Sabiha, Jesse and Brian.'

'And Brian is the gay one?' Mum raised her eyebrow. 'Is Jesse his boyfriend?'

'No.' I nearly exploded with laughter. 'Brian and Jesse are best friends.'

'Why don't the three girls just "hang out" together?' Mum used air quotations. Bosnians thought that boys and girls were friends for one reason and one reason only. In her words, because they were interested in "hanky panky."

'We do since Brian left school.' I stretched the truth. Jesse still met with us every morning, but lately he was spending lunchtimes with Charlie preparing his graphic book for publication.

'He isn't going to graduate?'

In Mum's world an education was all you could depend on. It was your chance to rise above and guarantee a better life. Anyone who didn't was a loser destined for menial jobs and a life of misery.

'He had to get a job when his parents kicked him out.' I hoped his hard-luck story would soften her up.

'Bloody Australians,' Mum muttered under her breath.

She pulled up a stool and sat, indicating I should do the same. I didn't know whether to be relieved. Mum was over her anger stage, but now she wanted to know everything about what happened at school and I hadn't thought about what I should and shouldn't tell her.

'Did they kick him out because of drugs?' Mum narrowed her eyes.

Of course, that was what she'd think. To her, gay people and drugs went hand in hand.

'No, it's because he told them he was gay. You'd have to be a pretty rotten parent to do that to your kid.'

'Oh.' Mum looked away guiltily.

Mum was religious, and she didn't approve of gay people because she thought they were deviants.

'Why did he tell them?' she asked, as if it was Brian's fault for rubbing his parent's noses in it.

'Because he got sick of lying.' I was annoyed. 'Anyway, his father always suspected. He kept making all these little digs about him not being a real man, and Brian said he wasn't really losing much anyway.'

Mum looked at the tiled kitchen floor. 'I used to know who all your friends were and what you were up to, but now I've lost touch.' Mum sighed.

I felt her despondence. I wanted to go back to a simpler time when I could share every part of myself and not keep it all compartmentalised.

'At least I don't have to worry about any of you being gay,' she said, as if this was a great bonus in her life.

'What does that mean?' I demanded.

'It's a blessing. I can't imagine what Brian's parents are going through.'

'What about what Brian is going through?'

'He brought it on himself.'

'Would you kick one of us out if we were gay?' I demanded.

Mum's eyes shifted to the side as if she was looking for a way out. 'That's something we don't have to worry about.' She stood and wiped the already clean countertop.

Mum refused to lift her gaze. I wished I'd never asked the question. I'd always thought Mum's love was limitless. That it was always going to be there, no matter what. This was the first time I'd seen that Mum's love could be a tap that was turned on or off at will. It made me feel terrible, like the only certainty in the foundation of my life was gone.

I stopped, my brain fuzzy from processing the terrible reality I'd learnt. For a moment I thought about the party and what would happen if they caught me. When I'd contemplated my punishment, I'd thought it would take the form of losing all computer rights, or not being able to watch television for a month. But what if the ultimate price was being kicked out? What if this was the tipping point that would make Mum abandon me?

Maybe Sabiha was right, and I shouldn't go to the party. Was it really worth risking Mum's love? I wanted to cry. I remembered everything Sabiha told me about her mother, the way she accepted her completely. Wasn't that what a mother was supposed to do? She was supposed to love you no matter what?

'Before you go, I wanted to talk to you about tonight. Are you sure you're up for the responsibility of being in charge?' Mum carefully folded the tea towel and hung it on the hook.

'I can make sandwiches with the leftover roast.' I ticked the points off my fingers. 'Sanela can stay up one hour extra, but she needs to be in bed by nine o'clock. Ali is to stay with us in the living room and help. And if there are any problems, we can call you at the hospital and have you paged.'

Mum looked relieved. 'The only reason I'm leaving you in charge is because I know you are responsible enough to handle it.'

'Don't worry,' I said. 'We're fine. I've been—'

I cut myself off before I finished the sentence that I'd been in charge plenty of times before. Mum wasn't supposed to know about all the nights that Dad didn't come home until after we were all in bed. As far as Mum knew, this was the first time we were on our own, when in reality it was the first time we were alone on a weekend when we didn't have the schedule of school to keep us on track.

'You know I'm responsible,' I said bitterly. I was responsible enough to be in charge of my siblings, but not to pick my own friends. The hypocrisy of the adults in my life made me burn. 'Did you know it was Sabiha's birthday next week?'

Mum dropped the aluminium bowl she was cleaning. It hit the tiles and made a deep clanging sound.

'It is?' Mum picked up the bowl and returned to the sink to rinse.

'I didn't realise there was only one year's age difference between us.'

Mum was hunched over the sink, her hands gripping the edge as she waited for me to ask the next logical question. I saw Mum's reflection in the window, fear on her face, and I knew I did not want the answer.

'I should probably buy her a present.'

Mum relaxed. 'You buy one from yourself and I'll buy one on behalf of the family.'

I ran up the stairs to my bedroom; the question poised on my tongue, ready to tumble out. "Mum, how is it you fell pregnant three months after Sabiha's mum did?"

Chapter 13

Mum called me downstairs to say goodbye before she left for work. I spent a few hours playing a board game with Sabiha, while Ali was in the study. Usually I would have chased him off the computer and forced him to help me take care of Sanela, but knowing what was awaiting him, I gave him a few hours' grace.

I rolled the dice and moved my figurine into the requisite number of squares. 'Ow.' I rubbed my temple. 'I'm getting a headache,' I said, setting in motion the first part of my plan.

I went to the kitchen and prepared sandwiches. Ali took his plate to the study. As I ate I was aware of the ticking clock.

I'd arranged to meet with Alex at eight and had over an hour to go. I did a quick checklist in my head. Sanela's usual routine was bath, brush, pyjamas, bed, book and lights out. Sanela had a bath earlier in the day, so that was taken care of. All Ali had to do was put her in pyjamas, read her a book, and leave her to sleep.

I placed the dirty dishes in the kitchen sink and sat on the couch. On cue, at seven o'clock I moaned gently.

'What's wrong?' Sanela stood beside me.

'I'm hurting a little.' As if I was holding my body together, I held my hands across my abdomen. I moaned again and gently writhed on the couch.

'Maybe we should call Mummy.' Sanela gently patted my hand.

'Mummy has to work tonight and we don't want to bother her.' I writhed harder.

Sanela ran out of the living room, yelling Ali's name. She returned, dragging him by hand.

'What's wrong?' he demanded.

'That time of the month.' I whimpered.

'Shit.' He stomped his foot.

I had to fight from smiling. Payback was a bitch. He was long overdue a turn babysitting.

'I'm going to lie down.' I sat up. 'You and Ali can watch dinosaurs together.'

Sanela tugged Ali onto the couch and eagerly curled up against him. I hobbled up the stairs, holding my stomach. I heard Ali asking Sanela if she could watch dinosaurs by herself. As I heard Sanela say no, I smiled. As soon as I was out of their sight, I stood straight.

I'd spent the afternoon in my room agonising over what to wear and pulled on the mini-skirt and v-neck top that wouldn't wrinkle while I lay in bed. I put my lipstick, eyeliner and mascara in my handbag and tucked it under the pillow.

I had just enough time to jump into bed when there was a knock on my bedroom door and Sanela walked in carrying her care tray that was a special treat for any sick family member. It was always a surprise what would be on it. Today it was orange juice and a chocolate that she'd pulled apart, eating a few bars herself and smearing the rest on the plate.

'This is just what I needed.' I took a bite of the chocolate.

Sanela beamed a big smile as I polished the tray. 'Can we stay here and play monopoly?'

'I need to have a little nap.' I curled up and let out a little moan.

'Oh.' Sanela was disappointed.

'But maybe you can watch Barbie Cinderella with Ali.' I had to fight from smiling when Ali winced.

After they left, I waited fifteen minutes. As I tiptoed across the hall and to the window opposite, the sound of the television downstairs reassured me. I psyched myself as I looked out the window. This was the hardest part of my plan. Our house was split-level, and the window overlooked the roof of the living area downstairs. I had to get out through the window, walk across the roof, and then slide down the trellis until I reached the ground.

In the light of day it had seemed like a reasonable plan, but now that I was facing the reality of walking on a roof at night and then hanging two metres off the ground, my overwhelming instinct was to return to my bedroom and burrow under the covers.

I looked at my mobile. Alex was due in ten minutes. I took a deep breath and clambered out the window, holding onto the ledge as I gained my balance on the tiles. I tried to gently slide the window closed, but my hand jerked and it latched.

I breathed in and out, attempting to control my panic. How was I going to get back inside? I leaned my forehead on the cool glass and looked at my mobile. I'd worry about it later.

Taking a shuddering breath, I turned around and slid down onto my backside, wincing as the cold tiles connected with my skin. There was no light in the backyard and the edge of the roof looked like it ended in a black void of nothingness.

I turned onto my stomach and hung my feet over the edge, moaning as the roof tiles cut into my stomach. Holding onto the gutter, I climbed down. As the wind blew, piercing my skin through my clothes, I looked longingly at the back door, fantasising about sneaking back into the house. Too late now.

I turned and limped to the locked gate dividing the front and backyards and double-checked my keys. Dad hadn't cut a spare key to the gate on my key chain. I wanted to cry, but in the end, there was only one way I was getting across. As I climbed down the other side, my hands slid on the cold aluminium gate and I fell to the ground.

Rubbing my bruised bum, I limped along the side of the house and down the footpath. This party had better be worth all the bruises I was collecting. I'd told Alex to meet me in the sidestreet so I wasn't seen by anyone in the house. The streets were dark. There were only streetlights on one side and they barely penetrated the gloominess.

I paced to keep warm. It seemed as if I was waiting forever. I checked the time on my mobile. Alex was late. When ten minutes passed, I tried calling him, but he didn't answer. I didn't know what to do? Should I keep waiting or try a taxi?

As I paced with indecision, trying to keep the cold away, I remembered Sabiha's face as she tried to warn me away and Mum's confession. I wanted to go to the party to get at them, show them they couldn't control my fate, but as the cold seeped into my bones, it became harder to sustain my burning rage and I began desiring my bed.

Another two minutes passed and the goose pimples on my skin decided for me. I was walking home, writing a SMS to Alex, telling him I couldn't get out, when a car turned into the street and stopped beside me. I didn't know what Alex' car looked like and hesitated before approaching it. How was I going to tell him I was bailing from going to the party? I stepped toward the passenger door and peered in. It wasn't Alex.

The driver wound down his window. 'Hey sexy lady, you want to make some money?' He leered at me.

I backed away, shaking my head.

The guy leaned over and opened the door. 'Get in.'

I looked around wildly. Would anybody hear me scream? I thought I'd faint from fear when I heard an explosion of laughter and Alex's head popped up in the backseat.

'Got you.' He slapped his thigh and looked at the driver. 'She looks like she's about to shit herself.' He shouted, and they both laughed.

I blinked back tears, feeling stupid and small.

'Get in.' Alex threw open the back door.

I walked past the car and headed home. Alex shouted my name, but I did not turn around. I heard his footsteps on the footpath behind me and he pushed in front of me. I went to go around him, but he grabbed hold of my arms.

'Let go of me.' I pulled away.

'I'm sorry, I'm sorry,' Alex said, tugging on my arm.

I pushed him away and continued walking.

'Okay, so it was a poor joke.' He shadowed me. 'But do you really want to spoil our night together?'

'I'm not going to the party.' All my fantasies about our night together had fallen to the ground like fairy dust billowing off a fairy, leaving her with no magic and wonder.

'Fuck.' Alex stopped.

I heard a loud bang and turned. He was kicking the neighbour's fence.

'Fuck, fuck, fuck.' He chanted as he kicked it.

'Stop it.' I pulled him away and peered at the windows. If the neighbour came out it would be all over for me.

'I always do this.' Alex squatted against the street pole, his hands in his hair. 'I always ruin things. This is what I need.'

I wanted to leave him where he was, but something about his voice tugged at me.

'Need what?' I was facing away from him, wondering how to sneak in through the back door unseen by Ali.

'I needed a night out. A night to forget all the bullshit.' He took a sip from the can of beer he was holding. 'My house is like a morgue at the moment.'

I finally turned to him.

'It's Lilly's anniversary,' he said between sips.

My stomach dropped. He hadn't told me. No wonder he was so wild and out of control.

'I'm all fucked up in the head and don't think things through.' He pushed himself back to his feet. 'Anyway, I'm really sorry about playing that joke on you.' He walked toward the car. 'I'll see you later.'

I looked at the sky in frustration. The moon hung low, big and yellow. A breeze fluttered over me and the edge of fear crept over me again as I thought of my parents and the betrayal I was committing. I turned to Alex. His back was hunched as if he was fighting off a blow. He needed me. I couldn't even imagine the pain he was in tonight. Pity drowned my anger out.

'Wait up,' I called.

He waited for me to join him and put his arm around my shoulders. When we got to the car, he opened the passenger door for me. 'Get in the back, Tim.'

'You sure?' Tim didn't move. 'You've put away a few.'

Alex threw his beer can on the nature strip. 'I'm fine.'

Tim got into the backseat while Alex walked around the front of the car.

I watched Alex with concern as he drove, but he seemed fine. He was driving fast, but he wasn't swerving or anything. When we got to Brian's, I put my hand on the door handle, but Alex restrained me from getting out.

'I haven't given you a proper kiss hello,' he said after Tim got out of the car.

I was still off-kilter as we kissed.

He lifted his head. 'I have a surprise. I've arranged for us to have Omer's bedroom all to ourselves.'

I was still angry about earlier and wasn't sure I wanted to be alone with him. 'Sabiha is expecting me,' I said.

'You're right.' He smiled ruefully. 'You deserve a night for yourself. You don't want to be dragged down by my cloud of grief.'

I felt like a total bitch. What sort of a girlfriend held a grudge in these circumstances? He got out of the car and I rushed out too. 'Sabiha can wait,' I said. 'I want to be with you.'

He smiled, his whole face lighting up with joy. 'Great. We'll sneak in through the window and no one will see us.' He locked the car door and took my hand. 'I'm so glad we're going to have tonight together.'

'Me too.' I twined my fingers with his.

We walked, and he tugged me down the side of the house. When we reached the second window, he pushed it open.

'Won't someone come in?' I stood on tiptoes and peered in.

He took hold of my waist and lifted me to sit on the window ledge. 'I locked the door.'

I hung suspended between the inside and outside. I remembered the last time we were alone in a bed together. Did he expect us to continue where we'd stopped? I looked at Alex. He was staring sadly toward the front of the house. Of course he wasn't expecting sex.

I put my feet on the bedroom floor. Alex pulled himself inside and closed the window. The room was utilitarian. A bed, a desk and chair and a stereo on the floor. The terrible techno music beat from the party thrummed through the wall.

He walked to the CD player and turned it on. 'This will give us something pleasant to listen to.' He took out the chair and gestured for me to sit on it while he sat on the bed opposite.

'So,' I said.

'So,' he said.

We both laughed at the same time.

'How are your parents doing?' I asked.

Alex shrugged. 'Not good. Mum mopes and Dad hangs out in the garage trying to fix cars.'

'Did you and your dad go to the footy last week?' During our last on-line chat, before we flirted, he'd told me he was really missing spending time with his dad. I'd urged him to try asking his dad to reignite their Friday night ritual of attending the footy.

'Nah, I tried, but the bottle was more interesting.'

'I'm sorry.' As I looked at his face, I felt guilty. I'd been sure that all father and son needed was some time together to heal the rift, despite his assurances they were past that. 'I guess I was hoping if it worked for you, then it would happen for me too.'

'Yeah, well...' He let the sentence peter out and a pregnant pause descended. He lifted my hand to his lips.

My skin broke out into goose pimples, and I shivered as he worked his way up my arm.

'I can't imagine how devastated my mum would be if something happened to my little sister.'

'Mmmm,' Alex murmured and aimed for my lips.

'I thought you needed to talk about things.' I moved away.

Alex looked annoyed. 'I said I needed a night out to forget things.' The CD flipped to a new track. He turned up the volume. 'I love this song. Dance with me.'

I remained seated, off-kilter at his change in mood. He began dancing with abandon. His smile was infectious, and I laughed. I stood and moved. Soon we were dancing together and Alex pulled me to him.

As we swayed together, butterflies fluttered in my stomach. It was my fantasy come true. He became serious and leaned down. I don't know how long we kissed for before we toppled onto the bed and he ended up on top of me. We kissed until my lips ached and I tingled between my legs with urgency. He inserted himself between my thighs and rubbed against me, causing delicious friction.

Alex leaned on his arms and groaned as he shifted his jeans.

'What's wrong?' I asked, scared I'd hurt him.

'I need a break or I'm going to explode.'

'Is there anything I can do?'

'You're a good girl.' He grinned at me. 'Good girls don't do the things I want you to do.'

'I'm not that good.' I wanted to be his match, not a little girl he dismissed.

'Really?' He lifted an eyebrow archly.

'I don't want to be a good girl anymore.'

He scooped me in his arms, kissing me so hard I lost my breath. 'Please touch me, baby.' Alex put my hand in his pants.

It again surprised me how soft it was. Alex groaned, dropping his head back. He put his hand over mine and instructed me how to stroke him. I gasped, feeling squeamish, and pulled my hand away. His eyes were closed, his face etched with pleasure as he attempted tugging my hand back.

'No,' I yelped.

He moved away and went to sit on the edge of the bed. 'Maybe you should go. You're obviously not ready for a boyfriend.'

'I am.'

Alex stared moodily at the door. When he said nothing, I rubbed my eyes as I headed for the door. My hand was on the doorknob when a sob broke through.

'Shit,' he said from behind me. As his hand covered mine, I felt him behind me. 'I'm sorry baby,' He put his arms around my waist and turned me toward him. 'I didn't mean to be a prick. You make me crazy with desire that I can't control myself. You're a work of art and all I want to do is worship you.' He dropped to his knees and buried his face in my midriff, his arms loosely holding me.

As he spoke, my tears dried and joy filled me. I was filled with tenderness. My muscles loosened and that familiar warmth came over me.

He lifted his head back. 'I keep forgetting you're a young one and I need to take it easy.'

'I'm not that young.' I ruffled my fingers through his hair, loving the feel. He nuzzled against my hand like a purring kitten, encouraging me to keep going. While I played with his hair, he nuzzled my breasts, taking my t-shirt between his teeth. He lifted it until he could press his naked cheek against my stomach, His raspy beard tickling my soft skin.

He pressed butterfly kisses on my navel, then licked me, peering at me with a sensual smile. My knees went weak. He put his hands under my buttocks and slowly lowered me to my knees. Once again, I was looking up at him.

He held my hands, and we exchanged an open-mouthed kiss. I was like the lead of a Hollywood rom-com who was being wooed on screen. One part of my brain kept squirrelling away details and I imagined telling the story.

I lost myself in the moment and only came back to the present when he undid my top and bent his head to my breasts. I gasped when he placed his mouth on my skin.

'Shhh.' He put his finger on my mouth.

He bent his head back to my breasts and undid my pants, stroking me between the legs. I tried to recapture the feeling of desire, but all I felt was squeamish embarrassment. I wanted the thrill of romance without the reality of bodily fluids. My brain wouldn't stop churning. I wondered if I'd put on enough deodorant? Were my legs smooth? Was I acting the right way?

The harder I tried to get back into the moment, the more random thoughts invaded. Was my breath ok? Did he think I was going to go all the way? Did I want to go all the way? I always thought I'd go all the way when I was in love? Was I in love? Was he in love with me?

'Are you ok?' Alex stroked the inside of my thigh.

His touch tickled, and I laughed, thrusting his hand away. He looked annoyed again and my laughter abruptly cut out. I put my hand in his pants and touched him. He kissed me and once again passion heated my skin, making everything look a little rosy and misty coloured. He took my hand in his and showed me how to move it and my passion stopped cold again.

He moaned, his eyes closed and face lit up with ecstasy. I was doing this. I was bringing him pleasure. He put his hands through my hair and kissed me, thrusting his tongue into my mouth as his hips pistoned off the bed.

His hand went to the back of my head, and he nudged it toward his lap. I was scared and excited in equal parts. I'd read about this in girly magazines. Once during a birthday party sleepover, the party-girl had suggested a game where we all put the magazine tips to test on a banana. We'd put on lipstick and engaged in a competition to see how good we were at performing the sexual act. I was the runner-up.

Alex was needy and vulnerable and made me feel powerful. I went down on him, practicing all the tips I'd read about in the magazine. I knew I must have been doing a good job, as his moans cut through the air. When I finished, he pulled me to lie beside him. As I lay my head on his shoulder, his chest heaved.

'You're not as good a girl as I thought you were.' He got up abruptly and did up his pants. 'I thought you were a virgin?'

I sat up slowly, the warm glow wearing off. 'I am,' I whispered.

Alex turned to look at me. 'How come you were so good?'

I didn't know what answer to give him. It embarrassed me to tell him the truth. Surely he'd think I was a social reject to have practiced on a banana.

'I read a lot of girly magazines.' He didn't look convinced. I took a deep breath and told him about the banana party.

He laughed. 'A banana?' Really?' When I nodded, he hugged me. 'You shouldn't be embarrassed about it. Losing your virginity is the most important experience you'll ever have. It's a moment you'll remember forever.' He gave me a kiss on the lips and looked into my eyes. 'It's a moment I want to share with you.'

I didn't know how we'd come to this point so fast. I'd been daydreaming about kisses and hugs, yet here I was having a conversation about when I was going to have sex. Alex must have seen my fear.

'But that's a long way off. You were amazing.' He kissed me softly on the lips.

I burrowed against his chest, trying to recapture the warm glow. 'We should go.'

Alex did up his zipper, and I turned away and straightened my clothes. Even though we'd been intimate with each other, it was confronting to be exposed afterwards.

'When will I see you again?' He turned off the stereo.

'I don't know.'

He hugged me again. 'I can't wait too long to be with you again.' His erection stirred. 'You bring it out of me.'

My parents kept a close eye on my movements. I'd have to fake another study date and my parents might get suspicious, but as Alex looked at me pleadingly, I didn't care about any of it.

'Ok,' I said. 'I'll meet you Monday.'

I'd figure out a way to keep our date. We walked to the window, and he lowered me down, his biceps straining.

'See you inside.' He leaned out the window and kissed me on the forehead.

I nodded and walked around the side of the house and to the front door.

Chapter 14

The party was a let down as soon as I walked in. I'd had images of sparkly outfits and glamour. Most of the partygoers were wearing denim, one even had on tracky dacks. I pushed through the crowd and spotted Sabiha and Dina in the living room.

'You came.' Sabiha sounded disappointed.

'Of course,' I said.

'How did you swing it?' Dina interrupted our stare off.

'I'm supposedly in bed suffering period cramps.'

'The Period Defence,' Sabiha smirked.

'It's what you use when you're trying to get out of a sticky situation with a guy,' Dina elaborated when I looked at her blankly.

'I thought this was going to be a small housewarming party.' I looked at the packed living room.

'It was.' Dina confirmed wryly. 'But then Brian's brother got in on the act and invited his mates and Omer invited his friends and here we are.'

I was uncomfortable. The ratio was skewed with more guys than girls. The guys were eyeing us like we were meat to be devoured. I looked for Alex, but he'd disappeared.

A guy who had left high school behind a long time ago detached himself from his compatriots and crossed the living room toward us. 'Hello there.' He held his hand out to me. 'I'm Billy.'

I automatically lifted my hand to his handshake, but Sabiha slapped it down.

'She's 15,' she told Billy coldly.

'I don't mind if you don't.' He practically licked his chops as he looked me up and down.

'Do the words statutory rape mean anything to you?' Sabiha asked.

Billy blanched and stumbled back to his friends, who slapped him on the back while he slugged back another drink.

'I don't need you to baby me,' I snapped at Sabiha. She thought she was such a know-it-all.

'Sorry,' she snapped back. 'I didn't realise you were so sophisticated.'

'Incoming,' Dina interrupted with a sotto voice.

We followed her gaze to two guys walking toward us, each carrying two cups in hand.

'We bring gifts,' one of them said.

I pushed in front of Sabiha and took the cups, placing them on the kitchen counter we were leaning against. 'Thanks. But we're not drinking tonight.' I gave Sabiha a supercilious look. As if my parents hadn't drummed into me not to accept drinks from strangers because of date rape drugs.

'You're going to miss out on all the fun.' The other guy did a silly dance. He got a rise out of Sabiha, who cracked a smile. 'Wow, your face didn't crack. Dance with me.'

He did some cool moves imitating Michael Jackson, and we all laughed. For a moment, it looked like she would relent, but then her eyes shifted to the door. I followed her gaze and saw Jesse had arrived.

'Thanks,' she said dismissively.

The guy followed her gaze and shrugged good-naturedly. They moved onto the next group of girls while Sabiha waved at Jesse.

'I didn't think we'd see you here,' Jesse said to me after we'd greeted each other. 'Sabiha said you weren't coming.'

'Sabiha doesn't speak for me,' I snapped, not looking at her.

'Hello my peeps.' Brian stumbled into us, breaking the tense silence. He hugged Sabiha and Jesse, then ended up leaning against them. 'Are you enjoying my little soiree? That's right, it's not a little soiree. It's a fucking frat party.' He spat out as he looked around.

In the short time I'd been there, the party mood had changed. Guys were shouting and egging each other on into drinking games and the few girls who were in attendance were leaving.

'Maybe we should leave,' Jesse said.

I welcomed his words, wanting to go home.

'No, please don't go,' Brian urged. 'Let's have our own party.' He collected booze. 'We'll hide in my room. It will be like Switzerland.'

We followed his lead and collected snacks, plates and drinks and followed him down the hall. I scanned the house for a glimpse of Alex and saw him in the kitchen, his arm on the kitchen cupboard as he chatted to a brunette. I slowed to catch a better glimpse, but Sabiha nudged me along. We piled into Brian's bedroom and put all our goodies on his student desk.

'Let's make sure we don't have any interruptions.' Brian lifted his chest of drawers and Jesse helped place them against the door. The doorknob rattled. There was a bang on the door and the interloper moved on.

Brian turned on his lamp, making the room more intimate. He hit a few buttons on his computer and music began playing. 'I prepared my own party mix. But the powers that be told me it was too gay for them. Who wants a hit?' Brian did an imitation of a bartender in a loud club who couldn't hear the drink's orders.

I was sitting on the bed and Jesse sat next to me. 'How have you been settling into the new school?' he asked.

'It's been really great,' I lied. The truth was, I'd never had a longer month. Every day was like walking underwater and fighting to get to the surface for a breath. There were currents and undertows and I constantly wished that I'd been able to stay in my old school and avoid the drama.

'Have seen little of you lately.' Sabiha sat next to Jesse and interjected herself in the conversation.

'I've been busy,' Jesse said. 'I'm revising my graphic novel.'

Sabiha nodded awkwardly and took a sip of her drink. 'Are you making a lot of changes?'

'Just smoothing out the structure so it reads better.'

'If you ever need another pair of eyes...' Sabiha said.

'I thought you didn't like graphic novels?' I needled her, still cut at her high handedness earlier. She'd made the admission at the family barbecue when she and Dad were talking about books.

'This is different,' Sabiha fumbled and her cheeks flushed. 'This is Jesse's comic book and I want to help in any way I can.'

'Who's your publisher?' I asked, to fill in the dead silence.

'Gordonio,' Jesse said.

'They published the Mikado Chronicles.' I named a popular graphic novel series that was in its tenth volume. 'My brother loves graphic novels, and I read some of them,' I explained at Jesse's surprised look. 'It's an amazing coup you got a main-stream publisher. Most people have to self publish.'

'That was Plan B,' Jesse said wryly. 'But it would have taken a lot longer to save the money.'

We spent the next few minutes talking about our favourite graphic novels.

'My brother Ali would love to meet you,' I said. 'It's his dream to write a graphic novel.'

'Let me know when and I'll be there.' Jesse took a swig of his drink and our eyes caught.

Sabiha shifted on the bed, and I saw her past Jesse's profile. She shot me a glance, and I quickly broke eye contact with Jesse and looked the other way.

I took a backseat as Sabiha monopolised the conversation with Jesse, talking about people they knew to purposely exclude me. Jesse acted like she was just a friend, while she nudged so close to him she was practically sitting on his lap.

I couldn't figure out if Jesse knew about Sabiha's crush and was purposely being cruel in ignoring her, or if he was honestly innocent in picking up her brazen signals.

Brian sat on the floor and leaned on the bed next to me. 'How's the job hunt going?' I asked him.

'It's not,' he said wryly. 'I'm going to be an entrepreneur.'

'What does that mean?' Dina asked. She was sitting on the floor across from Brian. 'You're going to entrap people and yell ner, ner in their face.' Dina laughed wildly and toppled onto her side.

'I'm cutting you off.' Brian took the bottle of beer that was in her hand, spilling a few drops on the floor as he placed it on the table behind her. 'Omer and I are going into business,' he said when he'd returned to his spot.

'What sort of business?' I asked.

Brian put his finger over his lips. 'Very lucrative business.' He opened a box on the bottom of the bookshelf he was sitting next to. 'It's my Stash of Cash.' Brian smiled proudly. He returned the lid.

'You should put that in the bank,' I said, amazed at the thick stash of cash. 'It's not safe to have cash lying around.'

'No one knows it's there,' he said dismissively.

I frowned, wondering how many other people he'd showed it off to. 'How did you get all that cash?' my curiosity peaked at his entrepreneurial acumen.

'It's top secret. Can't talk about it.' Brian laughed to himself. 'But if you ever need a movie to watch, I'm your guy.'

I shifted on the bed. I'd been drinking orange juice and after three drinks my bladder was getting full, but I didn't know how to broach the topic.

'Time to drain the lizard.' Brian stood.

I was relieved. I expected that he'd move the furniture from in front of the door. Instead he walked around Dina and opened his curtains.

'What are you doing?' Sabiha asked.

He pointed out the window. 'I'm going to water the roses.'

'Why don't you open the door?' Sabiha exclaimed.

He threw a foot over the window ledge. 'We have to keep the hordes out. Once we open that door, they'll descend on us like bloodthirsty vampires and won't leave until they've drained our bar.' He disappeared from view.

In the silence, there was a loud crash and raucous laughter. 'Sounds like they're pulling apart the house,' Sabiha said.

Brian returned and weaved as he jumped back through the window. He fell to the ground and reached for Dina to help himself up.

'Don't touch me with your pee hands.' She screeched and moved away from him.

'I washed them with the garden tap,' Brian said wryly as he stood.

'I need to go too.' Sabiha stood.

'I'll come.' I was going to bust. Once out of the house, I headed for the bushes while Sabiha went to the backdoor. 'Where are you going?'

'I'm not pissing behind the bushes like an animal.'

I finished in the toilet and found Sabiha in the bathroom.

'You and Jesse were looking cosy,' Sabiha said, staring me down.

'We're just friends,' I said, wondering where her jealousy was coming from.

'Don't read anything into it. He's just nice like that.'

'I'm not,' I snapped. 'I don't need to chase boys who are unavailable.'

Sabiha narrowed her eyes and made a big show of looking at her mobile. 'Isn't it your curfew?'

'I still have over an hour.' I looked at the time.

'Yes, but you have to get a taxi and they take ages.'

It wasn't hard to read between the lines. She wanted me gone. I wanted to stay to needle her, but she was right. It was better I left earlier and anyway Alex was giving me a lift home and this way we'd have extra time together.

'I'll call.' I looked at the towel as I carefully wiped my hands.

'I'll come with.' Sabiha made to follow.

'That's not necessary,' I said.

Sabiha flounced as she left.

I walked through the house, but couldn't find Alex. When I tried calling, his phone rang out. Where was he? I kept remembering him and the brunette in the kitchen, but told myself not to be paranoid. Sabiha showed me that jealousy wasn't a good look.

I picked up the house phone. Should I wait for Alex or call a taxi? I had 45 minutes until I had to be home. I dialled the taxi company. There was a half an hour delay. The party was wild and sleazy, so I returned to Brian's room to wait.

'Are you okay?' Jesse asked after ten minutes passed and I said nothing.

I nodded.

'Did something happen while you were alone outside?' Jesse asked.

'No, of course not.' I wondered where Alex could be. He'd promised he'd take me home and as time passed, I feared he'd forgotten about me. If the taxi took too long and I arrived home after Mum...

'Shit.' Dina turned green and swallowed.

'She's going to hurl.' Brian squealed like a little girl and backed away.

Sabiha helped Dina lean out the window and held her hair back as she vomited, looking like she was fighting her own gag reflex.

I decided it was a good time to leave. 'I have to wait for my taxi.'

'I can't leave Dina and come wait with you,' Sabiha said.

'I don't need you to.'

Sabiha looked annoyed.

'I'll come with you,' Jesse said.

Sabiha looked uneasily between the two of us. 'She'll be fine. Anyway, I can see the street from here.'

'There's drunk idiots everywhere,' Jesse snapped.

Sabiha shot me a furious look as we walked out. Jealous cow. As if the only thing I wanted was to poach her crush.

'So what's the deal between you and Sabiha?' I asked Jesse as we waited for the taxi.

Jesse shifted uncomfortably. 'We're just friends.'

'Does she know that?' I asked rudely, thinking about how she draped herself over him like he was her favourite armchair.

Jesse's face took on a look of consternation.

'You get that she's totally into you, right?'

He looked puzzled. 'We had a thing for a moment, but she moved on.' He still sounded cut up over it.

'I hate to burst your bubble, but she didn't move on.'

He looked at the house as if he were searching for her. His face creased as he processed what I told him.

I should have felt guilty for spilling the beans on a supposed friend, but I figured Sabiha had it coming. What you gave around, came around, and it was her turn to deal with the fallout of over sharing.

Brian opened the front door and shouted for Jesse. After an exchange, Jesse called out. 'I have to help Sabiha with Dina.'

Brian reluctantly walked to the front.

'What's wrong with Dina?' I asked.

'Girl can't hold her drink and I can't control my gag reflex.' He put his hands in his pocket and searched. 'Shit. I forgot my smokes. I'll be right back.'

After he left, I peered down the street. A commodore drove past slowly, the passenger window down, and a guy in a red singlet checked me out. I breathed easier when it passed.

A car parked in front of the house and Alex got out.

'Where were you?' I nodded to the car.

'I gave a mate a lift home,' he said. 'What are you doing out here?'

'Is your mate the brunette you were talking to in the kitchen?' I asked, the words passing through my lips without permission.

Alex frowned. 'Are you out here trying to catch me out?'

'Why? Have you got something to hide?'

'No,' he said after a beat.

'No,' I belatedly answered his question.

We looked at each other and laughed. 'I think we had our first fight,.' He hugged me.

He went to kiss me, but I pushed him away and looked at the front door. 'Someone could see us.'

As he moved away and stood under the streetlight, I saw he was wearing a fresh shirt. I was about to ask him about it when the Commodore passed by again, this time the driver did a burn out on the street as it chucked a U-turn.

'Is this Omer's house?' Red singlet guy asked.

'He's inside,' Alex said.

The driver parked the car, and the trio trooped inside.

Alex and I reached the car when the music cut out behind us and a scream pierced the air. Partygoers streamed out the front door, rushing into their cars or running down the street, all eager to put distance between themselves and whatever was happening.

'Get in the car and lock the doors.' Alex handed me his keys and ran into the house.

I unlocked the car with shaking hands. As I cowered in the passenger seat and peered out the window, shame descended. My friends were all inside while I was hiding.

I looked at my mobile and thought about calling for help, but I didn't know what was happening. There were bushes scattered on the front lawn. Before I had time to think about it I ran across the street in a crouched position.

I stealthily waded through the bushes and positioned myself in front of the living room window. As I'd guessed, the bushes provided the perfect cover from the street and I could hide from anyone leaving the house. I took a deep breath and bobbed up, peering through the window.

They pushed Alex up against the wall, one goon standing threateningly in front of him while Jesse and Brian were sitting on the couch.

'You've been hard to find, amigo.' Red singlet stood over Omer.

'I've been here the whole time, Louie.' Louie's other goon squeezed Omer's arm, and his eyes moved from side to side as if he was seeking an escape route.

'I thought maybe you forgot about me and you know that wouldn't be good for your health.' Louie's attention wandered as Dina stumbled in, weaving drunkenly as she dodged furniture.

Dina grabbed hold of Omer's arm to keep herself upright, moving him away from Louie's mate.

'So that's what's been keeping you busy, brother?' He smiled approvingly as he looked Dina up and down. 'And what's your name?'

Dina answered wearing a lop-sided smile.

Omer looked sick as he watched Dina flirting with Louie, but the way he was holding himself in check showed his fear. Jesse stood and reached for Dina, but Louie's goon pushed him back down.

'It's a shame Omer got to you first.' Louie gave Omer a sly smile.

'I'm not his girlfriend,' Dina said.

Omer approached them. 'About our business—'

'I'm his sister,' Dina said before Omer reached her.

It was like watching a car accident in slow motion. 'You're Omer's sister. Did you hear that, boys?' Louie asked the two guys that were with him. They took that as their cue and surrounded Omer, each grabbing an arm. 'If your sister and I go for a drive, I'll give you an extra three days to pay your loan.'

I hunted for my mobile to call the police, but the rustling of my handbag stayed my hand. Louie and his mates would hear me talking. The only way I could call the police is if I moved away. Louie moved closer to the window, Dina in his arms. I was trapped. If I moved, he'd see me. I hunched and watched the unfolding action.

Sabiha burst into the living room wearing Brian's jeans and a top. 'Dina, you owe me a new pair of shoes.' Her gaze sharpened when she saw Louie and his mates. 'What's going on here?'

'We're settling a debt owed by Omer,' Louie said.

Dina leaned limply against him. She looked like she'd fall down, but he held her up effortlessly, his biceps bunching up. He carelessly ran his hands through her hair, petting her like a dog. Dina leaned against Louie's shoulder, drunkenly smiling, oblivious to the danger.

'How much?' Sabiha demanded.

'Ten large,' Louie said. 'Are your sister and I going for a drive?'

Louie squeezed Dina's breast and hips. She struggled, but was helpless in his arms. Omer threw himself forward and aimed a punch at Louie's face. Louie dodged his punch and dropped Dina, who landed on the floor with a thud. The goon grabbed Omer and held him while Louie punched him in the torso.

Sabiha ran forward and pulled Dina toward the front door. Dina screamed and tried to return to her brother, but Sabiha relentlessly yanked her away. Jesse and Brian grabbed Dina's arms, and they ran. Omer's mate cut them off. Alex waded into the mêlée and bear hugged the goon, wrestling him to the ground.

'The back door,' Sabiha shouted.

I was frozen. I knew I should do something to help, but I was too scared to move.

Alex clambered on top of the goon and punched him. He lifted his head and looked at me. 'Run.'

I broke through my paralysis and ran down the driveway and joined my friends in the backyard. I looked around in a panic. There was nowhere to go.

Chapter 15

Sabiha reached the back fence. 'Jump over.' Sabiha lifted Dina's leg and put it on the beam. 'Hurry. We have to get help for Omer.'

Dina finally cooperated. Brian lithely jumped over while Jesse perched on top of the fence and helped the girls. We landed in someone else's backyard and ran down the side of the house.

'Who's got a phone?' Sabiha demanded when we hit the footpath.

'Me.' I rifled through my handbag and looked up in panic. 'I dropped it.'

'What are we going to do?' Dina sounded like a wounded animal.

'I'm thinking.' Sabiha looked up and down the street.

'I'll run to my house,' Jesse said. 'It will only take 10 minutes.'

'Too long.' Sabiha's gaze zeroed in on a house across the street. 'I'll ask to use their phone.'

'You can't go alone.' Jesse grabbed her arm.

Sabiha waited.

'Let's go.' He followed her.

Brian comforted Dina, who was sobbing. She'd lost all control and looked like a drowned raccoon as her eye makeup ran. Jesse and Sabiha knocked on the door and the owners allowed them to enter. Within a few minutes, they reappeared through the front door.

'The police are on their way,' Sabiha said when they rejoined us. 'They should be there by the time we walk around the block.'

'We have to jump over the back fence and help Omer,' Dina said.

'There's nothing else we can do.' Sabiha yanked Dina's arm and pushed her down the footpath. 'Walk.'

'Bitch,' Dina spat as she walked ahead, her gait still wobbly. 'You're acting like it's Omer's fault that this happened.'

The rest of us pretended we didn't hear her. Dina tried to tear ahead, but Sabiha carelessly grabbed her into a bear hug and covered her mouth when she protested.

'I think they're gone,' Jesse said, when we were a few houses up from Brian's house. He peered through the darkness, trying to see if Louie's car was gone.

'We should wait until the police arrive,' Sabiha said.

Dina violently protested, shaking her head as she tried to shake off Sabiha's bear hold.

I bit my nails and wondered if Alex was all right.

Jesse met Dina's panicked gaze. 'I'll see if it's all clear.' He began walking. 'You all wait here.'

'I'm coming.' Brian ran a few paces and joined him.

'This is bullshit,' Sabiha said with disgust, letting go of Dina. 'We're not waiting like some pathetic Victorian maidens that need to be saved.'

A police car drove past. 'They're here.' Dina ran.

When we got to Brian's house, I quickly ducked among the bushes and found my mobile.

In the living room, Omer was on the couch, his face bruised and his eyeball red. 'They were Asian,' he told the police officers, giving a wrong description. 'They crashed the party and lay into me.'

Dina sat next to him and cried hysterically. She tried to hug him, but stopped when he winced.

I looked around in vain for Alex.

'Did you see anything?' The police officer turned to where we were standing by the living room door.

'We were in the backyard,' Brian said smoothly. 'We jumped the fence when we heard screaming and called the cops.'

He looked at Sabiha, who eyeballed him for a moment.

'I'll get some ice.' She left the room.

'What about the rest of you?'

Jesse and I shook our head.

'We've had reports of a group of gatecrashers in the area.' The police officer gave Omer his card. 'Call us if you think of anything else.'

'Why did you lie?' Sabiha asked when the police left.

'Louie told me he'd cut up Dina if I went to the cops.' Omer had his arm around Dina. 'I have a week to come up with ten grand or else.'

'Ten grand.' Dina sounded like an echo.

'Don't worry, sis. I've got it under control.' Omer shifted and groaned.

'You have to go to the hospital,' Dina urged.

'It's not that bad.' He took a shallow breath.

I muttered the word toilet and headed down the hall. I heard the bathroom tap. The door was ajar, and I pushed it open. Alex was shirtless, his torso bruised. He was holding a wet towel against a cut in his eyebrow.

'Hey.' He smiled when he saw me in the mirror.

I threw myself into his arms, feeling a thrill as I touched the bare skin of his back.

'I'm all right.' He kissed my hair.

His smile faded as he looked at me tenderly. I remembered the way he'd put himself at risk to save me. Alex placed his lips on mine and kissed me like he was trying to pour all his emotions into it. He picked me up and carried me, pushing Brian's door open with his shoulder. He closed it with his foot and lay on top of me on the bed.

As my legs wrapped around his hips, there was a little voice of reason trying to penetrate through the fog of lust, but I blocked it and returned Alex' kiss with abandon. My mobile rang. The tone got louder and louder, cutting between us like a barrier. I yanked out my mobile and was about to turn it off when the flashing screen stayed my hand. I'd set the alarm to go off and warn me when I had to leave.

'Shit.' I shifted my eyes to Alex. 'My Mum is finishing work in fifteen minutes.'

Alex put his head on my chest and groaned. 'I'll take you home.' He went to Brian's wardrobe and took a shirt that he put on.

'I'll go out first,' I said.

Alex nodded.

As I walked out of the bedroom, my legs were weak and my skin tingled like it was alive. Jesse and Brian were half carrying Omer toward me. They ducked into the bathroom and I heard them helping him wash himself.

Sabiha held a garbage bag and was cleaning up.

'I have to go home,' I said in a panic. 'My Mum will be home in ten minutes.'

Sabiha stood straight. 'It's too late to call a taxi.'

Alex entered the living room.

'Can you give Alma a lift?' Sabiha asked him.

It wasn't until we were pulling out of the driveway that I realised I didn't say goodbye to Jesse and Brian. I looked at the dashboard clock and said, 'I'm dead.'

'Don't worry.' Alex jerked the wheel onto the road. 'I'll get you home.'

He sped down the road. The light ahead was amber. He stomped his foot on the pedal and shot through as the light turned red, leaving cars beeping in our wake. Alex burst into laughter. I held onto the roof handle.

Alex turned into a street without using an indicator, rubber wheels squealing. The wheels lost traction, and I screamed as the car slid out from under us. Alex aimed for the nature strip, making the car bounce hard as it climbed up.

'Whoops.' He put his arm on the back of my seat and reversed.

'Maybe you should slow down.' My throat was sore from screaming.

'How long?'

I glanced at the dashboard clock. 'Five minutes.'

He met my gaze. 'Do you want me to slow down?'

I knew I should say yes. We were playing with our lives, but I couldn't get the words past my lips. The good girl I used to be was asleep and the rebel inside was taking over. Alex waited. He'd do whatever I wanted.

'No.' I squealed as he hit the pedal.

The scenery passed by in a fluoro blur of lights. I was free in a way I'd never been before. The past and future ceased to exist, and there was only this moment. Alex howled to the wind as he sped through the streets. He pulled up a few houses away from my house with a squeal of rubber.

I threw myself sideways and kissed him deeply on the lips. 'Thank you.'

He put his forehead against mine.

'Monday,' I breathed and kissed him again.

'Monday,' he said with a promise when I reached for the door handle.

As I crossed the street, I looked over my shoulder and saw he was watching me. I swayed harder. His car roared away as I hid behind the bushes in my front yard. I looked up at the fence. My arms and legs were tired after all my exertions at Brian's party. With a sigh, I clambered over.

As I skulked past the living room window, I heard dead silence. Hopefully, Sanela and Ali were asleep. I carefully unlocked the laundry door and snuck into the house. Ali was in the study, engrossed on the computer. I did a Mission Impossible move and slinked past the doorway.

Sanela was asleep on the couch, the blue screen from the television lighting her up. I resisted the temptation to turn off the TV and remote. I nimbly climbed the stairs. In my bedroom, I changed into my pyjamas, wiped off my makeup and dived into bed, just as Mum's car pulled up in the garage.

There was a murmur of voices and the thump of footsteps on the stairs. A few minutes later, my door opened. I debated whether to pretend I was sleeping, but Mum came to stand beside the bed and smoothed back my hair.

'You're home,' I murmured.

'How are you feeling?'

The hallway light spilled into the room, and I saw her outline. 'Better.'

'Good.' Mum kissed my forehead. 'I'll see you in the morning.'

I stared at the ceiling and thought about Alex, desperately wishing he was here to hold me tight and make me feel good again. I'd been tiptoeing through life since Sabiha's existence was revealed. All my emotions were on mute as I battled each day, but Alex made all that go away. He made me come alive.

I kept replaying memories of our night together. Alex playing that awful prank on me, Alex apologising, Alex protecting me. It was like we'd lived out a lifetime in one night and we'd survived our first fight, our first make-up session, our first adventure.

My mobile beeped.

Alex: "Sweet dreams, Chiquita. Can't wait for Monday."

I hugged my mobile against my chest and imagined it was Alex. I tried to think of a way to sneak out and meet him. In the end, there was only one person who could help me with an alibi.

***

'Mum, can I visit Dina?' I asked the next morning after breakfast when everyone had dispersed.

'Oh.' Mum frowned from the sink.

'We're doing an assignment together.' I cleared the table, putting in place the first stage of my plan.

'I think we owe her parents a visit,' Mum said.

I held back my impatience and waited.

'I'll talk to your father and we might all go.'

'I was hoping to go now.' I glanced at the clock. I didn't want to be held ransom to their schedule. The sooner I talked to Dina, the sooner I could confirm my plans with Alex. 'I'll wash the dishes and you talk to Dad?'

'You're pretty eager to finish your homework.' Mum smiled.

'Maybe I want to talk to her too.'

'I'm glad you've made friends with Dina.' Mum cupped my shoulder as she passed. 'She's a good girl and the friend you ought to have.'

I nodded, an image of Dina sucking on a toke, making me look away guiltily.

Mum returned with an ok and I rounded up the troops. Ali stayed home. Sanela and I walked ahead, while Mum and Dad sauntered behind us. When we reached Dina's house, Dad had his arm around Mum's waist as we waited by the front door.

Anyone who saw us wouldn't believe that they'd spent the day at opposite ends of the house. It was like Sabiha's visit yesterday turned them into awkward strangers who didn't know what to say to each other, but now that they had an audience, they were doing their trademark performance of the respected doctor and his devoted wife.

Dina's mum, Suada, opened the front door and greeted us, her dad following soon behind. As Dina's parents moved out of the way, I saw Dina's pale face and the dark circles under her eyes. She looked like she hadn't slept all night.

'She's not feeling well,' Suada said, her hands on Dina's shoulders.

'Does she have a fever?' Dad went into doctor mode.

Dina shook her head. 'I must have eaten something that didn't agree with me last night.'

'Is Sabiha sick too? Didn't she sleep over?' Dad added when Suada gave him a blank look.

Suada shook her head.

'I must have heard wrong,' Dad said.

Dad forgot nothing. He always said that one of the most important things a doctor had was his memory. I gulped. Usually I'd be happy that Dad was catching Sabiha out in a lie, but if he uncovered Sabiha's deception last night, my unveiling wouldn't be far behind.

I gave Dina a hug, feeling her frailness as I put my hands on her back.

'*Sluša li te Babo*?' Dina's father asked Sanela behind us as I followed Dina to her bedroom, the Bosnian equivalent of a joke in asking a child if their father was taking orders from them. I was so glad I was past the age where I got asked stupid questions by adults.

'Fuck.' Dina closed her bedroom door. 'Do you think he bought it?'

I shook my head. 'Our only hope is that Sabiha is a convincing liar.'

'Then we're fine.' Dina lay on the bed. 'Sabiha could pass a lie detector.'

I wanted to quip that Dad was a lie detector, but Dina let out a pained sigh. 'How are you doing?' I asked and sat on the chair next to her bed.

'I've been better.' Dina stared at the ceiling. 'I can't get it out of my head.' She banged her hand on her forehead. 'I keep seeing Louie punching Omer and imagining what else could happen...' Her voice cut out, and she teared up.

I saw a tissue box on her vanity and held it out to her. 'Omer will figure something out. How's he doing?'

'He's at home doped up on painkillers.' She wiped her eyes with a tissue. 'And he's got no one to look after him.'

'He's got Brian. Has he got any plans on how to get the money?'

Dina kept staring at the ceiling. 'Maybe.'

'That's great then. Right?'

'Maybe.' Dina turned her head and looked at me. 'There might be a way, but... Never mind.' She looked back at the ceiling.

'What? You can tell me, after all we've already kept each other's secrets.'

'Okay.' She leaned on her elbow. 'You can't tell anyone what I'm about to tell you.' She waited until I nodded. 'We've figured out a way to get him the money, it's just really, really risky.'

'Risky how?'

'My parents set up a bank account for both of us when we were babies. They put in our birthday money and extra a few times a year. When they kicked Omer out, they closed his account and put the money in my bank account. Sometime back they began using internet banking to stop paying the bank fees, and I ended up helping them set up stuff so....'

'So you know their password and can steal the money?' I was shocked. I'd expected some outlandish proposition about stealing from the bank, not from her own parents.

'It's not really stealing,' Dina said. 'The money is technically mine.'

'Why don't you ask them for it?'

Dina dropped back onto the bed. 'Because they'd say no. They'd say that was their money that they were setting aside for me. For my wedding, or a car or university.'

'Then it's not really your money.'

'It's at moments like this I can really see you and Sabiha are sisters.' Dina groaned.

'Sorry.' I held up my hand in apology. I didn't mean to sound like a judgmental-know-it-all. When Sabiha lectured me, I knew how it got my back up. 'I can see why it's risky. Your parents aren't exactly the forgiving type.'

'Omer's already said that we could move in together. He wants me to leave before they have the chance to kick me out. There's money there to pay back Louie and then some, but I'm not sure.'

'You really are between a rock and a hard place. Either way, you're going to be facing some hard consequences.' I felt sympathy at her predicament.

'Exactly.' Dina gesticulated with her hands. 'I mean, I want to help my brother. I really, really do. But I don't know if I can trust—' She cut herself off.

'You don't know if you can trust him,' I finished her sentence.

'Neither side are saints. I didn't hear from him for two years. I didn't know if he was dead or alive because he never picked up the phone, or emailed me, or anything. Do you know what that's like? To always be wondering.' Dina was full on losing it and was crying in big, gulping sobs.

'Hey, hey.' I sat on the bed and hugged her. 'It's okay.'

'I shouldn't be laying all this on you.' Dina pulled away as she swallowed her sobs. 'Sabiha's my best friend. She's the one who I should talk to.'

'So why aren't you?'

Dina hesitated, not wanting to backstab her friend.

'Because you know exactly what she would say. She'd tell you that Omer doesn't deserve your loyalty. That he abandoned you and that this was his problem and he should deal with it.'

'Something like that.' Dina smiled wryly as she shredded a tissue.

'You're forgetting one thing,' I continued. 'Sabiha was raised with no siblings.' As I imagined how I'd feel if Ali were in the same position, I shivered like someone had walked over my grave. 'Sabiha doesn't understand that all those years of living together under the same roof, having that person in your life from birth, creates an unbreakable bond. At the end of the day he's your brother and of course you want to help him. But they're your parents and you love them too,' I sighed. 'You know this riddle has no solution. It's a matter of what you can bear.'

Dina looked down at the bed as she smoothed the coverlet. 'I can't bear the thought of my brother being tortured by some gangster because he owes him money.'

'Then you have your answer.'

'I do,' Dina said.

'But that doesn't mean that you shouldn't ask them first. If they say no you're still in the same boat.'

'That's true.' Dina's face lightened. She noticed the confetti scattered on the bed and picked it up. 'Thanks for talking to me. It helps to have a sympathetic ear.'

'I know.' I understood the need all too well as I wasn't able to discuss what was happening with Alex to anyone, and it was killing me inside.

'If there's anything you ever need, let me know.'

'Actually,' I intoned. 'There kind of is something.'

'Shoot.' Dina took the tissue shreds to the bin under her desk.

'I have a boyfriend.' I felt a thrill as I made my admission.

'You're shitting me.' Dina slapped me on the arm as she sat down again. 'Who is he?'

'He's someone you know.'

'Go on.' Dina gestured.

'It's only been a few weeks.' It surprised me how short a time I'd known Alex for. It felt much longer. 'I was hoping you'd cover for me tomorrow so I can see him. I'll tell Dad that you and I are studying at the library.'

'Of course.' Dina waved her hand in exasperation. 'Tell me about him.'

'He's really cute. And gentle. He makes me feel good.'

Dina interrupted. 'What does he look like? What's his name?'

'You can't tell Sabiha what I'm about to tell you.'

'Why?' Dina frowned.

'I don't want her to know—' I stopped when Dina shook her head.

'Sabiha's my best friend. I can't lie to her.'

'I'm not asking you to lie. I'm asking you not to share my personal business.'

'Why are you hiding him from Sabiha? Oh my God.' Dina put her hands on her chest. 'You're seeing Jesse.'

'It's not Jesse.'

'It has to be Jesse. Who else do you know? Sabiha is going to be devastated.' She looked at me like I was scum.

'It's not Jesse,' I shouted. I stilled, realising how loud I was. 'It's Alex.'

'Alex?' Dina repeated, like she was saying a foreign word.

'Alex Payne.'

'Alex? Really?'

'Yes, Alex Payne is my boyfriend.' Dina was acting like it was out of the realm of possibility that Alex would ever be with someone like me.

'But Alex, he's, well—' Dina cut out under my furious stare. 'He's cute,'

'What's your problem with Alex?'

'He's Alex Payne,' Dina said, like it was obvious. 'He has a terrible reputation.'

'He's not like that. He's sweet and nice.'

'Nice,' Dina repeated, looking at me like I was a mental patient.

'Yes, nice.'

'That answers my question?' Dina said coyly.

I gestured with my hands for her to continue.

'You haven't had sex with him yet. Once you do, well, nice won't be the operative word.'

I gasped. 'He's not like that.' I told her how he'd saved me at the party.

Dina looked confused when I finished. 'I don't know. That's not what I heard.'

'Well, you're hearing it from me. Alex is a good guy.'

'Okay, okay.' She lifted her hands in surrender.

'Don't tell Sabiha about him.'

'Why not? If he's a good guy, then you've got nothing to hide.'

'But my parents can't find out.'

'She's not going to tell on you,' Dina said.

The thought of telling Sabiha freaked me out. Even though I kept telling myself Sabiha's opinion didn't matter, there was something inside me that shrieked "Danger, danger," like Sabiha was going to take Alex away from me, the way she took away my father, and once again I'd be left lonely and invisible.

'She'll want to know when we got together and I'll tell her it was at Omer's house,' thinking of a way to get Dina to back off. 'You know, when Omer was passing around a joint and you got baked.'

'You're going to have to tell her eventually,' Dina muttered, realising my admission would do her no favours. Sabiha was already harping on about Omer's bad influence, she needed no more ammunition.

'Maybe.' The possibility was far off in the distant future and no threat to the present. 'Can I count on you for an alibi tomorrow?'

'I'm not going to lie to Sabiha.'

'But—' I cut out when Dina held up her hand.

'But I won't rat you out either,' she finished.

Dina was leaving me some wiggle room in the grey area that was a lie of omission. 'I can live with that.'

There was the sound of familiar running footsteps in the hallway. I opened the door to Sanela's grinning face. 'I found you,' she said, as if we'd been playing hide and seek.

'Yes, you did.'

'What are you doing?' Sanela peered into the bedroom.

'Talking. Go be with Mum.' I took her shoulders and tried to point her towards the stairs.

'No,' Sanela shrieked. 'I want to play hairdresser. Dina, can I tie your hair?' She evaded my grasp and burst into the bedroom.

'Okay,' Dina smiled.

I watched Sanela brush Dina's hair with a smile. I'd have to do some fancy footwork tomorrow to pull off seeing Alex, but it was all going to be worth it. Just to be alone with him, with no interruptions and distractions. I hugged myself with glee.

***

Later at home, I was watching television with Sanela in the living room when Mum asked me to get Dad for dinner.

'I'll get Ali,' Sanela said and ran up the stairs.

I walked to the study where Dad was doing paperwork. I'd just reached the doorway when his phone rang.

'Sabiha, I was getting worried about you.'

I ducked beside the door.

'I called hours ago. I wanted to touch base after yesterday's lunch,' he said.

I put my nails in my mouth. As I suspected, he was following up on Sabiha, supposedly sleeping over at Dina's. I was full of breathless anticipation. On the one hand, I felt vicious glee at Sabiha being caught out by Dad and that he would see who she truly was, but I was also terrified. If he caught Sabiha out, there was nothing to stop her from dobbing me in.

'I'm glad,' he said. 'Did you have fun at your sleepover at Dina's last night?'

This was it. The moment of reckoning. I bit my nail to the quick and sucked on the bloody stub as I waited.

'I'm glad you had fun,' Dad said. 'But next time get to sleep at a reasonable time. It's not good you spent all day in bed.'

He hung up. It took me a moment to process what had happened. He knew Sabiha was lying, and that she didn't sleep over at Dina's. I'd expected him to go off his nut. Instead, he'd let her get away with it.

I couldn't believe that Sabiha could get away scot free with lying and flouting authority and yet if my siblings and I made one minor infraction, we copped it both barrels. The injustice burnt through me and I smacked the wall with anger.

'Who's there?' Dad peered toward the door.

'Just me.' I popped my head in. 'Mum's finished dinner.'

'I'll be a moment.' Dad looked at the files on his desk with a troubled face.

Chapter 16

I lay in bed, waiting for the house to settle around me. My skin was itchy, like there were insects walking on me and I threw back the covers. As I paced, I kept remembering the undercurrent of disappointment in Dad's voice when he spoke to Sabiha, and yet he'd accepted her lie. His double standards disgusted me when I thought about the way he'd put me through the third degree when I was supposedly late from the library.

It was 10.00 pm. I lifted the curtain and looked out onto the dark street below. I wanted to be someone else and forget about all the things that were bringing me down, and Alex did that. He made me feel good. I typed a message and pressed send, but it was as if my hand didn't belong to me. I was discombobulated, like I was vanishing in the dark.

AlmaO "Chat?"

He replied straight away.

AlexP "Sure."

I hadn't realised how desperate I was to connect with him. He'd become my port in the storm, the one place I didn't have to worry about secret subtexts or hidden agendas.

AlexP "I was thinking about you. Can't wait to see you to-morrow. Be with you again."

AlmaO "Me too. It's all arranged."

We confirmed where and when to meet.

AlexP "Wish I could see you now."

AlmaO "Okay."

I turned on my lamp and took a photo of myself.

AlexP "Nice."

He sent a photo of himself. In it he was shirtless, his six-pack on display.

AlexP "What do you think?"

AlmaO "U r hot."

AlexP "LOL. Glad you like. Wish I could see more of you."

He included a smiley emoticon.

I peered at my cotton pyjamas. They wouldn't do.

AlmaO "Wait a sec."

I rifled through my wardrobe. I'd attended my high school formal in Hobart and Mum had bought me matching black panties and bra to wear under my black formal dress. After I put them on, I posed in front of the mirror, feeling sexy and daring. I put on a black chiffon shirt that Mum didn't let me wear because it was see-through, pleased to see I looked sexy, but still modest. After I brushed my hair and rubbed on lip gloss, I took another full body shot of myself.

AlexP "Wow. I'm so hard I can barely control myself. Do a striptease for me, sexy lady."

I hesitated, warning bells ringing.

AlmaO "You do a striptease for me."

I typed, trying to deflect.

AlexP "Okay."

I looked at the screen in confusion. Did he really say okay? My phone went quiet. When it beeped again, I opened the screen and laughed so hard I fell on the bed. Alex was posing in front of a full-length mirror. He was pouting as he hooked his thumbs in his jean tabs. His shirt was unbuttoned and draped around his torso. The phone beeped fast and furious as he sent one image after another.

He pulled off his shirt one-handed and photographed himself with the other. Click. He was shirtless. Click. His hand was on his zipper. Click. The zip was undone. Click. He turned and photographed his back as he yanked down his jeans, flashing his underwear-clad tight butt. Click. He smacked his arse. Click. The jeans were around his ankles, his hips askew as he danced. Click. He faced the mirror again, wearing nothing but his underwear.

My eyes zeroed in on this crotch. 'No, no, no,' I chanted as I squirmed on the bed. Even though I'd seen him nude, this was excruciating. Beep. I was equally embarrassed and curious to look at the screen. In the end, curiosity won. I laughed with delight when I saw the photo. He was completely naked, his hands cupping his genitals.

AlexP "Your turn."

I hesitated as I stood up. Was I really going to do this? I remembered my dad letting Sabiha's lie slide and a ball of rage hit my stomach. Hell yes. I stood in front of the mirror and undid my shirt, letting it drape open so it revealed my bra and underwear. Click. I pushed the shirt off. Click. I blew a kiss, wearing my underwear and bra. Click. I turned my hands on my bra clasp. Click. I undid the clasp. Click. I pushed the straps down my arms. Click. I threw the bra on the floor and turned to the mirror again, one arm covering my breasts. Click.

I imagined Alex was lying on the bed, watching me perform a striptease.

"More, more," he demanded.

The phone beeped, and I picked it up again.

AlexP "I want to see all of you."

The lamp was behind me and shadows played peekaboo with my body. Half my face disappeared into the darkness and I looked like someone else. A sexy, vampy supermodel who had nothing to hide.

I put down my hand and looked at my bare breasts. I hesitated before pressing the button on my camera phone. There was a half-formed thought trying to push through. Like a breeze, it passed by. I put my arm down. Click. I sent the photo.

AlexP "You are a work of art."

I smiled at my doppelgänger in the mirror.

AlexP "I wish you were here with me so I could hold you tight and whisper something in your ear."

AlmaO "What would you whisper?"

AlexP "I love you."

Tears came to my eyes, and I hugged the phone against my naked torso. I yearned to have him with me.

AlmaO "I love you too."

AlexP "I can't wait for tomorrow. To see you strip for me in real life."

AlmaO "Me too."

AlexP "Sweet dreams. I will dream of you until then."

AlmaO "Good night."

I sat on the bed, lost in a daze. He loved me. I was floating on a cloud. As long as I had Alex I was all right. My skin broke out in goose pimples. I put on my pyjamas and got into bed, the mobile in my hands.

I opened my sent items and viewed my striptease for Alex, feeling a strange mingling of embarrassment and pride. They were really wonderful photos. I looked like a model in a black and white artistic nude portrait. I smiled as I read Alex' responses again.

I wished I could keep these memories, but it wasn't safe. If my parents saw these photos, I'd be dead. As I deleted them, there was a bitterness seeping into me. I wondered how forgiving Dad would be of my secret life, but I knew the answer even before the question formed.

***

As I walked to school Monday, there were butterflies in my stomach at seeing Alex again. Dina and Sabiha were at the front gate, and I heard them arguing as I approached.

'He's coming home with me tonight when I finish with Alma at the library,' Dina said, slipping in my alibi. She looked like she hadn't slept since the party. Her eyes blinked every few seconds, making her look like a recovering addict. 'We're not giving them warning so they can refuse to see him.'

'Do you really think they're going to help?' Sabiha asked.

'I don't know,' Dina wailed. 'But Louie is going to hurt my brother. He could kill him even.'

'Omer will be fine,' Sabiha said. 'He got through all these years without your help.'

'You're so cold,' Dina said.

'I'm realistic. I doubt your parents are going to give him more money considering how many times he's hit them up in the past.'

'But this is different.' Dina's voice was full of hope. 'His life is in danger.'

Sabiha's expression spoke for her.

'What?' Dina demanded.

'Nothing.' Sabiha looked away.

Dina waited.

'It's just convenient.'

'You think he's lying?' Dina was shocked.

'I'm not saying that.' Sabiha motioned to stop with her hand. 'We don't know what the entire story is.'

'The only thing that matters is that my brother needs help,' Dina screamed.

I didn't breathe as I waited to see what Sabiha would do. Would she dig in her heels and argue with Dina or back off?

'You're right,' Sabiha said.

Dina looked militant. 'I'm going to call Omer.' She stepped away.

'Dina.' Sabiha took a step toward her.

Dina stopped, but didn't turn.

'I'm sorry,' Sabiha said. 'I didn't mean to be a bitch.'

Dina nodded and left.

'Fuck.' Sabiha kicked the park bench and yelped. She hopped on one foot while she clutched her sore toes with her hands.

I turned to hide my smile. When I had it under control, I turned back and saw Jesse approaching with a concerned look. Sabiha sat on the bench and waited, her face expectant.

Jesse walked past her and approached me. 'Did you get home okay on Saturday?'

'Isn't it obvious?' I smiled.

'Did you have any problems with Alex?' Jesse asked.

I shook my head in confusion.

'I told you she was fine,' Sabiha interrupted.

'You should never have allowed her to go home alone with him,' Jesse snapped without looking at her.

'She had a curfew,' Sabiha said. 'What was I supposed to do, babysit her?'

'Yes,' Jesse snapped. 'You shouldn't have let her near that sleaze bag.'

Sabiha recoiled with hurt. 'What's the big deal?'

'This.' Jesse held up his mobile.

In the brief moment before he snapped the mobile shut, I glimpsed a naked girl. It was the girl Brian did a makeover on, Rodney's ex-girlfriend.

'Alex' mate sent around this photo of his ex yesterday,' Jesse said.

I had trouble breathing. I'd sent photos exactly like that to Alex.

Jesse turned back to me. 'Did he try anything?'

I couldn't speak. Jesse put his hand on my arm. I clutched it, holding it like a lifeline.

'I'll kill him,' Jesse muttered.

I snapped out of my inertia. 'Nothing happened. He drove me home, and that's it.'

Jesse looked like he didn't believe me.

'It's shocking.' I waved at his mobile. 'That's all.'

Jesse hugged me, and I hunched into him. 'Are you sure?' he asked.

I had to find Alex. I lifted my gaze and saw Sabiha jealously watching us. 'I told you I'm okay.' I pushed Jesse's arm away.

He looked at me with reproach. I opened my mouth to say something, anything, but the words wouldn't come. The bell rang.

'I'd better get to class.' I walked away.

I sent Alex a text message to meet as soon as I was out of sight of Sabiha and Jesse. Alex replied at recess. He couldn't see me until after school. I rubbed my necklace.

After school, I walked to the side street where I'd arranged to meet with Alex. When I got in the car, my worries faded and a goofy smile broke out as he looked me up and down. He was wearing sunglasses, his hand hanging out the window. He looked cool and dangerous.

'Hello gorgeous.' He leaned in and kissed me, making my toes curl. He turned the car ignition and drove before I regained my senses.

'We need to talk.'

'Talk.' Alex pushed his sunglasses down his nose. 'Because once the car stops, that's the last thing we'll be doing.' He playfully leered.

'Your friend sent a photo of his ex around.'

'So?' Alex stopped at the red light and reached over to squeeze my boob.

I slapped his hand away. 'Would you do something like that to me?'

'Of course not. I wouldn't ever send photos of my girlfriend around.' He kissed me during a red light. A car beeped behind us. The light was green. He stomped on the gas.

'Could you delete the photos from last night?' I asked when I got my breath back.

'Sure,' Alex said.

I breathed a sigh of relief, reassured by his quick acquiescence. 'Where are we going?'

I'd thought we'd park the car somewhere and be together, but Alex was driving through the suburbs. A few more twists of the wheel and we were turning into Brian's street. He told me he'd arranged for us to use Omer's house.

'What about Brian?'

'He's not home.' He opened my car door. 'I've got a surprise for you.'

'I can't stay long.' Reluctantly, I followed him into the house. 'I have to be back before Dad finishes work.'

Alex grinned. 'He probably won't even notice you're gone.'

He said it to comfort me, but they were like a dagger through my heart. Was it true?

He pushed me up against the wall and kissed me again. My phone rang, piercing through the fog of my raging hormones. I went to answer it, but Alex snatched it out of my hand and turned it off.

'I need your exclusive attention for fifteen minutes only. After that, you can deal with the real world again.' He slipped my mobile back in my pocket.

As we passed by Brian's open door, I recognised the smell of marijuana seeping from it.

'Close your eyes,' he said.

Standing in the darkness, I noticed his smell and the feel of his palm against mine. I wanted to remain in this moment with this feeling of anticipation fluttering in my stomach.

'Open your eyes.' Alex breathed in my ear and my skin broke out in goose pimples.

He'd closed the curtains and made Omer's bedroom dark. There were candles on the chest of drawers, the golden flickering of the flame glowing in the mirror. Rose petals covered the white sheets on Omer's bed.

Alex left my side and turned on the CD player. Soft romantic music filled the room. 'May I have this dance?' He held out his hand.

I drifted into his arms. 'This looks beautiful.'

He nuzzled my neck. 'I wanted everything to be special for you'

His mouth worked its way up my jaw and to my lips. He kissed me deeply, tongue and all, holding me tightly against him. His leg was between my thighs and I was almost riding him. There was a delicious friction of his jeans against my panties, and I rubbed myself against him.

'You're a passionate one.' Alex pushed me onto the bed and took off his shirt.

As I looked at him ungracefully taking off his clothes, the passion faded and I realised what I was getting myself into.

'We don't have time for this.' I tried to stand, but Alex nuzzled me down.

'Sure we do.' Alex soothed as he took off his jeans. 'It's not ideal that we have to rush your first time, but it will still be special.'

'My first time?' I repeated.

Alex kicked his jeans off. 'You don't have to worry about anything.' Alex took off his underwear and was naked in front of me. 'I'll take care of you.' He lay on top of me and touched my breasts. 'I love you,' he whispered in a rush against my ear, and kissed me again.

I stilled in his arms. After we'd texted each other last night, I kept imagining what it would be like when we said our "I love you's" face to face for the first time. I'd imagined staring into each other's eyes, breathless with anticipation and that in that moment we would realise we belonged together forever.

In all my fantasies, I'd never imagined that I would feel this sense of wrongness. His declaration was so matter of fact, as if he'd said it many times before and it was now devoid of all meaning. This was the first time he'd said it to me, so why did it sound so rehearsed?

'Alex wait.' I moved my head.

'Why? You love me too don't you?'

He looked at me impatiently, waiting for a response. I didn't know what to say. When I'd texted him, I was sure that I loved him. That what we had was special, but now I was confused. He was in such a hurry, as if he was fearful I'd change my mind.

'You love me, right?' he said harshly.

'Right.' I felt I had no choice but to answer the affirmative. How could I suddenly tell him I'd changed my mind?

He covered me with his body, squashing me under his weight. Something was wrong. Until this moment, it seemed I was in a romantic movie where the two star-crossed lovers were about to make love. Now I was in a frat house movie with the sweaty, horny guy who wanted to get laid.

As I turned my head, I saw beside the bed where Alex had piled Omer's mess. It made me wonder if everything he did was like that, a big gesture that actually hid the seamy reality of life. I desperately wanted to be at Dad's medical centre, waiting for Mum, not here in this room with a naked guy grinding himself against me.

'No, don't,' I said when his lips moved to my breasts.

'What's wrong, baby?' He lifted his head and looked at me. 'Don't you want to be with me?'

I didn't know what to say. I wanted to be with him, but he'd tricked me. There had been no conversation about this. He'd presented it as a fait accompli.

'I thought you liked everything we did until this point?'

'I did, I do.'

'What's the problem? We're in a relationship. This is what boyfriend and girlfriend do.' His voice was full of exasperation.

'I know.'

'Good.' Alex smiled and nuzzled my chest again. 'I'll try to be gentle. I want it to be good for you.'

I panicked. He was right. Everything I'd done up til this point gave the impression I was ready and willing to have sex, yet now that it was happening it was the last thing I wanted. I'd been infatuated with the fantasy of having a boyfriend, without thinking through the reality.

There was something telling me to get out, to stop things before they got out of hand. Alex was right. The first time was supposed to be special. It was a moment I wanted to remember forever, and I knew with every fibre of my being that this was not the moment I wanted etched into my brain. His hands moved between my legs and he tried to take off my underpants.

'No.' I sat up.

'Why not?'

He looked at me, and his face had changed. Gone was the cheeky larrikin I'd fallen for. Instead, he looked predatory, as if I was prey on his menu. I remembered Dina's warning and my blood ran cold. This was the guy she'd been warning me about.

'Are you being a tease?' He was angry, his hands formed into fists as he watched me moodily.

I realised how vulnerable I was. We were all alone in the house. I was completely at his mercy. 'Of course not.' My survival instinct kicked in. 'I have my period.'

Alex' face turned to disgust, before he quickly rallied. 'That's okay, baby.' He reached for me again. 'I don't mind.'

'I do.' I dragged myself away from him. 'I want our first time to be special.'

I walked to the door, full of relief.

'Aren't you forgetting something?' Alex said.

I turned. He was sitting on the edge of the bed with his legs apart. He got a pillow from the bed and threw it on the floor. I had to fight my feet from running to the front door, but there was a shivery feeling inside me. A little voice that warned me not to make him angry. As I bent my head and covered his lap, his hands went to my hair. When he moaned as he came, I was repulsed and relieved in equal measure.

'You're fantastic at it.' He smiled. 'Like a little hoover.'

His taste was in my mouth, and I had to hold back from dry reaching. I ran to the bathroom before I vomited in front of him. As I washed out my mouth in the basin, I looked in the mirror.

There was something different in my eyes. The sparkle was dulled, and I looked like a sad little girl. How had things changed so quickly? I walked out without looking at him.

'What's wrong?' He lifted my chin.

I stepped back.

'Don't be sensitive. I was joking about you being a hoover.'

I nodded. 'I have to get back.'

'I'll be a sec.' He left the bathroom door open, and I held my arms and shivered as I listened to the loud and vulgar sound of his urine splashing the toilet bowl.

'How long until it's finished?' Alex asked as he drove me.

'What?' I was confused.

'Your period?'

'At least a week,' I lied.

'Then I'll see you next week.' He stopped on the main road and gave me a quick kiss on the cheek.

I froze as he leaned over me, having to fight my instinct to throw myself away from him. When I got out of the car, he sped off, car tyres screeching.

Chapter 17

I hurriedly walked to Dad's medical centre. The front door was locked and the reception lights turned off. My heart raced, and I looked at my watch. Did Dad leave without me? I found my mobile in my pocket and turned it on. There were three missed calls from Sabiha and two messages.

Sabiha: "Where the hell are you?"

Dina: "Sabiha knows."

I moaned pitifully. While I'd been in the thrall of my infatuation with Alex, it had seemed an impossible reality that my parents would find out. Now I couldn't believe that I'd been so stupid to believe in a fantasy. Sabiha was going to gleefully embrace this opportunity to sell me out. I tried to think of a lie to save me, but my brain was frozen. I saw a flash of movement and looked up.

Sabiha walked through the reception area. 'Where the hell have you been?' She yanked open the door and pulled me inside, wrenching the delicate skin of my arm.

Before I could say anything, Dad walked in.

'I told you she was on her way.' Sabiha forced a smile. 'Dad was about to send a search party to the library.'

'Yes.' Dad was annoyed. 'I sent Sabiha to get you half an hour ago, and she said you were finishing up an essay.'

I paused, in shock that Sabiha covered for me. 'I'm sorry. I got caught up.' As he was looking for me, I remembered what I had been up to and guilt punched me in the stomach.

'I'll switch off the lights. You two wait by the car,' Dad said.

Sabiha and I walked into the car park behind the medical centre.

'Talk.' Sabiha demanded as soon as the door closed behind us.

'I went to the café—'

'No, you didn't.' Sabiha interrupted.

'Yes, I did,' I said. 'I needed a break from studying.'

'How did you get the hickey on your neck?'

I held my hand to my neck. Dad exited the building. While he had his back to us locking the building door, Sabiha flicked my hair forward.

'Let's get going.' Dad clicked the remote lock and both of us reached for the passenger door.

'You go,' Sabiha said. 'I'm getting dropped off first.'

We spent the drive to drop Sabiha off in silence. I felt a storm brewing from Dad in the driver's seat.

'Talk to you tomorrow,' Sabiha said as a warning as she got out.

'What essay were you writing?' Dad asked abruptly as we drove off.

He'd started his classic interrogation technique, feeling me out with an innocuous question to check inconsistencies.

'It was for English about *How to Kill a Mockingbird*. I chose the topic on education and got caught up reading papers about the benefits of home based learning.' I continued prattling about the essay I'd already submitted, knowing that the best way to drown out Dad's suspicions was to overwhelm him with an avalanche of details.

'Sounds good.' Dad turned into our driveway. 'I'd like to read it.

I unclipped my seatbelt. 'You can proofread after I type it.'

I rushed upstairs before Mum's sharp eyes latched onto the evidence of my misdeeds. I locked the bathroom door and frantically checked my neck. The hickey was barely visible. I dabbed on concealer.

I spent a sleepless night thinking about what happened with Alex and trying to figure out how it all went wrong. Was it my fault? Was I being a tease? I'd given him all the signals that we were heading down the sex road. I just thought we'd take our time getting there.

I had to talk to him. Make him understand I needed more time. *"And that you're not a hoover who will perform on demand?"* said a voice in my head that sounded suspiciously like Sabiha.

***

I'd almost forgotten about Sabiha's interrogation until I rocked up to school and she practically launched herself at me. 'Where were you yesterday?'

'With a friend.' I sidestepped her.

'Which friend?' She stood in front of me again.

I stopped, barely avoiding crashing into her. 'What's with you?'

'What are you hiding?' Sabiha burst out.

'Nothing.'

'You were with a boy, weren't you?'

'And what if I was?'

'Who is it?' she demanded.

'None of your business.' I shouted.

'Of course, it's my business. We're sisters,' Sabiha said.

I halted, my fiery rage cooling. 'You hypocrite.' My voice tight with rage. 'You've been treating me like crap since I came to St Albans High. The only reason you're pretending to be friends with me is because Dina asked you to and anytime someone asks about us, you refer to me as your "relative."' I used air quotations for emphasis. 'You're not my sister. You're an acquaintance I have to endure for the sake of courtesy. Nothing more, nothing less.'

It was such a buzz to say all the unspoken words that I'd been holding inside. I felt like I could float away with the lightness of my relief.

Sabiha looked shocked. For once, she was speechless.

'What's going on?' Jesse ran up and stood between us.

'I was just asking Alma about her boyfriend—'

'And I was saying it was none of your business,' I cut her off again and stared her down.

'You have a boyfriend?' Jesse asked with surprise.

I swallowed hard. Once he found out who it was, he'd lose all respect for me and the thought bothered me. He was the only one who made genuine overtures of friendship, and I felt bad that I'd messed that up.

'Yes.' I cleared my throat. 'But it's my private business and not something I want to discuss.'

I heard Sabiha shouting my name, but didn't turn around. Footsteps sounded and Sabiha reached me again.

'I'm sorry. I thought it was Jesse.' When I looked at her blankly, she repeated, 'I thought you were seeing Jesse.'

'I'm not.'

'Please come to the front so we can talk.'

'I have nothing more to say.' I walked away.

I spent the day avoiding Sabiha's overtures. Dina didn't show up at school and Sabiha was on her own, too. We both ended up at the library during lunch, but I kept my head down in my book, ignoring Sabiha's circling around me as she pretended to search for books.

While I was pretending to read, I heard the rumours about Rodney's ex-girlfriend. Her parents were pressing charges against Rodney for sending the photos around, and she'd stopped coming to school. My hands crumpled the cover as I remembered the photos I'd sent to Alex. *But he's deleted them*, I reassured myself.

I kept sending Alex messages, desperate to clear things up. I was trying to convince myself that Dina's warnings were all a lie, but a chill of warning seeped in my bones.

During fifth period English I got a toilet pass. I hesitated in front of the third floor toilets, rubbing my sweaty hands on my skirt as I gathered my courage to enter. I finally pushed the door open and walked through the sink area and to the cubicles.

'Alex.' I said his name and waited. I heard him breathing.

Finally, he threw open the cubicle door, his face wreathed in a Cheshire grin. 'Come on.' He gestured for me to join him inside.

I shook my head. 'We need to talk.'

His grin faded. 'Don't say that.' He slammed the door shut and stepped out. 'Nothing good ever comes from that sentence.'

I cleared my throat, trying to remember the speech I'd rehearsed all day. 'I might have given you the wrong impression about us having sex.'

'I don't think so.' Alex leaned against the cubicle door. 'We're boyfriend and girlfriend and there are certain expectations that come with that.'

'I think we're rushing into things—'

'What things?' He approached and took my hands in his, and gazed at me with his beautiful blue eyes. 'I love you. You love me. Having sex is a natural thing that you do when you're in love.' He sounded so sincere. He didn't break eye contact as he delicately kissed my wrist. The butterfly soft touch of his lips made me shiver.

I pulled away. 'When we were together last time…' I hesitated. 'You made me feel dirty.'

'I'm sorry.' He hugged me and spoke into my hair. 'Maybe you're sensitive because you haven't been in a proper relationship before.' He pressed a soft kiss on my lips.

I closed my eyes and let him kiss me. Everything was swimming in the blackness behind my eyelids. Was he right? Was

I being too sensitive and immature to not understand how a relationship worked? Had I built up a huge fantasy about how he would declare he loved me and then felt let down? All the certainty I'd felt before speaking to him faded.

'I'll be on-line tonight.' He gave me a tight squeeze and left.

I spent the rest of the school day examining every word we'd exchanged. Trying to find the truth of things between us, but all it left me with was confusion and a sense of wrongness.

It was a relief that I walked toward the school gates. I wanted to put as much distance between Alex and me as possible. My steps slowed when I saw Sabiha was waiting for me. It was polite for us to talk together. After all, we were going to the same destination, but I didn't want to endure her probing questions.

As I dawdled, Brian approached Sabiha. Their arms gesticulated as if they were fighting. I didn't realise my footsteps had quickened until I was within hearing distance.

'Dina was away sick today,' Sabiha told Brian.

'Shit,' Brian said.

'Why?'

'No reason.' Brian tried to sound careless, but his voice was imbued with worry.

'Is this about Omer?' Sabiha asked.

Brian shrugged.

'What's going on?'

I'd stopped beside them without conscious thought and waited, a bad feeling dropping in my gut.

'He has the rent money,' Brian said. 'He was supposed to pay last week, but I got a call from the real estate agent and it isn't paid.'

'Did you try calling him?' Sabiha asked.

Brian nodded, reaching for his phone. He dialled again and put it on speaker phone. An automated message blared from the speakers that the phone was out of service.

'I'll try calling Dina.' Sabiha reached for her phone.

I remembered my last conversation with Dina and her terrible plan to steal from her parents. I'd given her the advice to do it. What if Dina's parents kicked her out? I'd be responsible for not talking her out of it.

'She's not answering. Does anyone have her home number?' he asked.

'Not on me,' Sabiha said.

'I do.' I rifled through my backpack and pulled out my address book.

Sabiha dialled Dina's home number. She shook her head when no one answered. 'Is anything else missing?' Sabiha asked.

'No.' Brian shook his head.

'Did you check Omer's wardrobe?'

'No. Why would I?' He demanded.

There was a beat of silence.

'Shit,' he said. 'My Stash of Cash.'

'Okay, okay.' Sabiha clutched her head while Brian jiggled his leg impatiently. 'Aren't you supposed to take Dina her homework?' she asked me.

We were in science together and the teacher had asked for someone to pass on notes, and since we lived close to each other, I'd volunteered.

I nodded.

'Okay, you do that and see if she's home. I'll go with Brian to see what else is missing. We'll SMS each other with updates,' Sabiha issued orders with the confidence of a general.

Usually I'd be annoyed at her high-handedness, but I was too worried about Dina and my complicity in her troubles. I'd been so happy to have a go at Sabiha, I'd given Dina terrible advice.

We split up in front of the school and went in opposite directions. I was in the car with Mum when I received a message from myself. Sabiha and I had swapped phones.

Alma: "Stash of Cash gone. Clothes gone. He's split."

I kept one eye on the clock as I waited for Mum to pick me up. Even though I had my homework strewn on the table in front of me, I couldn't concentrate.

'Where's Sabiha?' Dad looked around the empty kitchen area.

'Um.' I was blank. We'd been in such a panic about Dina's predicament we forgot to come up with an excuse. Panic gripped me as Dad's gaze narrowed in suspicion. In the end, there was only one thing to do. 'Brian's having a crisis and she's helping him out.'

'What crisis?'

I shrugged.

'Give me your phone.' Dad scrolled through the address book with a look of consternation.

'Sabiha and I swapped phones,' I said.

Dad nodded and called my number. 'Where are you?' he asked Sabiha when she answered.

I waited in tense silence.

'What's wrong with Brian?' Dad asked.

I let out a breath of relief. Good, our stories matched up.

'You should have called if you weren't coming to work. When you have a job, you can't not show up whenever a friend has a crisis.' He put extra emphasis on the word crisis.

Dad listened for another minute and hung up. His face was stony as if he hadn't liked what he heard. Dad loomed over me for a few minutes before leaving. I packed up and waited for Mum at the front of the medical centre.

'I have to drop off Dina's homework,' I said as I got in the car. 'She was sick today.'

After Mum drove off, I walked up Dina's driveway with trepidation. I was scared to knock and find out Dina no longer lived there, but curiosity was twisting inside me, propelling my feet forward.

I rang the doorbell, and it echoed in the house. A curtain upstairs moved. As the silence stretched, I was embarrassed.

They would not open the door. I was walking away when the door opened. I turned around and saw Dina's eye through the door crack.

'You're here,' I said, happily. Thank God. I was now off the hook.

'Where else would I be?'

'Um, well, I wasn't sure if your parents...' I gulped and stopped my rambling. It was probably best I didn't share my suspicions. 'I brought your homework.'

Dina put her hand out.

I began rifling through my backpack, but my contents were a mess.

Dina sighed and opened the door for me to come in. She had dark circles under her eyes and her hair was unwashed. I followed her to the kitchen. As Dina served herself orange juice from the fridge, pouring me a glass that she pushed across the countertop, I found her homework.

'Are you feeling better?' I handed it to her.

Dina shrugged.

My mobile phone beeped. It was another message from Sabiha. I gasped as I read it. They'd found an out of service phone in Omer's room and had found text messages between him and Louie organising the fight at the party.

'You know he's gone,' Dina said matter-of-factly.

I hesitated, not knowing how much of the truth she knew. 'Brian said he's taken all his clothes.'

'I'm guessing he took more than that,' Dina said wryly.

I sat up straight. 'You know he's a thief?'

'He's much more than that. He's a drug fiend impersonating my brother.' She said it matter-of-factly, with no inflection in her voice, and it scared me. It was such a change from the last time we spoke about her brother, where she was terrified for his life.

'What happened? When we spoke at school yesterday you and Omer were going to try talking to your parents together and now....' I didn't know how to finish the sentence and let it peter out.

Dina drew circles with her fingers on the countertop. The silence stretched out, and I didn't know whether I should leave.

'Omer drove me home, and we walked into the house together. Mum saw Omer first, and she eyed the bruises on his face, looking worried. I thought we had a chance that she'd help us, but Dad was behind her. He told Omer to leave. When Omer didn't move fast enough, Dad manhandled him out of the house.'

Dina pushed her hair. 'We had a massive fight. I said many things to them, tore them apart because they wouldn't help their flesh and blood, but they didn't budge. So I implemented our back-up plan. After they went to sleep, I logged onto the internet and transferred the money into Omer's bank account and then I packed my bags.'

Dina's voice faded, as if she was struggling to get the words out. 'I was carrying my bag when I bumped into Mum at the top of the stairs on her way to the toilet, her eyes half closed. Mum's eyes caught on the suitcase and then worked their way up my body, taking in that I was fully dressed.'

Dina looked up out the window, her lips drooping in the corners from sadness. '"I'm leaving," I told Mum. I held the suitcase so tightly it cut into my hand.' She looked down at her clenched hand as if she were still expecting it to be there. '"I'm going to live with Omer." Mum said nothing, and I thought she was giving me the silent treatment. I went to walk past her, but she grabbed me.'

Dina splayed her hand on the countertop, covering the top with her palm as if she was recreating her mother's touch. '"Did you give him the money?" Mum asked. "If you did, then he's already gone." I'd just completed the internet transfer and there was no way she could have known.' She took another deep breath, and a tear seeped out of her eye.

'Mum led me into my room and told me he'd approached her before, telling her he was in danger from a gang member and that he needed money to pay back a loan. She went behind Dad's back and gave him money.'

Dina took in another shuddering breath. 'He'd been going through all of our family and his old friends over the years, tricking them out of money, or stealing from them if they were naïve enough to let him stay. He'd finally exhausted all his options, and I was the last resort.'

She laughed bitterly at her naïve past self. 'I didn't believe her, of course. I told her Omer was waiting for me. "Then go," Mum said. I couldn't believe she was practically kicking me out of the house. Mum waited with me in the living room. We didn't speak for an hour. Mum sat there on the couch.' Dina nodded at the living room, the black leather couch visible through the doorway.

I pictured the scene. The house was dark and silent, the open window letting the streetlight flood the living room. Mother and daughter frozen in silence as Dina paced up and down, peering out of the curtains every time a car passed. A mother waiting for her daughter to accept the truth.

'I tried calling him, but his phone was switched off. After an hour, I stopped checking the window. When dawn was lighting up the sky, Mum took me upstairs and unpacked my suitcase. I heard her on the phone to the bank while I lay in bed, staring at the ceiling. She was trying to get the money back, but Omer had already transferred it into another bank account. She woke Dad, and he came to my bedroom. I expected him to yell at me. It was what I deserved. But he didn't. He sat on the bed and stayed until I fell asleep.'

She began crying. I stood beside her, hugging her as her body shuddered from deep, gasping sobs.

'Where are your parents now?' I asked.

'They're at the bank.' She wiped her face with a tissue. 'Technically my brother pulled a con job, but because he's a member of the family and not a conman, we don't know if they will help.'

'I'll stay until they get back.' I didn't want to leave her alone in this state.

'It's okay. I think I'll go lie down.' She was weaving from tiredness.

I nodded and began walking out.

'It's funny.' She walked me to the front door. 'There were signs all along about who Omer was. And it wasn't as if I didn't have any warning. I mean, Sabiha has been practically shrieking her alarm bell, and yet denial is an amazing thing.' Dina opened the front door. 'I wanted him to be better, and I rewrote history. My parents were the villains, he was the innocent victim, and it didn't matter what he did, the things that I saw that didn't match this reality.'

I stepped through the door, Dina's words setting off tingles of awareness. I looked over my shoulder and caught sight of her broken smile.

'There's a saying that when a person shows you who they are the first time, you should believe them.' Dina's smile disappeared. 'Now I know. You don't need a second or third look. Believe that first glimmer you see and get the fuck out.' Dina gazed at me, as if trying to force the power of her words into my skull.

'But what if there are extenuating circumstances? Like they're going through a loss.'

'Or what if they're using drugs? Or what if they're drunk? These are excuses we cling to in order to deny reality. People are who they are. If they're going through something tough, they may act out badly, but the core of who they are doesn't change no matter what the circumstance. Look at my brother.' Dina gestured. 'He was a selfish person with a sense of entitlement before he became a druggie. The only thing that changed was the scope. People don't change,' she said with finality, and closed the door.

I walked home in a daze. There was a thrumming inside me you get when you hear an undeniable truth. As I replayed my relationship with Alex, I remembered all those brief moments of disquiet and wrongness that I'd wilfully ignored, but now they all added up to something more.

While I could make excuses for Alex about his vulgar jokes, the way he ambushed me for sex yesterday and expected me to pleasure him with no concern about my feelings, that couldn't be chalked up to grief. That's who he was. A selfish guy who only wanted sex.

I had to get out. Break it off with him. The only question was how? I'd never had to break up with anyone before. In the high school etiquette book, I'd dispatch my bestie to do the deed, but I didn't have anyone to take on the role. Dina was the only one who knew about him, and I couldn't ask her now.

When I thought about doing it face to face, my skin shrunk on itself. There was only one way. I'd have to do it on-line. My phone rang, and I saw my name.

'Did you see her?' Sabiha demanded.

'Yeah,' I said. 'It's not good.'

'I'll put you on speakerphone so Brian can hear.'

I told them what happened with Dina.

'Fuck, fuck, fuck,' Brian chanted.

'Okay, thanks for helping. Listen, about before—' she said, trying to talk about this morning.

'Don't worry about it.' I cut her off and ended the call. The only thing I cared about now was getting away from Alex.

I practiced my break up speech as I walked home.

Chapter 18

I heard Mum shouting when I opened the front door and hesitated in the doorway to listen. Mum was ripping Ali a new asshole. What could he have possibly done to get such a reaming? Ali was the goody-goody two-shoes who hardly ever got into trouble.

I quietly shut the front door and stepped in. They were fighting in the kitchen. Sanela was at the top of the stairs and she put her finger over her lips, and waved for me to come up.

'What's going on?' I asked.

'Ali failed his science exam,' Sanela whispered.

I was shocked. Ali was a prodigy. He aced all his exams, and my parents decided early in his childhood that he would follow in Dad's footsteps and be a doctor.

'Tell me the truth, Ali,' Mum shouted. 'Why did this happen?'

'I don't know.' Ali sounded defeated.

This was obviously a question Mum had lobbed at him numerous times. She was a terrier like that.

'There must be a reason that you've suddenly changed. That you have failed for the first time in your life. Is it your new friends?'

'You'd think that,' Ali snapped. 'Maybe it's you and Dad not being home.'

'What are you talking about?' Mum was exasperated. 'I've picked up a few extra shifts, but your dad or I are always home.'

'You're right.' Ali backtracked. 'I wasn't applying myself.'

Ali had nearly blurted out the truth and was now trying to skirt away from the abyss. If Mum found out about how lax Dad really was in his duty as a father lately, World War III would begin.

'Your Dad has been home during the weeknights supervising your homework?' Mum's voice was full of suspicion.

'Of course.' There was a telltale squeak in his voice. I could just imagine how flushed his cheeks were.

There was dead silence.

'You can tell me the truth,' Mum played the good guy to catch him off guard. 'Does your Dad come home late?'

'No.' He didn't fall for her alternative approach.

I gripped the banister, mentally urging him to hold out.

'Can I go now?' he asked too eagerly.

'Of course.' Mum sounded distracted.

I hit my forehead onto the hardwood. The game was up. Ali climbed up the stairs, his eyes full of panic. Sanela and I followed him to his bedroom, where he threw himself across the bed and screamed into his pillow. 'Fuck.'

Sanela patted his back. 'It's okay.' She mimicked how we comforted her when she hurt herself.

Ali shrugged her off. 'No, it's not.'

'Don't take it out on her.' I hugged Sanela.

'Sorry,' he muttered.

'How did this happen?' I asked after I'd sent Sanela to her room to get her dollhouse ready for us to play.

'How does anything happen? You make a series of small decisions that lead you to certain consequences.'

'But you're a straight-A student.'

'And now I'm not.'

'You're acting like this isn't a big deal.' I was confused. Ali once got a B, and he cried, and never again scored a grade below A.

He shrugged.

'But you failed!' I exclaimed again, not understanding his *blase* attitude. While I was conscientious and concerned with my grades, Ali was obsessed. He put everything on the line to achieve his dream of being a doctor.

'So what?' Ali threw his pillow. 'Lots of people fail and the world doesn't end.'

'But that's not who you are.' I was confused at his turnabout.

'And who are you? The girl who fakes period cramps and then sneaks out of the house.'

I gaped at him.

'Did you really think I wouldn't come into your room?'

I stood still, afraid if I blinked, I'd be admitting the truth.

Ali sat back on the bed. 'The truth is, we're all being someone else. We're living different lives.'

I'd been feeling the same way, but still he was missing the point. I felt a shiver of fear as I thought about what would happen when Mum realised the truth about Dad.

'Don't you care they're going to fight again?'

'It's not as if they need an excuse to fight, anyway. And maybe he deserves it.' There was simmering anger in his eyes like he hated Dad.

'But what if they get a divorce?' I told him my secret fear.

'What?' Ali jerked with surprise. 'They're the perfect couple. They're just fighting more than usual.'

I wasn't convinced. Wasn't that how people ended up getting a divorce? They fought more until things slowly got bad enough to end it completely. At least that's what my friends, who had divorced parents, had told me.

'But—' I began, wanting to feel him out more.

'I'm tired.' He lay on the bed, his back toward me.

As I left his room, I wondered if he truly believed Mum and Dad were the perfect couple or if he was trying to convince himself.

I spent the next few hours in a state of nervous anticipation, jumping at the sound of every car driving down the street.

When Dad came home, we had a tense dinner. After Sanela went to bed, Mum asked Ali and me to go upstairs, while she spoke to Dad.

I'd expected she'd wait until we went to bed, but she was chafing to have it on, rushing us through dinner. We pretended to go into our bedrooms and then snuck back to the top of the stairs to eavesdrop. I was tense, expecting another slanging match.

'Here's Ali's test,' Mum said, as soon as she thought we'd cleared the stairs.

A beat passed as Dad read the paper. 'An F,' he exclaimed. 'Where is he?'

'I've already spoken to him. Now we need to ensure this doesn't happen again.'

'He obviously hasn't been studying hard enough,' Dad exclaimed. 'Once he's grounded, he'll pick up his game.'

'He probably hasn't been studying at all. Since neither one of us has been supervising him.'

'He's old enough to do his homework without supervision,' Dad said. 'Alma's changed schools twice this year, and she's still getting A's.'

'Yes, but it's Ali's weakest subject and one that he needed your help on. I told you you had to be home with the kids if I was going to work.' Mum's voice held an edge of anger.

Dad's silence spoke for itself.

'How late were you? One hour, two hours?' Mum demanded.

'They're old enough to take care of themselves.' Dad was defensive. He hated admitting he was wrong and did everything he could to avoid it.

'Would you advise one of your patient's to leave a 15-year-old in charge of a five year old child?'

This was always where Mum won the argument—by challenging Dad's authority as a doctor. If it was something he wouldn't tell others, then he couldn't do it.

There was a screeching of table legs and a thud, as if a chair hit the floor. 'I had no choice,' Dad said. 'I opened a new practice. You know better than anyone how much work is involved.'

'If we'd stayed in Hobart—'

'We're not rehashing that argument, Jasminka,' Dad thundered. 'We're here. Make peace with that and move on.'

'How can I?' Mum shouted. 'When every day I'm reminded of the past?'

'You know what my solution is—'

'No,' Mum cut him off. 'We're not telling them.'

There was dead silence.

Ali and I looked at each other quizzically. What was it they weren't telling us?

'This isn't about the past,' Dad said. 'It's about the present.'

'That's right,' Mum cut in. 'This is about our children needing more attention. I'm reducing my work hours and you need to be home before I leave for work.'

There was a pause.

'Fine,' Dad said. 'We'll have to cut back our expenses since our income is dropping.'

'I'm not the one who's blowing out our budget,' Mum said, scathingly, having a go at Dad for the house we lived in that she'd thought was out of our price range.

There was the sound of footsteps and the slam of a door. Dad retreated to his office, while Mum remained in the kitchen where she banged pots and pans.

We snuck back over the landing and into my room.

'Do you think things are going to change?' Ali asked.

'I think Mum will make sure of it.' I remembered the determination in her voice. 'What do you think they were not telling us?' I felt disquiet at the possibility of yet another secret. Mum had been full of fear when Dad raised it.

'Don't know, don't care. If we have another long-lost sibling, I'd rather not know about it, ever.' Ali left my room.

I wished it was that simple to switch off and forget my the question, but there was a premonition building that there were worse surprises coming down the track. There was only one way to distract myself. I sent Alex a message while I was on-line. There was no response.

***

I was walking to school, a little skip in my step. Maybe the fight between my parents wasn't all bad. This morning we all sat down and had breakfast like a normal family, touching base about our day. Even though there was a tense vibe over the proceedings, both my parents made an effort to check in with us. It was as if Ali's science exam had shocked them out of their self involvement. I was enjoying the heat of the sun on my skin when a car pulled up.

Alex peered at me from the driver's seat, his eyes red. 'Get in.'

I looked around. It was quiet on the street. I'd left Dad as soon as he arrived at the medical centre and it was still too early for any parents to be dropping off their children. As I closed the car door, the overwhelming smell of alcohol and cigarettes hit me.

'I thought this was too early for you,' I said, buying myself time to remember the break up speech I'd practiced for two days. Now that I had the opportunity, I couldn't remember a word of it.

'It is. I'm heading home from an all nighter.' His eyes were red, and he was jittery, jiggling his leg as he parked.

'We didn't chat yesterday—'

'I had a hot party to go to. You're not going to be one of those nagging girlfriends who thinks her boyfriend shouldn't have fun. I can't hang around waiting for the one in a million when you can break your curfew.'

'Of course not.' I was surprised. 'I wasn't able to, anyway. My brother—'

'Good. Then it's no great loss.' He leaned over to kiss me.

I pulled away. 'There's lipstick on your collar.' I noticed a bright red lip smear.

Alex adjusted the rearview mirror to look at it. 'Shit. This is my lucky shirt.'

'How did that happen?'

Alex rubbed the stain. 'Some bird planted one on me.'

'You kissed someone else?' Maybe this was my out. I didn't have to make up an excuse. I just had to play the jealous girlfriend card.

'Of course not. She kissed me, but I put a stop to it because I have a girlfriend.' Alex put his arm around me.

There was a long dark hair caught on his shirt button. It was obviously a girl's hair and there was only one way it could have gotten wrapped around his button. 'Why is her hair all over you?' I moved back in my seat.

'Seriously,' Alex snapped. 'Stop giving me the third degree. I told you nothing happened.'

He stared me down, his hands splayed open. He'd given me the same look after Brian's party when he'd given his "mate" the brunette a lift home. Clarity descended and the little moments of disquiet culminated in this one moment of truth. He'd slept with someone else last night, just like he'd slept with the girl at the party. I turned to look out the windshield, feeling shell-shocked.

While I'd decided to use his indiscretion as an excuse to break up, now that I knew it was the truth, I felt sick. The night of Brian's party, we'd been a couple. It was the best night of my life, but now I knew it was all a lie. He'd been having sex with someone else a few minutes after we were together.

Alex tried to turn me toward him, but I resisted.

'You slept with her,' I muttered.

Alex tapped his fingers on the steering wheel.

'Didn't you?' I needed him to admit it.

'I already told you no.' He sounded bored, as if he'd been through such arguments before. I opened the car door, but he yanked it shut. 'Don't be like that.'

'I think we should take a break—'

'Are you trying to dump me?' Alex' easygoing expression faded. 'Because no one dumps me.'

I wanted to burn my bridges and get away from him. Put him in my rearview and forget about him, but the menace in his voice gave me pause. Even though we were parked on suburban street, we were in front of a park with no one nearby. 'I think we should take a step back,' I backtracked. 'Get to know each other better.'

Alex leaned his back against the door and watched me moodily. 'What's there to know? What you see is what you get?'

I realised the truth of those words. I looked out the window, feeling like I was trapped. My brain was thick and I couldn't form a coherent thought. I knew that I should have the upper hand, after all, I was the wronged girlfriend, but once again he'd shaken me up and eroded all my certainty.

Silence filled the car, thick with my despair and his frustration.

He yanked my head toward him. I gasped, scared at the rough touch of his fingers on my skin. He stared into my eyes instead of kissing me. I had to force myself not to look away. Whatever he saw in my eyes made his face tighten with disgust.

'I should have known better than to get involved with a youngin'.' Alex pushed me away. 'It's much easier to go with someone who's already broken in. No need for the romantic bullshit. A few drinks and you're in.'

I began sobbing, the buildup of fear exploding into a mass of hysteria at his cruel words.

Alex was exasperated. 'Cry to your Mamma.'

He reached over, and I flinched, thinking he was going to hit me.

'Get out.' He opened the door.

I stumbled out, forgetting my backpack. He threw it after me and swerved away erratically. I sat on the curb and cried into my knees. How could I have been so stupid? I'd received warnings from everyone about what he was really like and yet I'd still fallen for him, allowed him to use and debase me, and all because he'd said those three paltry words, "I love you." Other students appeared on the footpath, and I reluctantly pushed to my feet and headed to school.

I thought about going home and claiming I was sick, but I was afraid Mum's newfound resolve as an involved parent would test my ability to keep things to myself. I felt so open and vulnerable, like if one person asked how I was, I'd spill my heartbreak in a stream of word vomit.

As I walked, I tried to process what happened with Alex, but my brain shied away from the memory. It was like the trauma had burst through all my emotions, leaving me numb and lethargic. My only goal was to get through the school day without drawing attention to myself.

When I got to the toilets, I held onto the sink and panted as I forced down my sobs. I felt weak and headachy, like I could fall asleep. 'Get it together,' I muttered as I washed my face.

No one could know what happened with Alex. I was finally out of that situation and didn't have to worry about getting caught. Now I just had to recover from the wounds he left.

I didn't know how I was going to face him. Would he tell people we were a couple to get back at me? Or would he give me dirty looks or ignore me like I had never happened? I didn't know what was worse.

After I dried my face, I checked my reflection. I was pale and my eyes were red-rimmed, but at least now no one could tell if it was because I pulled an all-nighter or had a crying fit. With a deep breath for courage, I headed back to the front.

I kept an eye out for Alex, but I didn't see him all day. When we walked around the school, I saw his friends and concluded he was spending the day at home, sleeping off his all-nighter.

The school day flew by and I almost forgot about my heartache in the jostling of our clique. Sabiha and I avoided talking directly to each other all day, until we had to walk to Dad's work.

'You've been quiet today,' Sabiha said.

I shrugged.

'Boy trouble?' she pried.

I gave her a dirty look.

'I'm worried about you. If you need to talk, I'm here. If not, I'm still here.'

We walked in silence the entire length of Main Road. I didn't know if she was sincere or trying to catch me out.

'We broke up.' I said, testing to see if Sabiha would jump on me.

'Are you okay?'

I shrugged. 'He wasn't who I thought he was.' A flash of memory from our fight in the car sliced through me, leaving a thickness in my chest. I swallowed harshly, pushing it down.

Thankfully, we'd reached the medical centre and the end of our alone time.

'At least you found out before it got too deep.' Sabiha opened the glass door.

'It got deep enough.' Bitterness seeped into me like septic in a wound. I felt like I was soiled. Sabiha gave me a sharp look, but didn't probe.

'I'm sorry. My offer still stands,' she whispered as we walked to the kitchen.

'Thanks.'

We set up in our regular fashion. Sabiha at one desk with the shredder while I got out my books and began my homework at another. I tried to do homework, but gave up quickly and waited for Mum in stunned silence.

As Mum drove home, I was happy to be in this moment, surrounded by my family. So much had happened, so many things changed. When I thought about how things could have been if my parents found out about Alex, I shuddered. I'd come close to disaster and was pulled back from the brink just in time.

When I got home, I ended up lying on the bed and staring at the ceiling, thinking about Alex and where things went wrong. How could I have missed what a creep he was? It made me doubt all my instincts.

I kept treating Sabiha like a threat who was trying to take something away from me, yet all she'd done was to warn me about Alex and cover up for me. I curled under the doona as tears seeped out of my eyes. My door burst open.

'What'cha doing?' Sanela demanded.

'Go away.'

Sanela crawled over my body. 'I want to sleep too.'

Sanela lifted the doona and clambered over me, digging in her elbows as she used me like a mattress.

'Ouch.' I rubbed my nose.

'I'll kiss it better.' Sanela kissed it.

I closed my eyes to hide my tears.

'I'm sorry, I'm sorry.' Sanela put her little arms around my neck and patted me as I begun crying in earnest.

I hugged her to my chest. 'It's not your fault.'

I was drowsing when I heard Mum's voice.

'What are you two doing here?' Mum asked.

'I hurt Alma's nose and she was crying,' Sanela said. 'But now she's sleepy.'

'Okay, let's leave her then,' Mum said.

Mum lifted Sanela out of bed and tucked the covers around me. As they left, I heard them whispering. I drifted into sleep and when I woke, my room was dark. I glanced at the clock. It was after six. When I got downstairs, I found my family eating dinner.

'Are you better?' Mum asked.

I nodded.

'You look flushed.' She put her hand on my forehead. 'Maybe you're coming down with something.'

I leaned in, putting my head on Mum's shoulder. She hugged me, kissing my forehead. 'Come here and eat dinner.' She led me to the dinner table and sat me down. 'I set a plate aside for you to eat later, but I'll bring it now.'

I ate dinner slowly, getting each bite to my mouth an effort.

Dad looked at me. 'I'll examine you in the morning and if you're not better, stay home tomorrow.'

I nodded, fighting tears at my parents' concern. I listened to the surrounding conversation, everyone sharing their day, and it was like we were back to how we used to be.

After dinner I sat on the couch, Ali beside me playing his gamer, while Sanela lay on the floor hugging a cushion.

'Okay Ali,' Dad said from the doorway. 'Get your science books and meet me in the study.'

Ali's face mirrored my surprise and delight. Maybe Dad really was telling the truth, and he was going to change. This was the first time he'd left his paperwork untouched in months.

'You'd better hurry.' I took his gamer off him. 'You've got a lot of catching up to do.'

Ali practically bounced out of the room. I didn't think anyone had ever been happier to do homework.

Chapter 19

The next morning I woke feeling blue. As I opened the curtains and looked out at the sunny day, heaviness weighed me down. I returned to bed and watched the sky when my mobile beeped. It was a message from a blocked user. I'd received a photo. I saw a montage of body parts, arms, breast cleavage, a haughty smile. Then it all came together into a clear image. It was one of the striptease photos I'd sent to Alex.

He told me he'd deleted them. He'd promised that he'd never send photos around of his girlfriend. His girlfriend. Oh God, if I was his ex, he'd have every reason to send them. I called him, but his phone rang out. I typed a message with shaking fingers.

AlmaO "You promised you would delete them."

I tried the blocked number, but it went to message bank. My phone beeped. Another photo from a blocked user. I jumped out of bed and dressed myself. I had to see him, make him understand what was at stake. If these photos got out... I had to sit down as a sharp pain cut across my stomach. If they got out, my life was over.

'I thought you were staying home.' It surprised mum when I joined them in the kitchen.

'I remembered I had a test.' I fidgeted nervously as I waited for Sanela and Ali to finish breakfast.

I planned my entreaties to Alex as Dad drove me. When I got to school, Jesse was sitting on the bench by himself.

'Are you feeling better today?' he asked.

I smiled weakly, not commenting. Jesse was wearing a Cheshire grin. 'You seem happy.'

'I have a surprise.' Jesse smiled widely. 'We have to wait for everyone else and then I'll bring it out.'

Sabiha arrived and when she heard about the surprise she demanded, 'tell me, now,' trying to tickle it out of Jesse.

'My lips are sealed until Dina comes.' He fended her off.

'Dina's coming?' I'd expected her to take a few days off with everything that happened.

'I spoke to her yesterday,' Sabiha said. She looked at me questioningly.

'How's Brian?' I asked Jesse, turning away from Sabiha's probing gaze.

'Here's Dina?' Jesse waved her down.

Dina walked toward us slowly, as if she was a hospital patient learning to use her legs again after a broken bone.

'Hey.' Sabiha put her arm around Dina's shoulders and led her to the bench.

'Now that everyone is here, I can reveal my surprise.' Jesse rubbed his hands together. 'Close your eyes.' There was the shuffling sound of footsteps. 'And open,' Jesse shouted a minute later.

I opened my eyes. Brian was standing before us, but it wasn't a Brian I'd ever seen before. This wasn't the hobo Brian I'd first met with the un-kept hair and creased clothes, or the gay Brian with his glittering see through outfits. This Brian was an amalgamation of the two. His hair was slicked back, faint eyeliner and lip-gloss on his lips, and he wore tight jeans and a glittering t-shirt.

'Surprise,' he said in a sing-song voice, making jazz hands. 'I'm back as a student of this illustrious institution.'

'Get out of here.' Sabiha shoved him. 'I thought you said you were never coming back.'

Brian shrugged. 'My brother Greg let me move in with him as long as I returned to school.'

Dina covered her mouth and sobbed.

'This wasn't the reaction I was expecting,' Brian said dryly.

'It's my fault my brother ripped you off. If I hadn't talked you into moving in with him—'

'It's okay.' Brian hugged her. 'I'm fine.'

'But your money,' Dina cried.

'Most of that money came from dodgy gains.' Brian waved his hand.

'What dodgy gains?' Sabiha demanded.

'Omer and I were peddling black market DVDs. Most of the money in my Stash of Cash was from that.'

'What about your savings?' Dina asked.

'I spent all of that on my wardrobe, which I still have. So you see.' Brian kissed her cheek. 'I'm all good.'

'Aren't you angry with me?' Dina asked.

'Why?' Brian laughed. 'I had the best month of my life. No rules, no parents, no school.'

'So it's a good thing Omer ripped you off.' Jesse clapped his hand on Brian's shoulder.

'I wouldn't go that far,' Brian said.

'I would,' Jesse said. 'You were off the rails, man.'

'And now I'm firmly back on the rails. I have an entire week of detention to make up.' Brian scrunched his face as if someone shoved dog shit under his nose.

Sabiha and Jesse laughed. Even I broke out in a smile.

'Poor baby.' Sabiha patted his cheek. 'All good things must end.'

I tuned out as they continued their catch up and kept a lookout for Alex.

'Is everything good?' Sabiha asked as me as I stared at each school arrival.

'All good.' I kept an eye out for Alex' car.

He hadn't arrived by the time school began and I dragged myself to class. I saw him in the corridor at recess and fought my way through the crowd. He watched me approach with a smirk, holding his mobile.

My phone beeped. He sent another photo. Beep. Another photo. My vision swam. His smile was predatory, anger still glittering in his eyes. He wasn't happy I'd dumped him. The corridor cleared, and he waited by the window in front of the stairs, his gaze set on a spot above my head.

'Please don't do this,' I whispered. 'Please delete the photos.'

He continued looking over my head.

'Please,' I begged. 'Please help me.'

He deigned to look down, tilting his head to look down a nostril. 'What do I get out of it?'

I traced his face with my eyes, trying to see the boy I fell in love with, the boy I thought I knew. But he was gone. Before me was the guy they warned me about.

'Where's the Alex I fell in love with?' I asked, not able to stop myself.

'He's here,' Alex said.

I waited for compassion to shine through and for him to be the loveable scoundrel with the cheeky smile.

'He's there. He's nowhere.' He smiled snidely.

I ran into the girls' toilets before I lost it. My phone rang. My legs collapsed when I saw the image. I was in undies and nothing else, my hands cupping my breasts as I pouted. My hand loosened its grip and my phone clattered to the floor.

'Alma.' Sabiha burst through the door. 'What were you talking to Alex about?' Seeing me huddled on the floor, her face furrowed in concern. She bent and picked up my phone.

'Don't.' I reached for it, but I was too late.

Sabiha's mouth gaped open as she looked from the screen and back to me. 'Who sent you this?' Her knuckles were white as she gripped the phone.

'No one.' I wiped my eyes with toilet paper and forced myself to my feet.

'Don't.' Sabiha rubbed her hand over her face. 'Please don't lie to me. Let me help you.'

'How? By telling Dad?'

'Maybe,' Sabiha said. 'Maybe not. I can't tell you until I know.'

'I don't want your help.'

My phone rang again. I tried to snatch it from Sabiha. She turned her back and stiffened when she opened the message. The fight went out of me and I had to lean against the wall.

Sabiha turned to me. 'Oh Alma, what did you do?'

I couldn't keep it together anymore. The pity in her voice undid me. I covered my face with my hands and cried.

Sabiha shuffled closer and hugged me. 'It will be all right. I promise.'

'No, it won't. My life is over.'

'Snap out of it.' She shook my shoulders. 'We'll figure it out. You just have to trust me.'

Her eyes bored into mine. My gaze slid away.

'Have I done anything to make you doubt my sincerity to help you,' she demanded.

'No,' I said, but—' I stopped, scared to put words to the ugly thought in my head.

Sabiha waited, not letting me off the hook.

'I don't know if your loyalty to Dad is stronger,' I finally said. 'He knows you didn't sleep over at Dina's. He knows, but he didn't call you on the truth.'

'He does?' Sabiha was surprised.

I explained how he'd figured it out after our visit to Dina's.

'I doubt that I'd get the same free pass.'

'It's not because he loves me more or anything like that,' Sabiha said, verbalising my greatest fear.

I hesitantly met her eyes.

'It's because he feels guilty about not being a father to me.'

I didn't know if I believed her. The way Dad changed when she showed up shook me to the core and made me doubt everything.

'What can I do to make you trust me?' she asked.

In the end it wasn't my change of heart in trusting her that got me talking. It was the fact that I was choking under the weight of all the unsaid words pressing on my chest. I desperately needed a confidante to clear out the poison left by Alex.

We ended up sitting side by side on the floor, our backs against the wall. It was easier to talk without looking at her. I started at the beginning—my first day at school and the first time I met Alex.

As I retraced our relationship I cleared the dark muddled mess in my head. For the first time I was able to look at our relationship and see the truth.

'He manipulated you,' Sabiha said after I told her about the first time we were together sexually. 'He made you feel like you had to prove yourself.'

'It wasn't like that,' I denied, even though a tiny crack had formed in my certainty. 'He cared for me.'

Sabiha brushed my hair. 'What happened then?'

As I told her about Brian's party Sabiha hissed between her teeth.

'It's not his fault,' I jumped in before she could say anything. 'It was the first anniversary of his little sister's death?'

Sabiha went still as if she'd stopped breathing.

'What is it?'

'Nothing.' Sabiha refused to meet my eyes.

'Tell me,' I shouted.

'What's his sister's name?'

'Amy.'

'Shit.' Sabiha hesitated.

The silence stretched out and I got scared. I knew that Sabiha had something huge to say. I was about to tell her I'd changed my mind when she spoke.

'His Mum brought her daughter Amy to Dad's surgery the other day.'

'Maybe he exaggerated. He said that she had leukaemia.' I looked at Sabiha hopefully.

Sabiha shook her head. 'Ear infection.'

I shut down. Everything he said was a lie. Who did I pour out my heart and soul to?

'How can you be sure?' I clung to a dying hope.

'I read the chart,' Sabiha said.

This was forbidden by Dad, but I knew the impulse. I'd flicked through the charts of my crush in Tasmania until I learnt he had *phimosis*, condition where his foreskin couldn't be retracted and he had to be circumcised. He'd told everyone at school he had an ingrown toe nail and I was never able to look at him the same way again.

'Is Alex the one sending you the photos?' Sabiha asked when my sobbing subsided.

I nodded. 'He's angry that I ended it.'

'How did he talk you into posing for him?'

I hid my face in my knees. I couldn't tell her the truth, that I'd been stupid enough to strip off and photograph myself.

'He'd had plenty of practice talking girls into doing things,' Sabiha said ruefully.

I lifted my head.

'No, I wasn't one of the masses,' Sabiha said to my questioning look. 'I was tempted until I saw him chatting up another girl.'

It made me feel better that I wasn't the only one taken in. 'I don't know what I'm going to do. He could send the photos to everyone and if my parents find out—' I couldn't even finish the sentence.

I'd never disappointed my parents before I got expelled. I was always the good daughter, the perfect child. I didn't know how I'd come to this point. During the past few months I'd slowly crossed the line one step at a time and now I didn't know who was left.

'A few months ago I would have looked at a girl like me with disgust and thought she was stupid. I keep thinking if only I could go back, make a different decision, but I don't know when. When I first came to this school, the first time I caught him out in a lie, the first time he treated me badly.' I grabbed my hair and yanked at it in chunks, the pain of my strained hair follicles soothing me.

'The moment you moved, the moment you found out about me,' Sabiha said.

'I've got no one to blame but myself. I'm the one who made bad choices.'

'Before me.' She squeezed my hand when I was about to protest. 'It's no secret that since you found out about me my life got better and for all of you it got worse. I was so happy to have a father that I didn't care what you were going through.'

I'd never considered it from Sabiha's point of view and thought that she deserved what any other child had. What my siblings and I had all our lives—two parents who loved and were there for us.

'It's not your fault. You should have had a father with you as you grew up.'

'But then we wouldn't be here.' Sabiha took my hand and stared ahead. 'And I wouldn't have a sister.'

I blinked back tears. I'd been resentful of Sabiha and hadn't seen that all she'd wanted was to have a normal family with brothers and sisters, something I took for granted.

'Okay, enough with the maudlin act,' Sabiha stood and paced.

I stood too, but I was woolly-headed and heavy from crying.

'What are our options.' Sabiha counted on her fingers. 'Tell Dad.'

'I can't. He would never forgive me and then there's the other thing.' I hesitated. I'd hid the truth for so long, but Sabiha already knew my deepest, darkest secret, she may as well know the rest. 'My parent's marriage is in trouble.'

Sabiha looked at me disbelievingly. 'But they look happy.'

'Things have been really strained since we—' I didn't finish the sentence, not wanting to pile more guilt on her.

'No wonder you hate me.'

'I don't hate you.'

'How could you not.' Sabiha brushed her hand quickly across her face, like she was wiping a tear.

I gulped. It was the first time I realised I could hurt her.

'I thought you guys were like this normal Brady Bunch family.' Sabiha's voice trembled with emotion. 'And by being connected with you I finally had the chance to be normal, and not be the girl from the wrong side of the tracks with the trashy Mum, and now I find out that I was right. That families like that don't exist outside of TV.'

She sounded cut up. I wanted to comfort her. Give her hope.

'They do. We did. We used to have family lunches every week rotating at our aunt and uncles house. We went out together for movie nights and Mum and Dad took turns driving us to extracurricular activities so they could spend individual time with us.'

Sabiha listened to me with rapt attention, like I was telling her a fairytale.

'And then I came along,' Sabiha said wryly. 'The wicked witch who wrecked everything.'

'It wasn't you. Things just changed. They were both so angry at each other.' I remembered Mum telling Dad how they couldn't tell us something. Maybe there was something else going on and it wasn't all about Sabiha appearing in our lives.

Sabiha took my phone and pressed the buttons, wrenching me out of my musings.

'What are you doing?'

'I'm sending these photos to my phone.'

'Why?'

'Let's go.' Sabiha headed for the door. 'We're going to talk to Alex.'

'No, you can't.'

'Why not?' Sabiha quirked an eyebrow. 'Can I make it any worse? You said it yourself, it's only a matter of time before he sends the photos around. Worse case scenario I speed him up.'

'Okay.' I was unconvinced.

'Don't worry.' Sabiha patted my hand. 'I've got this.'

'What's your plan?' I demanded as we walked.

'Shhh.' Sabiha was staring ahead vacantly. 'I'm thinking.'

We found Alex at his hangout on the oval. His mates noticed us coming and pointed as we approached. Alex kept his back to us. His disregard was like a physical blow. I slowed and would have backed up, but Sabiha put her arm around my waist and pushed me forward.

Sabiha stopped five metres away from Alex. I looked at the distance between us and Alex in confusion. It was too far away to talk to him. We could only shout. I waited for Sabiha to call his name, but she stood still and stared at his back.

When his mates kept snickering and elbowing each other, Alex turned his head to look at us, his body stiff with irritation. Sabiha still didn't say anything. Another 30 seconds passed. I waited, feeling like a lifetime passed.

Alex violently turned away from his mates and stalked to us. 'What?' he snarled.

'Give me your phone?' Sabiha said as if she were asking him to pass the salt at a dinner table.

'Why?' Alex did a double-take.

'There's some photos on there that don't belong to you.'

He smirked. 'They were sent to me, so they're my property.'

He gave me a lecherous once-over. I would've run away, but Sabiha held me. I expected Sabiha to reprimand me or at least give me a dirty look for not setting her straight about the photos, but she just ploughed on as if Alex hadn't said anything.

'Give me your phone so I can delete the photos.'

'Why would I?' Alex snarled.

'If you don't I'll report you to the police and you'll be up for child pornography.'

'No,' I gasped, grabbing her arm.

Alex smiled. 'I don't think your sister is too keen on everyone finding out about her penchant for lingerie.'

I held my sweater tighter across my chest and looked down at the ground.

Sabiha sighed.

I knew I'd let her down by not backing up her bluff, but I couldn't risk my parents finding out.

'What does my sister have to do with it?' Sabiha asked. 'I'll be making the complaint to the police about *my* photos.'

Alex laughed. 'But they're not yours.'

'Who says?'

It was a pleasure to watch him as he worked it through. The resemblance between us was striking in real life, but in the photos my face was in shadow and it was almost impossible to tell the difference.

'Everyone would think you're a slut.'

'As opposed to now thanks to your little prank.'

Alex looked sickly. He was responsible for vandalising Sabiha's locker and spreading the blowjob gossip. Sabiha was right. Everyone already thought the worse of her. I knew the exact moment when Alex realised he was in a catch 22.

'I'll tell them that I was dating Alma,' Alex threatened.

'Do you know what happens to 18 year old men who date 15 year old girls?' Sabiha asked. 'Do the words child sex offender mean anything?'

'Fifteen,' he yelped. 'But you're in Year 10.'

'She was put up a year in primary school,' Sabiha said, sounding bored. 'But hey, if you like the thought of being a paedophile...'

Alex looked shell-shocked as he looked from me to Sabiha. He fumbled through his pockets and found his mobile, placing it in Sabiha's outstretched hand. Sabiha bent her head and pressed his keypad.

'I can't believe you lied to me that you were 16,' Alex said crossly.

'I can't believe you lied to me that your sister died.' I expected him to at least look embarrassed to be caught in a lie, instead he shrugged as if I'd made a comment on the weather.

'Are there any photos anywhere else?' Sabiha demanded when she finished.

'That's it. I swear.' He added when Sabiha gave him a disbelieving look.

'Like your word is worth anything.' Sabiha handed back the phone. 'Remember, you do anything with those photos you're risking jail. A pretty boy like you would do well in there.' She smiled evilly. 'I'll make sure to send you lots of mouthwash.'

Alex snatched his phone back and stalked off.

Sabiha was smiling widely as we walked off. 'Payback's a bitch.'

'What did you do?'

'I subscribed him to a few extra services.' She laughed maniacally.

'I can't believe your bluff worked.' I was floating like an untethered balloon caught by the wind. 'That he believed you would go to the police and complain it was you.'

'Who said it was a bluff?' Sabiha said quietly.

I stopped and turned to look at her properly.

'I meant everything I said. I would have reported him. I have nothing to lose, you do.'

'But what about Dad? What if he didn't forgive you?'

'Then he's not a real Dad,' Sabiha said. 'Because he abandoned me and I forgave him.'

'But he didn't know about you.'

'He's a doctor and he didn't notice his wife was pregnant. Either he's a lousy husband or a lousy doctor. Either way he's guilty of something and is in no position to judge anyone else.'

It was the first time I'd thought about it in those terms. Dad had always been this mythical, perfect person. When Sabiha came into our lives I'd accepted his version of the story unquestioned. Swallowed it whole like a baby bird receiving its feed.

But after Alex something shifted inside me. I wasn't a little girl who could accept one side of the story. There were so many things that didn't add up. Whenever I thought about it my mind shied away like I was stepping around a well. Whatever the story was, my parents weren't blameless. My conception was too close to Sabiha's for it not to suggest a suspicious nature of their relationship. I remembered the snatches of conversation I'd heard between them.

'Affair,' I muttered, a thought circling my brain, but I couldn't grab hold of it.

'You've figured it out. Your parents were having an affair when you were conceived.'

Something clicked into place. I remembered the fight I'd overhead, the way they avoided talking about how they met, the whispers in the community after everyone found out about Sabiha.

'If Dad has a problem with anything you or I do then he's the biggest hypocrite in the world,' Sabiha said.

I remembered all the times Dad spoke about doing the right thing, and the whole time he was the worst kind of liar. Any other day I would have been raging at his duplicity, but now I was numb. I wondered if I was being inoculated to finding out people were liars.

'Anyway, it's a moot point. Alex won't be giving you any trouble and Dad will never know.'

I should have been happy about the fact that I'd escaped scot-free and that my parents would never find out, but I wasn't. I wanted to make Dad feel bad, hurt him like he'd hurt me the past few months. Then I remembered Mum and the desire retreated.

I spent the rest of the school day in a daze. I glimpsed Alex once more in the corridors between classes, but he ignored me. I couldn't believe that a few days ago he was the boy I thought I'd lose my virginity to and now he was somebody I used to know.

After school Jesse asked to speak to Sabiha alone. Dina was picked up by her parents and it was only Brian and me.

'Ah, young love,' Brian sighed, his hand on his forehead like he was swooning.

'What's that about?' I asked.

'I told Jesse about her heroic deeds with Alex,' Brian said as we watched them.

I told Brian and Dina the abbreviated version about what happened with Alex at lunchtime. I didn't want Dina and Sabiha's friendship to be affected because of my secret, and I gave Brian the okay to tell Jesse who wasn't there.

'So?' I asked.

Jesse kissed Sabiha.

'I guess he's decided she's worthy of his affections again,' Brian said.

A few minutes later they parted, lingering as they held hands. Brian and Jesse went one way down Main Road, and Sabiha and I another.

Sabiha smiled dreamily as she walked.

'That was weird. You and Jesse getting together like that.'

'Not really,' Sabiha said. 'It's take two. The first time I fucked it up, but this time I know how lucky I am. How are you doing?'

She let me vent my anger about Alex' duplicity. It was such a relief to be able to have to unload.

'Call me when you get home,' she said as she left me at Dad's medical centre. 'You need to let all this poison out so it doesn't fester.'

'I can't do that,' I said. 'I'm talking your ear off about this crap.'

'That's what sisters are for.' Sabiha waved and walked away.

Chapter 20

I was home again, relieved to be amid normality as I set the table while Mum cooked. Sanela came into the kitchen.

'I want to wear a bikini.' Sanela tugged on Mum's arm.

'Why?'

'I want to play model like Alma. Please, Mum get my swimsuit.'

I turned. Sanela was holding my mobile, her fingers clicking as she scrolled through photos.

'Alma isn't wearing a swimsuit,' Mum said.

'She does in the photos.' Sanela held up the phone out to Mum.

Time stopped. Mum was distracted. She pretended to look at the screen and was thrusting it back to Sanela. I knew it was my fault. If only I hadn't reacted in that moment. If only I hadn't exclaimed and rushed forward to snatch it.

Mum looked at me with narrowed eyes. Her interest peaked, she turned her attention away from the pot she was stirring. Her gaze arrested by the image on the small screen she pressed the buttons and scrolled through.

'Alma, what is this?' Mum looked at me with disbelieving eyes.

'What's wrong?' Sanela asked.

'Nothing.' Mum pushed her to the door. 'Go upstairs.'

That was the moment Dad came home.

'Why did you take these photos?' Mum demanded.

I was frozen. I didn't know what to say.

'Who did you send them to?' Mum was shaking my arms, trying to dislodge an answer.

I didn't understand how the photos were back on my phone. I'd deleted them all. Did Alex send them again? I saw the star sticker on the back of the phone and realised we'd swapped phones when Sabiha was forwarding the photos to herself.

Mum pressed a few more buttons. 'You have internet.' Her face cleared. 'This is Sabiha's phone. So these are photos of Sabiha.' Mum put her hand on her chest like she was recovering from a heart attack.

Mum wanted to believe it was Sabiha, then she could sweep it all under the carpet and protect her sanitised image of our family.

'What photos?' Dad asked. Mum handed him the phone. His eyes went wide with shock. 'Why would she have these?'

Mum sat on a chair like her legs couldn't hold her. 'To send to a boy.'

The phone rang, flashing up my photo. Sabiha was calling to tell me we'd swapped phones.

'Don't.' I took a step forward, trying to stop the train wreck.

'Yes, we know,' Dad said when he answered. 'We're looking at your photographs. What were you thinking?'

I heard Sabiha's voice, then Dad cut in.

'Obviously your mother has failed once again in her parental duties. This is unacceptable. I'm coming over.'

'Alma, go to your room,' Mum told me.

My feet automatically obeyed, and I found myself outside of the kitchen, standing in the recess by the doorway.

'What did she say?' Mum asked when he hung up.

'She said she made a mistake.' Dad rubbed his hand over his face. 'She trusted a boy when she shouldn't have.'

My vision swam. Sabiha told me she'd take the rap, but I thought she said that to make me feel better.

'What are you going to do?' Mum asked.

'I have to go there and find out who she sent the photos to and be there for her.'

Mum was holding Dad's arm, and they looked united. Maybe I shouldn't tell the truth. Maybe I should leave things as they are and let Dad think it was Sabiha. After all, Sabiha said it herself. Her reputation was already damaged and it couldn't hurt her anymore.

'She needs a firm hand, boundaries and an understanding of consequences,' Mum said. 'Something her mother obviously can't provide.'

'You're right,' Dad said. 'This proves Bahra doesn't have what it takes to be a parent. I need to take custody of Sabiha and give her structure and discipline.'

'I don't feel comfortable having our children exposed to her bad influences.'

'What do you want me to do? Turn away from her?' Dad asked.

'That's not what I'm saying,' Mum argued.

'I've had enough of you letting me decide and then blaming me later,' Dad shouted, his voice hoarse from frustration.

'And I'm sick of you deciding without consulting me,' Mum snapped.

'Fine,' Dad said. 'Tell me what you want me to do and I'll do it.'

Mum was quiet as she thought. 'If you think it's best that we fight for custody, then that's what we'll do,' she finally said.

All I had to do was walk away. Let my parents believe these were photos of Sabiha. But how could I look Sabiha in the eyes again? I'd spent the past month crossing the line, getting further and further away from who I was. Did I want to make one more poor decision?

I looked at Dad's disgusted face and imagined how I would feel if he looked at me like that. The sense of loss and devastation I expected wasn't there. Something broke inside me when Sabiha told me about my parents.

My father's god-like status died, and I was finally free of my desperate need to ingratiate myself. I was his flesh and blood. Either he loved me no matter, or he didn't.

My parents talked about hiring a lawyer and taking Sabiha's mother to court.

'How will this affect Bahra?' Mum asked.

'I can't think about that,' Dad said. 'I have to prioritise Sabiha.'

I shut my eyes. This would destroy Sabiha. Her mother was the most important person in her life. I had to tell. As soon as I decided, a feeling of wellbeing filled me. I was sick of the burden of secrets. Sick of being in fear that at any moment, I would be discovered. I wanted to be free once again.

I knew that if I took this step and admitted the truth, my life was going to take a turn for the worst. I would disappoint my parents. It might even make them fight again, but that was a price I was willing to pay to do the right thing. To become the girl I used to be who knew right from wrong and had a clear conscience. Most importantly, I'd be able to look Sabiha in the eye and finally be the sister she deserved, the sister she was trying to be for me.

I stepped out of my hiding place and into the kitchen. 'Mum, Dad, I have something to tell you.'

'Not now, Alma.' Dad picked up his keys.

'Those are photos of me.'

Dad stuttered to a stop, his hands on the doorhandle. He hesitated. 'It's okay. You don't need to lie for Sabiha. We'll take care of her.'

'Look at the shoulder. It's my birthmark.'

Dad clutched the phone tighter in his hand, not looking down. Mum snatched it from him and flicked through the photos. Her face went white and her knees listed. 'Alma, how could you?'

Dad turned around, helped Mum to a chair before looking at the photos himself. He sat next to Mum. 'Why?'

'I had a boyfriend. I fell in love and I thought he loved me. He didn't.' I clutched the back of the chair as tears seeped out of my eyes.

'We taught you better than this,' Mum slammed the phone down on the table, cracking the glass.

'Yes, you did. But people make mistakes.'

'Not in this family, we don't. We know better.'

'Do we? How did you and Dad meet?' I demanded, rage growing at her hypocrisy.

'That is not what we're discussing right now,' Dad interjected.

'Why are our birthdays only three months apart?'

Mum and Dad looked at each other.

'How did you not know that Bahra was pregnant with your child?'

'We are not discussing this today!' Mum stood.

'How could you have abandoned your child? And how could you have slept with a married man? You both make me sick. You're both liars and hypocrites, and you have no right to judge me. I made a mistake. I trusted the wrong guy. I put myself in dangerous situations and could have been hurt, but you don't give a shit about that, do you?'

'Of course we do.' Mum reached for me.

'No, you don't. All you give a shit about is the community and how we look in their eyes. You don't give a shit about anything else.' I headed for the door. 'Well, you don't need to worry. I had one family member actually looking out for me. Sabiha took care of it. Sabiha is the one who made sure that the creep who had my photos didn't send them around. And I don't think you need to worry about the parenting she received. Bahra did a good job, with no help from either of you.'

I stomped upstairs, locking my door and placing my chest of drawers against it. Mum and Dad attempted knocking on my door separately and together, and Sanela knocked and pleaded for me to let her in. I lay in bed, sobbing until I had no more tears left.

I woke early in the morning, my stomach twisting on itself in hunger as I hadn't eaten dinner. I dressed in my school uniform and tip-toed downstairs. There was a phone on the kitchen island, the screen intact. I picked it up and taped the screen. It was my phone. Dad must have gone to see Sabiha. I made myself toast and checked the bus schedule for St Albans. After I wrote a note for my parents that I was catching the bus, I left, eating my toast as I walked. I knew I would have to face my parents and talk about Alex with them, but not yet. I wanted time to process before I saw them.

It was a bright, and sunny morning as I walked to the bus stop. I somehow felt light and optimistic. Even though I knew I had to face a reckoning with my parents about Alex, I was unburdened for the first time in months. All my secrets were out in the open and I had nothing to fear.

I texted Sabiha while I was on the bus and walked down Main Road West. She'd suggested coming to her house, but that seemed intrusive. Instead, I waited for her at the park near her house. I climbed to the top of the cubby house that had a slide attached and was reading while I waited.

Sabiha arrived half an hour later, throwing her backpack onto the platform below and climbing up the stairs. 'What happened with your folks last night?'

I told her about them finding the photos on my phone and how they thought they were her photos.

'You didn't have to tell them the truth.' She hugged my shoulders. 'It wouldn't have made any difference to me. If Dad tried to sue for custody, I would have just cut off contact with him.'

'No. We're sisters. I want you to be in my life.'

Sabiha kissed my head. 'Me too.'

I handed her a tissue. 'What happened when Dad came over?'

'I told him about Alex the creep, without using his name. He wanted to go to the police. I told him that was your decision.'

I nodded. 'I think it's the right thing to do, so Alex doesn't do this to any other girls.' I hadn't slept all night, thinking about what happened. Alex had known exactly how to prey on my vulnerabilities and was prepared to use my photos to blackmail me into performing sexual favours. He needed to be stopped, so no other girl was ensnared in his charm again.

'Are you sure? It's going to be messy and public.'

'I know.' I'd seen what happened to Rodney's ex-girl-friend when the photos were spread around. She'd started home-schooling afterwards because she couldn't deal with the stares and comments. When her father pressed charges, it had stemmed the tide of photos being shared, but she still didn't return to school. I'd heard she was getting counselling because she'd had a breakdown. I wasn't going to let Alex and his friends do this to other girls.

We headed to school, leisurely walking as we had plenty of time. It was the first time Sabiha and I chose each other and there was a fresh feeling between us. We couldn't stop talking and found so many things we had in common. I had a constant feeling of *déjà vu* as I recognised myself in her facial expressions and voice. It was like having a doppelgänger.

When we arrived on the school grounds, Jesse, Brian, and Dina were already at our table. 'I sent them a heads up,' Sabiha said.

'How are you holding up?' Brian came forward and took hold of my hands.

'Okay. Better than okay. Relieved. No more secrets.' Sabiha and I shared a look. We'd talked about our parents on the walk to school, compared notes about what we knew about our father's marriage with our mothers.

Dad's marriage to her mother was an arranged one. Dad had returned to Bosnia to visit family and was quickly paired up with Bahra. He fell for her, but quickly realised that she'd only married him because she was rebounding from her Serbian boyfriend, Darko. When they arrived in Australia, she told him she thought she was pregnant with Darko's child. Dad confided in his receptionist Jasminka, my mother, about his troubled marriage, and somehow their conversations turned to something more. Soon Mum was pregnant with me and so Dad left Bahra, and my parents moved to Hobart, to start fresh. The only contact he had with Bahra after that was divorce papers. As he heard nothing different from Bahra, he'd gone on with his life, assuming that Sabiha was Darko and Bahra's child, until three months ago when he learned the truth.

I wondered what would have happened if he knew about Sabiha. Who would he have chosen? Bahra or my mother? Either way, one of us would have been a loser in the family stakes. When I'd shared this thought with Sabiha, she told me that things had worked out the way they were meant to. That Dad's marriage to Bahra wouldn't have survived her illness. I clung to her certainty, wanting to believe that my parent's marriage was a genuine love match. It was the only way I could believe that they would weather this current storm, and the future one that was coming when I pressed charges against Alex.

'I'm glad to hear it. Let's toast to no more secrets.' Brian lifted his bottle of coke and toasted with Dina, who tapped her metal water bottle to his.

Jesse approached Sabiha and curved his arm around her waist. She nestled into him effortlessly, lifting her face up to his, and they shared a short, sweet kiss. I wondered if I would ever have that again? Before Alex, I had daydreamed about scenarios of having a boyfriend. Now the thought made me recoil.

Brian noticed my look and curved his arm around my shoulder and pulled me to his side. 'We may not have boyfriends, but we have something better.' He hugged Dina with his other arm.

'What do we have?' Dina demanded.

'Each other.'

'God, you're so corny.' She slapped his torso, laughing as she did so.

'You're one of us now, Alma. You're one of the Sassy Saints.'

'I am.' I smiled, feeling a sense of wellbeing.

'Yes, you are.' Sabiha and Jesse joined, and we all stood in a circle, hugging.

'Sassy Saints Forever,' Brian shouted.

'Sassy Saints Forever,' we shouted in unison together.

For now, it was enough.

***

Glossary

Ajvar Bosnian. Bosnian relish

Burka Arabic. An outer garment that covers a woman's face

Ćevapi Bosnian. Pronounced chevapi, skinless sausages

Džezva Bosnian. Pronounced djezva, coffee pot

Fildžan Bosnian. Pronounced fildjan, demitasse cups that coffee is served in

Hijab Arabic. Scarf that covers a woman's hair and nape

Pljeskavica Bosnian. Pronounced plyeskavica, spicy Bosnian beef patties that are flatter and thinner than hamburgers

Kajmak. Bosnian. Pronounced kaymak, churned cream

Kefir Bosnian. Fermented yoghurt-like drink

Šopska Bosnian. Pronounced shopska, salad with tomato, cucumber, roasted peppers, onion, topped with grated white brine cheese and parsley sprinkled on top

Alma's Loyalty

BONUS

Reckoning (short story)

Alma's Real Talk about Sexting

Sign up to my newsletter for bonus gifts

https://www.amrapajalic.com/my-newsletter.html

Sassy Saints Series

Sabiha's Dilemma was my debut novel that was traditionally published under the title *The Good Daughter*. This story was inspired by my own experiences of being from a Bosnian background, growing up in the Western suburbs of Melbourne (a low socio-economic suburb) and being brought up by a mother who suffers from Bipolar.

I loved the characters that I created and kept imagining their lives beyond the pages of the book I wrote. The year after publication I wrote a follow up novel about another character, Alma, who finds out she has a half sister she never knew, Sabiha, and through Alma's story I continued Sabiha, Jesse, Brian, Dina and Adnan's stories.

When I embarked on my indie publishing career and was preparing *Sabiha's Dilemma* for release I was hit by a wave of inspiration. What if I expanded this universe and created a series where each character had their own book? This would give me the opportunity to recreate so many of the experiences that happened off-page for each of my characters and to extend their storylines.

And so the *Sassy Saints Series* was born.

Sassy Saints Series
Follow the lives of six sassy teens coming of age in St Albans, as they navigate their sexual and cultural identity and search for belonging.

These books will be an inter-connected series that can be read out of order (I'll be keeping any spoilers off the page). If you want to follow the *Sassy Saints* journey join my mailing list and stay in the loop.

Sabiha's Dilemma

Sabiha's dilemma is being the good daughter so that her mentally ill mother is accepted back into the Bosnian community.

Alma's Loyalty

When Alma finds out that she has a half sister she never knew, she is faced with competing loyalties.

Jesse's Triumph

After Jesse's debut novel is published while he's a high school student, he contends with becoming popular.

Brian's Conflict

Brian's dreams of being a designer are in conflict with his father's hopes he'll join the family business as a bricklayer.

Dina's Burden

Dina carries the burden of living up to her parent's expectations to make up for her brother's errant ways.

Adnan's Secret

Adnan is the perfect son carrying the weight of his migrant parent's expectations, who lives a secret life.

Pishukin Press

Sabiha's Dilemma

AMRA PAJALIĆ

Can Sabiha play the part of the good daughter
so that her mentally ill mother is accepted back
into the Bosnian community?

Unbelievable Discounts

https://www.pishukinpress.com/

Pishukin
Press

After Jesse's debut novel is published while he's a high school student, he contends with becoming popular.

Unbelievable Discounts

https://www.pishukinpress.com/

Jesse's Triumph Chapter 1

I was walking down the corridor, fixating on the scene in my novel, when my protagonist was lost in the woods. The world around me was slightly hazy and out of focus. I knew I was in my high school corridor and saw the students milling at their lockers around me, but they were distant, ethereal, my body on autopilot as I floated in my make-believe world.

Ow! Pain in my shin and I fell forward, hitting the linoleum floor hard, my palms stinging and my knees burning. I looked up to find Joshua King standing above me. He attempted a concerned mask ruined by the smirk tilting his lips. 'Sorry mate, didn't see you there.' He offered his hand under the guise of helping me up.

I knew better and ignored his proffered hand, standing up and wiping my jeans. His mates guffawed behind him. My cheeks burnt. I knew my milky skin showed all my emotions and, when I got embarrassed and red-faced, my blue eyes looked watery, like I was on the verge of tears. Sarah, my sister, teased me. I had a tragic face, and as a child I'd used it to sucker many an adult out of sweets. As I got older, it was a liability, especially in the cut-throat atmosphere of St Albans High.

I collected my books off the floor and walked around King and his idiot posse, staring at the floor. My rage built as I walked away. I was so sick of King and his bullshit. My mind turned to another scene, one of death and carnage. I ran to my safe space on the ground level of the three-storey building—the library.

When I walked in, I saw Brian, my best friend, sitting at a table. I rushed over, dropping to my knees in front of his desk.

'Joshua King,' I said. 'I'm putting him on my hit list.' I took out my notebook and took Brian's pen.

A girl was sitting next to Brian. I glanced at her and saw she was reading my page upside down. Her face blanched when she saw the heading, *People to kill.*

'Why?' Brian asked.

'He tripped me in the hall,' I said.

Brian read the next Maths answer from his notebook, but the girl beside him was stiff and unresponsive.

'Sabiha, this is my best friend, Jesse,' Brian introduced me.

I looked at the girl, recognising her as the new student who had begun a few weeks ago. She looked between me and Brian, obviously struggling to understand how we were best friends. Brian's brown hair was slicked back perfectly, and he wore black pleated pants and a dazzlingly white crisp shirt. He looked like he was going to a job interview. I wore loose jeans and an even looser sweatshirt, and both had seen better days. I'd never cared about my appearance until I saw myself through her eyes.

'We're in Phys Ed together,' I said, then regretted it as I saw the moment she remembered me, wincing as she flash-backed to our last lesson.

When our teacher, Mr Robinson, left the gym to go to his office, all the boys in class played dodgeball with me as the target. I'd flinched, trying to catch the balls, but I didn't have a chance in hell with multiple players targeting only me. Everyone laughed as the balls connected and bruised. I knew I'd become red-faced and watery-eyed again as rage worked through me, giving the bullies more hilarity as they revelled in thinking they'd made me cry.

When Mr Robinson returned and saw the balls on the floor around me, he'd asked me what happened. Mr Rob and I had a deal. I'd told him I couldn't nark on the kids anymore. He'd tried to punish the bullies for their idiotic behaviour in the past, which only led to more of the same. When I said nothing, Mr Rob ordered me to put the balls away. When we began playing soccer, he subtly punished King and his crew by not giving them their favourite positions. Their team lost, and mine won. It was a minor victory as victories went, but it was enough.

I noticed the book she was holding, Tara Moss' book *Split*. 'That one's great.' I took the book.

'You've read it too?' Sabiha sounded surprised.

'I can read.' I threw the book on the table. Did she equate me with King and his neanderthal brethren, incapable of stringing together a legible thought?

She grabbed my hand. 'I haven't met many boys who read.'

Sabiha smiled at me and my heart lightened; her green eyes sparkled, and her golden hair framed her face. My heart sped up for another reason.

'I was just surprised to find someone who shared my passion,' she explained.

'Jesse's the book-lover,' Brian said. 'I just read what he tells me to.'

She let go of my hand, and I clenched it, still feeling her touch. To hide my emotions, I looked at my watch. 'I've got to stock up on my rations.'

Seeing Sabiha's confusion, Brian translated. 'He needs to get reading material for the weekend.'

I quickly stood and went to the stack, peering at Brian and Sabiha through the gap in the shelf. As she stood and bent over to pack up, my skin heated as I noticed how her camouflage cargo pants curved around her waist. She straightened, revealing her bare midriff and curved waist.

'How long have you two known each other?' Sabiha asked.

'Since primary school.' Brian put his Maths book away.

'Has he always wanted to kill people?'

'Jesse's not a weirdo or anything. He uses fantasy to deal with the bullying. He couldn't hurt anyone.'

'Good to know,' she said.

My stomach dropped. Of course, she thought I was dangerous. What kind of weirdo talked about killing people at a school? I gently hit my forehead on the books in front of me. Shit! I glanced around, checking if anyone could see me. I had to be more careful. People already thought I was weird. I didn't have to help them.

I quickly pulled a few books from the shelves, needing a comfort read, returning to my favourites of John Green and Melina Marchetta. Sabiha and Brian had packed up and were waiting by the counter.

I placed my books on the counter next to Sabiha. 'This is a new title,' Miss Swan, the librarian, said as she scanned the latest John Green book. 'Write a recommendation since you're the first lender.'

I smiled, excited by the thought. As a writer, any byline helped boost my confidence. I placed my books in my book-bag and caught sight of Sabiha's face. She was frowning as she eyed me and the librarian. I looked away. She hated me. What did I expect? I'd thought I had an ally. As if?

Brian and Sabiha walked ahead of me as we walked out of the library and up the stairs to the second storey. We had History together.

Sabiha followed Brian to the back of the class and threw her backpack on the table next to him. I hesitated next to her, meeting Brian's gaze. Usually, Brian and I sat at the back. I doodled on the edges of my notepad as the teacher spoke while Brian stared out the window, caught up in his own world. If the teacher called on Brian, I'd quickly jot down the answer he could read out, maintaining the impression that he was engaged in class.

'Let's move one down so Jesse can sit on the other side.' Brian waved to her right.

Sabiha looked at me, flushing slightly, as she moved one seat down. I sat in the chair next to the window. 'So altruistic of you to give up your favourite seat,' I murmured.

Brian shot me a frown but said nothing as he sat between us.

The teacher asked us to discuss whether World War I or World War II was the war that affected the world the most. Brian moved his seat back so that he included Sabiha, as no one was sitting next to her.

'World War I because it's the first war that involved the entire world,' Brian said.

'I agree because it's also the fact that it changed the class system. It brought about the demise of the aristocracy, and there were millions of deaths, both during the war and afterwards, from the Influenza,' I added.

'It might have been responsible for more deaths, but it was steeped in the traditions of trench warfare,' Sabiha said. 'The second world war was much more brutal and bloody because it was about genocide and extermination. Hitler's ideology has become a blueprint that keeps repeating. Just look at what's happening in my corner of the world.'

I frowned, not understanding what she was referring to.

'I'm Bosnian. Ethnic cleansing is a new term, but it's the same concept. Exterminate an entire race of people for a land grab.'

The penny dropped. It was years ago, but I'd seen news reports about the Balkan Conflict as the country that was once Yugoslavia tore itself apart, with each state seeking independence after their dictator Tito, who had ruled for forty years, died.

'Can you really compare the ethnic cleansing of Bosnia and the Holocaust, though?' I questioned, my intellectual brain engaged. Usually, Brian made a one-sentence announcement and then attempted to segue the conversation into his social life. This was the first time I'd actually had someone to debate.

Sabiha's jaw tightened. 'I wasn't comparing. I was justifying my argument that the second world war was more brutal.' She turned away, crossing her arms on her chest as she stared straight ahead at the whiteboard.

'Don't be a sore loser,' I stirred.

She looked at me, her green eyes flashing ire. 'I'm not,' she spat. 'To you, this is an intellectual discussion about war. To me, this is real life. My family were brutalised and chased out of their homeland. So excuse me if I don't want to trade details to win an argument.'

I flushed, looking down at the table as I scratched the edge. I'd been so engaged in the discussion I hadn't thought through that I was pushing emotional buttons. The teacher asked us to share, but our group remained stubbornly silent.

'Apologise,' Brian wrote on the edge of his notebook and held it to me. When I read it, he quickly scrawled over it and transformed it into a love heart.

Sabiha was frosty for the rest of the double, barely looking at me.

'I want to apologise,' I said as we packed up a few minutes before the bell. 'I didn't mean to be insensitive.'

'That's fine,' Sabiha snapped.

'Sabiha, Jesse apologised. Now you accept his apology,' Brian intervened.

She glared at him. Brian maintained eye contact. She wilted.

'I accept,' she muttered, swinging her backpack onto her back.

The bell rang, and we drifted out of the classroom and down the stairs.

'See you tomorrow.' Brian kissed her on the cheek at the bottom of the stairs. The boys' lockers were at the other end of the corridor.

She smiled, her face transformed. 'See you.'

'Jesse,' Brian prodded, looking at me.

'See you tomorrow,' I muttered, waving quickly.

Sabiha's smile faded. 'See you.'

I opened my locker, carefully checking my diary for all the homework and collecting the notebooks and textbooks I'd need. Brian emptied his backpack of textbooks and notebooks.

'Really!' I exclaimed.

'I don't need those when I've got you.' Brian smiled widely and put his arm around my shoulders. He came over every night after I'd finished my homework and used my notes and homework to complete his.

'Eventually, the teachers will figure out you're not doing any of your own work.' It surprised me it hadn't happened already. While Brian could complete the homework using me as a resource when we were doing the exams, he had to pass on his own, and somehow he always did.

'Please. They'll only figure it out if I over-reach. But I know my speed. I'm a bare-pass student.' He preened in front of the mirror he'd attached to the inside of his locker door, using his comb to slick back his dark hair.

'The fact that you pass all the exams means you've got a great memory. If you tried, you could get a great grade.'

'What do I need good grades for?' He slammed the locker shut as his face darkened. 'I know where my future is.'

I gently closed my locker door, not saying anything. Brian's father was an immovable boulder.

We walked home together. When we reached my house, Brian continued, waving as he called out, 'See you soon.'

I took my key from my pocket and unlocked the front door.

Mum was in the living room, sitting in her wheelchair in front of the TV. The bright colours of the TV show The Price is Right lit up her face in the darkened room, the sun setting early in winter.

I flicked on the light switch. Mum turned to look at me, a smile brightening her face.

'You shouldn't be sitting in the dark,' I chastised.

'Reggie, you're back from work,' she exclaimed, calling me by my father's name. He'd been dead since I was four years old, hit by a drunk driver, but lately, Mum sometimes confused me for him. I hardly had any memories of him. Just a vague impression of a show, maybe Moomba, as there was a river and water-skiers. I couldn't see, so he lifted me on his shoulders. He towered above the other partygoers at six foot four, and I'd reached my hands up, convinced I could touch the sky.

Sometimes when I looked at the scant photo album charting my life with him, the ten photos of just me and him, I had a glimpse of a memory, a shimmer that quickly faded. My fourth birthday and the car birthday cake Mum made. Him lighting the candles, urging me to blow them, feeling his breath next to my ear as he helped me blow. I'd examined myself in the mirror, trying to see the resemblance. Something in the way the stubble covered my skin highlighted my square chin and high cheekbones. The one thing I'd wanted from him was his towering height, but alas, my mother's genes had dominated, and I was only 5 foot 10.

Mum's face cleared as she recognised me. 'Jesse, tell me about your day,' she demanded.

I placed my backpack on the shoe shelf in the hallway and wheeled her to the kitchen. 'First up, I had English,' I told her, as I opened the fridge and took out carrots, celery, capsicum, and the eggplant dip that was her favourite. 'We had a class debate about the ethics of cloning for language analysis.' I closed the fridge and took out the chopping board. 'My team won, of course.' I chopped the vegetables and placed them on a platter, fanning them out around the eggplant as I told her the Disney version of my day. There was a debate, but Joshua King was in my English class and made it a point to torment me by interrupting me every time I spoke. The teacher attempted to stop Joshua at the beginning of the year, but now was completely worn down and just let the class bully suck all the attention from the room.

I pushed Mum's wheelchair to the kitchen table and sat across from her. As we ate our snacks, she laughed at my jokes, her full cheeks wobbling.

'I love you, Jesse,' Mum said, her hand patting mine.

I held her hand in mine. Her fingers were thick and swollen, her knuckles barely visible. She'd had breast cancer five years ago and, as part of her treatment, had her lymph nodes removed, which affected her thyroid. At first, the doctors thought she suffered from depression. She was tired and slept most of the day, and her short-term memory deteriorated. She attempted to keep up with her job as a nurse but cut back her hours more and more as fatigue hit her. Her memory began failing, and she made a few mistakes on the job. She was put on sick leave. Without a job, she drifted increasingly into lethargy, sleeping all day, gaining more and more weight. By the time she was diagnosed with hypothyroidism a year later, her career was in ruins, and she was morbidly obese and struggling to function.

I wheeled Mum back to the living room and parked the chair in front of the TV. She smiled as I turned the television screen back on. I returned to the kitchen, washed the dishes, and then checked the casserole I had started in the slow cooker this morning. I put on the rice in the rice cooker, glancing at the clock. I had an hour and a half until my sister Sarah returned from work. I went to my bedroom. I turned on my computer, flicking through my notes and working on my English home-work. When I finished, I went to the backyard with a washing basket, collecting the washing from the clothesline I'd put up in the morning. I folded it as I went, returning to the house and placing the dried clothes in our wardrobes and drawers.

I checked on the rice cooker and the slow cooker. Both were finished and on warming. I served the table, putting out three dinner plates and cups, and the cutlery, then returned to my bedroom and started my history homework. I heard the front door open, and Sarah called out. Her murmurs from the front room as she kissed Mum hello, followed by footsteps down the hall and a quick knock on my door before she peered in. 'Hello, baby bro.' She blew a kiss.

I smiled at her. She looked so much like me. The same blonde hair and blue eyes, the shape of the face. We both took after Mum. Looking at Sarah was like looking at Mum twenty years ago. Sometimes it made me sad. If Mum had been diagnosed earlier, how different would our lives have been?

'See you in ten.' Sarah went to her bedroom, and I heard the shower.

It was the first thing she did when she came home, jump in the shower and get rid of all the clothes she wore. Nursing was grimy work, and she felt she had to decontaminate hers. Sarah was twenty-two, six years older than me. After Mum went into remission, we expected life would return to normal, but it didn't. The thyroid medication that she used wasn't effective and had some pretty nasty side-effects.

Those were tough years. We survived on a pension Mum received from the government. We had to go to the food bank, and all my clothes were secondhand and frayed. Our extended family had to chip in regularly to help with large bills, and every time there was a visit from the Department of Human Services, our Aunt Cara came to stay overnight, pretending that she was living with us, to fend them away. When Sarah turned eighteen, she did a nursing course and started working full-time. At least the financial struggle eased a bit, but I had to take on more household duties to relieve the burden from her. I didn't mind. I was just relieved that those days of stress and scarcity were behind us.

While Sarah was showering, I served up the food and placed it on the table. Mum wheeled herself from the kitchen. As I brought over a jug of water, Sarah walked in, wearing grey tracksuit pants and a matching top, her hair tied up loosely in a ponytail.

'You're a lifesaver.' She sat down and lifted the serving ladle. 'I didn't have time to take a lunch break.' She heaped her platter and began eating, shovelling in four spoonfuls by the time I had served Mum and me.

'That's better,' Sarah said after a few more spoonfuls. 'My stomach has stopped attempting to eat itself. How was your day? Anything interesting happen?'

'We had a class debate.' I sipped water.

'You did. How did you go?' Mum asked me. She had forgotten. Even though I'd told her the story two hours before. Another side effect of her condition.

I told the story again, this time for Sarah's benefit. We always began with my day. Sarah could only tell her work stories when we weren't eating, as most of the ones she found interesting or funny involved bodily fluids.

'Oh, also I met the new girl,' I added, serving myself another portion.

'New girl?' Sarah's spoon paused on its way to her mouth. 'Name, description, attributes?'

'Sabiha, blonde, blue-eyed, Bosnian Muslim. And I guess her key attribute was angry.'

'So she's the angry new girl?' Sarah smiled as she spoke.

'I guess she has reason to be. She's Bosnian Muslim, and her family came from the war.'

'Mmm. You forgot to mention she's pretty.' A wicked smile lit up Sarah's face.

'What? I don't need to say that.' Even as I was speaking, I felt my cheeks flushing. I had been awestruck the first time I saw her, and as we argued in history, I had felt more than the stirrings of intellectual debate.

'Oooh, so she's really pretty,' Sarah prodded.

My cheeks got hotter, and I flashed her an angry look.

'Stop teasing your brother,' Mum intervened. 'Just because Jesse finds the new girl pretty doesn't mean we have to tease him.'

'Muuuum,' I wailed.

Sarah and Mum chuckled. This was the problem with being the only male in the house. I was constantly outnumbered and outmanoeuvred.

'What was your day like?' I asked Sarah, desperately hoping for a tale of horrible bodily fluids to take the attention of me.

'Oh, have I got a story for you.' Sarah cracked her knuckles, a gleeful look on her face. She loved telling excruciating stories. 'A man came in. Or should I say, hobbled in. After he'd checked in, claiming an excruciating stomach ache, he wouldn't sit down.'

I closed my eyes and shuddered. It was going to be one of those excruciating stories about an obstruction in the bowel. Sarah gestured and mimed as she revealed details of the interview and investigation. When she shared details of the extraction, I had to breathe through my gag reflex. This was the problem with getting your wish. It was always a regret.

After we ate, I collected the dishes.

'Shoo.' Sarah took the plate off me and shooed me. 'I'll do the dishes.'

'It's okay. I've got time.'

'You've done enough for today.' Sarah went to the kitchen and filled the dishwasher while I returned to my bedroom. Sarah still had to bathe mother before bed, but she always wanted to be fair.

As I was completing my Maths homework, there was a brief knock, and the door opened. I knew without looking it was Brian. He had a distinctive knock of refusing to wait for the all-clear before barging in.

He threw himself on my bed and sighed. I spun in my chair and turned to him. 'Do you want to talk about it?'

He was lying on my bed with his hand over his face. He shook his head. 'No point.'

I turned back and left him. He must have had another argument with his father. Nothing else laid him as low.

'Okay, I'm ready.' He sat up.

I handed him my notebooks. He scrawled on sheets of paper. I finished my homework and flicked to the document where my mate, Charlie, and I were working on a graphic novel. Charlie was autistic, and while he was high functioning and so could endure the hallways of a public high school, he had found ways to cope. One of them was wearing headphones every day.

Another was fictionalising the school into a post-apocalypse world where everyone was a zombie or survivor. We'd started the project as a lark in our graphic design class when we were paired up, mostly because we were the class rejects.

At first, Charlie hadn't wanted to speak to me at all, but I'd watched him with his sketchbook. I began writing captions for his drawings that I showed him. He loved it, and pretty soon we were collaborating. One day, he showed me a blank page. He wanted me to write the story, and he would draw it. And so that's how we started. Now it has become a therapeutic after-school activity. I would write about what happened to me during the day, but re-setting it into my imaginary world and email it to Charlie. He'd send me the images the next day.

Charlie drew in black and white pencil and then scanned it. He got a fancy scanner that his extended family had pooled money for his last Christmas present, wanting to give him a chance for self-expression.

After I received the new pages, I'd lay them out using the publishing software we had access to at school. We impressed our graphic design teacher with our progress and story. Somehow he hadn't twigged that all the zombies were based on my classmates.

I looked at Charlie's photos and laughed as I saw Joshua King's zombie clone being killed with a hammer pounded to the head. I heard Brian shifting on my bed behind me. He stood and leaned over my shoulder.

'How many times have you killed Joshua King now?' he scoffed.

'Not enough,' I muttered as I saved the images to my computer.

'Listen,' Brian cleared his throat. 'About what happened in the library today—'

'I know,' I interrupted him. 'I completely freaked Sabiha out.'

'Yeah. She doesn't really know you yet. So we should probably keep all this on the down-low from her.'

I looked at the images before me. I was so used to them that the gruesomeness didn't register. There were images of body parts being hacked off, hands twitching as zombies were dismembered and blood, guts and gore spilling out in a multitude of ways.

'Yep, you're right.' I vowed not to mention anything to Sabiha, then I paused. 'Hang on, so she's going to be a regular girl hang?' I looked over my shoulder at him. Brian had gravitated towards girls as friends, but usually these were short-term goss sessions that didn't last longer than a few days. This was the first time he'd expressed interested in a girl.

'Yeah, she's special,' Brian smiled. 'I want her to stick around.'

I nearly said, I thought you were into guys, but bit back my words just in time. Brian had never officially come out, and I'd never asked. 'This is the first time you've had a crush,' I said instead.

'Maybe I just hadn't met the right girl,'

'Yeah, maybe you're right?' I turned around, a stone sinking in my stomach. Why did I care Brian liked Sabiha? 'I'm happy for you, man,' I forced out past my lips.

'Thanks bud. I knew I could count on you.' Brian patted my shoulder and headed for the door. 'Tomorrow.'

After he left, turned back to my graphic novel. At least this was one constant.

About the author

 **Amra Pajalić** is an award-winning author, an editor and teacher who draws on her Bosnian cultural heritage to write own voices stories for young people, who like her, are searching to mediate their identity and take pride in their diverse culture. Her short story collection *The Cuckoo's Song* (Pishukin Press, 2022) features previously published and prize-winning stories. Her debut novel *The Good Daughter,* was published by Text Publishing in 2009 and won the 2009 Melbourne Prize for Literature's Civic Choice Award and is re-released as *Sabiha's Dilemma* (Pishukin Press, 2022).

Her memoir *Things Nobody Knows But Me* (Transit Lounge, 2019) was shortlisted for the 2020 National Biography Award. She is co-editor of the anthology *Growing up Muslim in Australia* (Allen and Unwin, 2014) which was shortlisted for the 2015 Children's Book Council of the year awards. She works as a high school teacher and is completing a PhD in Creative Writing at La Trobe University.

Amra Pajalić publishes her dark fiction using pen name A. P. Pajalic. She also publishes romance novels under pen name Mae Archer.

g goodreads.com/author/show/3310015.Amra_Pajalic

f facebook.com/AmraPajalicAuthor/

instagram.com/amrapajalicauthor/

https://twitter.com/AmraPajalic

bookbub.com/authors/amra-pajalic

tiktok.com/@amrapajalic

youtube.com/c/AmraPajalicAuthor

SIGN UP FOR AMRA'S AUTHOR NEWSLETTER

For news, giveaways, bonus material, and sneak peeks, please sign up to her newsletter below.

www.amrapajalic.com

PLEASE LEAVE A REVIEW

If you enjoyed this book and would like to show Amra your support, please consider leaving a star rating and/or review on the website you purchased the book from.

A guide for international readers

This book is set in Australia and uses British English spelling. Some spellings may differ from those used in American English.

Australia's seasons are at opposite times to those in the northern hemisphere. Summer is December–February, autumn is March–May, winter is June–August, and spring is September–November. Christmas is in summer.

In the Australian school system, primary school is for grades Kindergarten to Grade 6, and high school is for grades Year 7–12. Secondary college is a name frequently used for high school. Tertiary education after high school is either at universities and TAFE (technical and further education) institutions.

In Australia, each school year starts in late January and finishes mid-December.

The legal drinking age in Australia is 18 years old.

AUSTUDY is financial help if you're 25 or older and studying or completing an Australian apprenticeship.

www.ingramcontent.com/pod-product-compliance
Lightning Source LLC
Chambersburg PA
CBHW020913130726
47904CB00006BA/1892